THE ROYAL WEDDING

Felicity Philips Investigates Book 10

Steve Higgs

Text Copyright © 2024 Steven J Higgs

Publisher: Steve Higgs

The right of Steve Higgs to be identified as author of the Work has been asserted by him in accordance with the Copyright, Designs and Patents Act 1988

All rights reserved.

The book is copyright material and must not be copied, reproduced, transferred, distributed, leased, licensed or publicly performed or used in any way except as specifically permitted in writing by the publishers, as allowed under the terms and conditions under which it was purchased or as strictly permitted by applicable copyright law. Any unauthorised distribution or use of this text may be a direct infringement of the author's and publisher's rights and those responsible may be liable in law accordingly.

'The Royal Wedding' is a work of fiction. Names, characters, businesses, organisations, places, events and incidents either are the product of the author's imagination or are used fictitiously. Any resemblance to actual persons, living or dead, events or locations is entirely coincidental.

Contents

1. Chapter 1 – Felicity … 1
2. Chapter 2 – Albert … 7
3. Chapter 3 – Cody … 10
4. Chapter 4 – Patricia … 14
5. Chapter 5 – Buster and Amber … 20
6. Chapter 6 – Felicity … 25
7. Chapter 7 – Eddie … 32
8. Chapter 8 – Felicity … 34
9. Chapter 9 – Elizabeth … 37
10. Chapter 10 – Albert and Rex … 44
11. Chapter 11 – Patricia … 55
12. Chapter 12 – Buster and Amber … 58
13. Chapter 13 – Cody … 62
14. Chapter 14 – Albert Smith … 64
15. Chapter 15 – Rex and Eric … 66

16. Chapter 16 – Patricia — 70
17. Chapter 17 – Albert — 73
18. Chapter 18 – Cody — 77
19. Chapter 19 - Rex — 79
20. Chapter 20 – Buster and Amber — 82
21. Chapter 21 – Albert with Cassie — 85
22. Chapter 22 – Patricia — 88
23. Chapter 23 – Felicity — 93
24. Chapter 24 – Rex and Albert — 96
25. Chapter 25 – Lord Edward — 99
26. Chapter 26 – Blue Moon Investigations — 102
27. Chapter 27 – Cassie and Albert — 106
28. Chapter 28 – Cody — 109
29. Chapter 29 – Felicity — 111
30. Chapter 30 – Albert and Cassie — 115
31. Chapter 31 – Felicity and Patricia — 119
32. Chapter 32 – Amber and Buster — 121
33. Chapter 33 – Albert — 124
34. Chapter 34 – The Distraction — 126
35. Chapter 35 – Edward — 130
36. Chapter 36 – Albert and the King — 132
37. Chapter 37 – Buster and Amber — 137
38. Chapter 38 - Tempest, Patricia, and Felicity — 140
39. Chapter 39 – Felicity and the Dogs — 143

40.	Chapter 40 - The Aftermath	148
41.	Chapter 41 – Felicity	151
42.	Chapter 42 – Felicity and Primrose	155
43.	Chapter 43 – Felicity and Patricia	162
44.	Chapter 44 – The Reception	168
45.	Chapter 45 – Buster and Amber	171
46.	Chapter 46 – Patricia and Blue Moon	180
47.	Chapter 47 – Mindy	184
48.	Chapter 48 – Felicity	188
49.	Chapter 49 – Barbie, Jane, and the Rest	192
50.	Chapter 50 – Felicity	195
51.	Chapter 51 – Lord Edward and Mindy	201
52.	Chapter 52 – Blue Moon and Patricia	205
53.	Chapter 53 – Felicity	207
54.	Chapter 54 – Mindy and Edward	215
55.	Chapter 55 – Felicity	218
56.	Chapter 56 – Amber and Buster	223
57.	Chapter 57 – Mindy and Eddie	228
58.	Chapter 58 - Felicity	233
59.	Chapter 59 - Barbie and Jane	235
60.	Chapter 60 - Vince	238
61.	Chapter 61 – Elizabeth	240
62.	Chapter 62 – Felicity	242
63.	Chapter 63 – Jane and Barbie	245

64. Chapter 64 – Felicity and Primrose 250
65. Chapter 65 – Albert and Rex 252
66. Chapter 66 – Lord Edward 254
67. Chapter 67 – Felicity and Primrose 258
68. Chapter 68 – Barbie et al 263
69. Chapter 69 – Mindy 266
70. Chapter 70 - Elizabeth and Vince 268
71. Chapter 71 – Albert and Rex 270
72. Chapter 72 - Mindy and Lord Edward 272
73. Chapter 73 – Elizabeth 276
74. Chapter 74 – Tempest and Patricia 280
75. Chapter 75 – Felicity and Primrose 284
76. Chapter 76 – Elizabeth and Lord Edward 286
77. Chapter 77 – Lord Edward and DI Cassie Munroe 290
78. Chapter 78 – Three Days Later 294
79. Author's Notes: 299

Chapter 1 – Felicity

I could feel my palms sweating. I rubbed them along my trousers, trying to convince the tension out of my body. It was so unlike me. I don't get nervous before a wedding. Those days are far behind me.

Yet I knew why I felt overwhelmed by stress. Today was to be the pinnacle of my career. The greatest achievement by far.

Or my greatest failure depending on how things went.

I'm not normally one to think in negative, pessimistic terms, but things have not been running smoothly of late and that's about the biggest understatement of my life.

My name is Felicity Philips. I call myself 'The' wedding planner because I cater to the rich and famous, providing the grandest, finest ceremonies one can find anywhere. Well, anywhere in England at least.

For decades I have built my business, leading the way as the one to call if you and your intended want the most lavish of events. Want a gaggle of swans to lead the bride down the aisle? No problem. Thinking you might like the Royal Air Force to perform a fly-by? I can cover that. Is it your desire to have Rod Stewart sing as you lead the first dance? I have him on speed dial.

Yet recently my weddings have been beset with drama. When I say drama, I of course mean murder, kidnap, runaway brides, gangsters, thugs, corrupt police, and anything else you think couldn't possibly happen to the same person.

Don't feel sorry for me. There's nothing to be gained by wallowing in self-pity. But maybe pray a little.

Why?

Today I host a royal wedding. The King's youngest son, Marcus, is getting married to his long-term girlfriend and I am one hundred percent certain someone is going to try to mess with the event. Admittedly, it's not quite the same thing as arranging a wedding for the future King of England, but royal weddings have been handled by the palace for longer than I can remember. This is the first time in living memory, possibly even in known history, that an outsider has been allowed such access.

Prince Marcus, as the King's youngest son, stands almost no chance of ever ascending to the throne. The old adage of an heir and spare could not have been truer, for with two spares plus his older siblings already having kids, he was now ninth in line. It would be a sad day indeed if the crown ever came to rest on his head.

I believe there was a small sense of rebellion in his decision to have the wedding not at St Paul's Cathedral in London, but at Canterbury Cathedral some fifty miles to the south. He didn't want the same level of pageantry – no royal coach, no procession through the city with millions of adoring royal supporters lining the streets.

THE ROYAL WEDDING

It was to be a smaller affair, and yet still the largest, most lavish wedding I had ever pulled together. The guest list reads like a who's who of the celebrity world but the names attending are not just from popular culture, but includes heads of state from around the world, our own Prime Minister, and of course the King of England.

And it's happening today.

Security is tight, as one might expect, but tighter than usual because there has been an unfortunate run of deaths in the royal family. Not from the immediate line of succession, but from those just outside it. It started almost a year ago when the eldest son of the Duke of Westborough died in a bizarre accident at the palace. Since then, there have been seventeen deaths. All of whom were persons listed on the line of succession.

None of the deaths, beyond the first one I mentioned, are considered suspicious, but the number of them is. Viewed as a whole, it appears as though someone is attempting to eliminate their way to the throne. I use the word 'eliminate' rather than 'murder' because not one of the deaths has been recorded as such. Despite that, a detective inspector assigned to the palace believes they are all indeed precisely that: Murders.

Her name is Cassie Munroe, and she even thinks she knows who is behind it: Duke Westborough's youngest son and surviving heir. She has not, however, one jot of proof despite months of investigation. Her bosses do not support her theories, and she is treading on thin ice to even still be conducting her investigation.

Banned from continuing it officially, she recruited a private investigation firm to help her. I know them personally having hired their help myself a short while ago. Four of them are working for the palace so they may spy and learn and perhaps ensure today's event does not end in disaster.

I will see them later in Canterbury, but the potential for a murderous royal isn't my only concern. My recent run of problems did not come at the hands of whoever is behind the royal deaths, but is there another player in the field? Or have I just been unlucky?

I wish I knew the answer.

My archnemesis, Primrose Green, arguably the second most capable wedding planner in the country, has waged a campaign of guerrilla tactics against me for years. She was initially awarded the coveted contract for the royal wedding only to lose it when scandalous pictures from her early modelling career emerged. She blamed me for the leaked photographs, but knowing I am innocent means there is someone else out there with an axe to grind.

When the prince and his fiancée pulled the wedding forward, giving me four weeks to have everything arranged, it was a tactic insisted on by the palace. They feared that if there was a person behind the recent run of deaths, they might see the gathering of so many family members in one place at one time to be too much to resist. The change of date was not announced until just a few days ago. The sudden change was expected to disrupt and defeat any plans that might exist.

The shortened timeframe certainly messed with mine. Putting our past differences behind us, I hired Primrose along with the woman I consider to be the third candidate for the top spot. Elizabeth Keats lacks the finesse Primrose and I bring to our events, but she is a capable wedding planner, and with four weeks until the big day I needed all the help I could get.

"Are you ready, Auntie?" called my assistant Mindy, sticking her head through the door to my bedroom.

She moved in with me some time ago, wanting independence from her parents. She's about to turn twenty and has been working for me for a little more than a year. She is surprisingly good at her job, but today she created an additional complication I could very much do without.

She's dating Eddie Chamberlain, the heir to the Dukedom of Westborough. Yes, that's right, the same man DI Cassie Munroe believes to be the person seeking to murder his way to the throne.

Initially, Mindy listened to Cassie's thoughts on the subject. She even agreed to place a listening device in his chambers and wore a wire. However, when DI Munroe could find no evidence to support her suspicions, and Mindy spent more and more time with Eddie, it became obvious she saw him as an innocent.

Yes, there were a few coincidences that warranted Cassie's suspicion, but in Mindy's opinion that's all they were. She's in love and who could blame her? Edward Chamberlain is handsome, rich, and lives in Buckingham Palace. It would be hard to find a better suitor. I recall how fiercely that emotion ran when I was her age. It was too powerful to resist.

She was working with me today, but only for the ceremony. She would join her beau at the reception and was giddy with excitement. Working in such close proximity made talking to Cassie about Mindy's boyfriend nigh impossible.

I closed my eyes and tried to shut out the voices in my head. I would gain nothing from listening to them. Forcing the tension from my body, I opened my eyes, nodded to myself in the mirror, and turned around.

"Yes, I'm ready."

Mindy grinned, her enthusiasm and excitement for the day ahead bubbling over.

"Great! Buster and Amber are already in the car. We should get going."

She wasn't wrong. It was just a little after five in the morning and we had a big day ahead. It probably would have made more sense to stay in Canterbury last night, but after weeks of living in hotel rooms there, managing every element of today, I wanted to withdraw for a night. I'd hoped it would allow me to sleep better and that I would feel refreshed this morning, but nothing could have been further from the truth.

Regardless, I couldn't stop the ticking clock, so a few hours from now, no matter how it went, it would all be over.

Chapter 2 – Albert

Albert pursed his lips and frowned.

"I don't think it works all that well, truth be told. What do you think, Rex?"

Rex tilted his head, not fully understanding the question. His human had wrestled him into a waistcoat and bow tie. They were both made from Royal Stewart tartan to match Albert's own waistcoat and bow tie.

As an official guest of the King's, he'd been given options for what he could wear in a formal letter from the palace. A man in a fine suit then visited a few weeks ago to discuss his choice and to make sure his outfit for the day would not only fit but would be delivered on time.

The palace, while they were not organising the wedding, had plenty of influence still and were going to ensure the guests were correctly dressed.

Albert wasn't comfortable in his hand-cut morning suit complete with tails, waistcoat and pocket watch, but he could put up with it for a day. His invitation to the wedding came from King Charles in person after he knighted him. Later life was proving to be full of surprises.

Ruffling the fur atop Rex's head, he wandered to the kitchen where a cup of tea was going cold.

Rex padded after him, wondering what all the fuss was about. The clothing didn't bother him all that much. He'd worn something similar during his time as a police dog, and the bowtie around his neck was no more constricting than his collar and he'd worn that, or a version of it, his entire life.

They were going out today, he knew that much, but if he understood his human accurately, they were soon to resume their travels. Many moons ago – Rex had no concept of weeks or months – they had set off walking around the British Isles. Rex had no real sense of geography either, but he knew his home and they weren't there for a long time.

He'd enjoyed it. Every few days they went somewhere new, often finding adventure to fill their days. After some time at home, they set off again. However, they found themselves back home quite quickly the second time, following his human suffering injuries at the hands of a man running a cult.

Albert had recovered, more or less, but forced to participate in a sword fight, he was lucky to be alive and had the scars to prove it.

Albert drained his tea. The car would be here soon. His sons and daughter questioned his decision to go alone when there was a plus one on the official invitation that followed the King's verbal one, but of course, he wasn't. They all thought he would choose one of them, but Albert was taking Rex. Sir Rex, in fact, since King Charles saw fit to knight his dog too.

THE ROYAL WEDDING

Sir Rex and Sir Albert were partners and the press, who were being managed and restricted, but would nevertheless be in attendance, were used to seeing them together.

Waiting patiently for his ride to arrive, Albert hoped the day would go smoothly. It was his experience, especially in recent months, that trouble seemed to find him wherever he went. Even when he went to Buckingham Palace to be knighted there was an incident. On that occasion his granddaughter Apple-Blossom solved the crime alongside Rex, but surely they could get through today without any drama.

Surely?

Chapter 3 – Cody

Cody Williams couldn't decide if he felt sick from the anticipation of what he was about to do or from the knowledge that no matter how it went there would be no tomorrow. Dying for what he believed in was never the plan, but it was better than a life behind bars.

The statement he was going to make would reverberate around the planet and echo for centuries. Would it end the monarchy? No, probably not, but that was why he was doing it and maybe his stand, his act of selfless sacrifice, would light the flame for the rest of the nation. There were plenty of others who felt the same as he.

The monarchy was an outmoded, ridiculous concept that had no place in 21st century society. Who did they think they were that they could stand above anyone else? People were supposed to bow and call them 'your majesty' or 'your highness' as if they didn't need to use the toilet like everyone else. He would sooner die.

And that was precisely what would happen in just a few short hours.

Months of planning. Months of pretending to be someone else. He stumbled across Gershwin George in a dark web online chat group dedicated to anti-royalists. The similarity in their appearances was uncanny. Not that they would be confused as twins if placed next to each other, but a haircut, a few pounds lost, and a little practice to lose his west country accent was all Cody Williams needed to fool the people at the palace.

Gershwin had taken the job at the palace aged eighteen. Back then he'd thought it a grand thing to do but quickly became disillusioned when he saw how the royals spoke and behaved when the public wasn't there to watch them. He could have quit. He thought about it many times but chose not to. Instead, Gershwin believed he could capture how the royals really were. He planned to blow the whistle when he had enough evidence and was on the dark web telling everyone what he knew and what he planned when Cody dropped into his life.

Gershwin talked a good conspiracy, but Cody Williams was the real thing. A man on the run from the police after committing multiple murders in the pursuit of bringing down the monarchy. Where Gershwin planned to embarrass the crown, Cody was going to end them.

Together, they recruited more people, using the imminent wedding and its demand for additional, temporary staff to get them inside the palace. As a team they plotted, looking for the perfect way to murder as many of the supposed elite as possible. Cody's original plan had been to poison them at the engagement party. It had been genius in its simplicity and would have surely succeeded had it not been for Albert Smith.

The old man with his dog appeared in Cody's hometown of Looe in Cornwall at precisely the right time to foil his plan. According to Cody, Albert Smith didn't even realise what was going on. Not really. His dog found a body and the old man insisted on sticking his nose in. The body was one of Cody's co-conspirators, a man who had to die, according to Cody, because he was going to blow his carefully crafted plot to kill the King.

Well, no one was going to get in the way this time.

Four of them would be in position to create the perfect distraction just when Cody needed it. The police would panic as would the press and the guests. But those charged with keeping the King safe would keep their heads and do as they ought. It was through their predictability that Cody would get close enough to do what had to be done.

Gershwin admired him. Worshipped him in a way that many do with their idols. Yet Cody was no popstar with posters to put on a wall. He was a real person with drive and passion beyond that which many could claim.

Gershwin questioned if he would be able to go through with it if the key role was his. He doubted it. He just didn't have the backbone to swap his life for another's. Even if it was the King.

The one danger that existed today was that he and Cody would both be working at the same time. For months, Cody had swapped shifts with Gershwin, pretending to be him so he could learn the role and blend in. It had worked better than either could have ever predicted but they had never been in uniform performing official duties at the same time and now they would.

They only had one pass between them, but they'd figured out how to get around that. The danger lay in someone seeing one of them and then the other immediately afterward in a different place doing a different thing. They agreed the likelihood of discovery was slim, yet it existed and therefore had to be considered as a factor.

Then there was Albert Smith. He was going to be at the wedding ceremony. He would also be at the reception, but that didn't matter. It would all be over by then and if things went to plan, neither the ceremony nor the reception would take place.

THE ROYAL WEDDING

The last time Albert Smith was in the same location as Cody, he recognised him. They had to hurry to get Gershwin to the palace that day so he could be the one they found. It worked, but it had been such a close call.

Surely, they wouldn't be so unlucky a second time. However, yet again, the possibility existed and therefore they had to consider it.

Like so many of the palace staff, Cody/Gershwin was to be working at Canterbury Cathedral today. There had been many practice sessions with Sir Cuthbert and the other pompous fools. It made them smile to think how they were fooling everyone and to imagine what expression their faces might pull when they delivered the blow the nation so badly needed.

The desire to be the one striking that blow fuelled Cody. Yes, he would almost certainly die today. If not instantly, then in his bid to escape prison. He would become the first regicide in centuries, his name immortalised, and the press would receive copies of his manifesto in the mail tomorrow morning. It would explain it all and he knew they would read it.

The world would want to hear why the crazy man murdered the King of England, and the truth would he heard. The nation's eyes would be opened and as one they would see the royal family for what they were – arrogant fools perched atop a class pyramid that had existed unchallenged for centuries. A system underpinned by wealth so ingrained in the subconscious of the people that they don't even blink when they see the King's face on the very money that keeps them enslaved.

Using his hand to brush the creases from his tunic, Cody Williams checked the silicone dagger was secure and turned away from the mirror.

It was time to die.

Chapter 4 – Patricia

"Madam." Jermaine passed Patricia a cup of tea.

"Thank you, sweetie," she said, gratefully accepting it.

They were in one of the administrative areas in the library adjacent to Canterbury Cathedral. Drawn to England by Felicity's request for help, the renowned sleuth had been in the country for a week, observing Felicity and the people around her.

An acquaintance of Felicity's for more than thirty years – Felicity opened her wedding planner business with Patricia's wedding – they had become closer in recent months when a chance encounter brought them back together. Felicity assisted when Patricia needed a high-end wedding planner on board the cruise ship on which she lives and works, so when the chance to reciprocate the favour came just a few weeks later … well, let's just say Patricia was only too happy to help. Not least because the favour included an invitation to a royal wedding.

However, tasked with figuring out if there was a malevolent force behind Felicity's recent run of ruined weddings, and if there might also be someone targeting the royal family, Patricia Fisher had so far drawn a total blank.

Felicity harboured a nagging doubt that her main rival, and now chief assistant for the royal wedding, might not actually be the saboteur. One might question the decision to employ Primrose Green, but the theory of 'keep your enemies close' came into play. With Primrose operating under her nose, Felicity believed she would catch her if indeed her rival was up to no good.

So far, Patricia had observed nothing to raise even the slightest suspicion. Even Felicity admitted that Primrose might be entirely innocent but that wasn't helpful news because it left the field open to everyone else. And there were a lot of everyone elses.

Felicity moved in a circle of dozens of firms and business doesn't always run smoothly. Felicity knew that with so many years of operation each firm would be able to claim at some point she'd held back a contract they wanted or leveraged her position to obtain a discount they didn't want to give. Did that mean one of her suppliers was behind her run of bad luck? Possibly.

That being the case, Patricia needed to watch all those who had been granted access to the wedding and the reception that would follow.

Patricia sipped her tea and thought about the royal conundrum. Now that she was here, her pseudo celebrity status – something that happens when your name and face are plastered across the world's papers – meant a disaster at the wedding would result in a finger pointing her way. If a member of the royal household died, why hadn't the great Patricia Fisher figured things out in time to prevent it happening?

While the question was unfair, Patricia knew she would be asking herself the same thing should such a terrible event come to pass. She was her own harshest critic and rightfully so.

Felicity had a vague suspicion that a member of the royal household might be behind the rumoured plot, but it was based upon the unfounded opinion of a disgraced detective inspector. Patricia wasn't going to dismiss DI Munroe's concerns out of hand, but there was no evidence to substantiate her speculation.

Edward Chamberlain came across as a playboy. Born with money and a title, he was well educated, very handsome, and almost certainly more interested in leisure pursuits than murder. Besides, he owned a dachshund. How bad could he possibly be?

The china cup clinked as she set it back into its saucer and again when she set them both on the table. The sun was high in the sky outside and the grounds of the cathedral were beginning to bustle. Rising to her feet as Jermaine swept the empty cup and saucer from the table with practiced flourish, Patricia saw a duo of florist vans pull to a stop.

Canterbury Cathedral was to be transformed over the next few hours. Some work had taken place the previous day, but flower arrangements, like food, needed to be fresh.

To Patricia's way of thinking, the surest way to spot what didn't fit, was to observe as much as possible. With that in mind, she left the room, heading outside to see who was doing what.

The cathedral sat fifty yards away across an open expanse of mostly grass. It was enclosed on three sides by buildings built long before the concept of a brick had occurred to the construction industry. Hewn from rock taken from a local quarry, the cathedral and all the lesser buildings around it were erected more than a thousand years ago.

The third side of the square wasn't open but enclosed by a series of arches wide and tall enough to permit vehicles to pass through. Obviously, that wasn't a design consideration made when they were built, but a happy coincidence to be employed now.

Felicity was due to arrive in the next thirty minutes or so, but Primrose was already here. Patricia could see her greeting the florist like they were old friends. Which, she supposed, they probably were.

Heading outside, she spotted Felicity's second extra set of hands, Elizabeth Keats. Another wedding planner of some repute, if Felicity brought her in to help manage a portion of the work, Patricia assumed she must be good.

Elizabeth was easier to get on with than Primrose, that was for sure. Primrose presented a smile, but there was no sense of genuine warmth behind it. In fact, Patricia always got the impression the tall, elegant, blonde woman was looking down her nose at those around her.

Her looks commanded the attention of all the men operating in the cathedral, including those in the clergy. Unfortunately for Primrose, Patricia brought her own bombshell with her.

"Hey, Patty!" Barbie called from across the open area. As so often with Patricia's young, Californian friend, a beaming smile dominated her features. She was laughing with a duo of young men as they unpacked uniforms from a van. Each was covered in a thin plastic sheath to keep anything from soiling the ornate outfits.

They were to be worn by the men and women of the palace household staff. They were decoration as much as anything else, but had key roles to play as ushers, doormen, footmen, valets, et cetera.

Barbie waved. "Have you seen these outfits?" she asked, her voice still a little above conversation level so Patricia would hear as she closed the distance between them. "Everything is so incredible in England."

"In Great Britain, dear," Patricia corrected her. "We may be in England right now, but you will find equal splendour in any Scottish castle."

"This is Ryan," Barbie introduced one of the two men unloading the van. "Gershwin." She indicated the second man, blithely oblivious that both men were drooling. "Is that an unusual name over here?" she asked. "I've never met a Gershwin before."

"And I've never had a Barbie," said Gershwin, his cheeks colouring slightly at his double entendre.

Barbie grinned, but said, "Cheeky. Turning her attention back to Patricia, she said, "I offered to help them, but they said they can handle it."

Barbie wasn't just being generous. The best way to see things was to be involved. Also, staff quickly become background scenery so being a person doing a job provides a degree of invisibility.

Patricia smiled at the two men but drew Barbie away.

"Catch you later, guys," Barbie shot them another grin. "Have fun today."

Once they were out of earshot, Patricia said, "Felicity will be here soon, and I want us all to attend her briefing. It will help us to understand who should be doing what and that might help us see when something is not as it should be."

Barbie pursed her lips and frowned. "It's hard to believe someone would mess with such a wonderful occasion."

"I very much hope they don't, and this proves to be a wasted trip for us."

Barbie let out a sad laugh. "Not much chance of that. Not with you here."

It was Patricia's turn to frown. Barbie liked to tease about the regularity of bedlam whenever Patricia went anywhere. She might have fired a retort were she not so worried it might turn out to be true.

Chapter 5 – Buster and Amber

Amber cracked one eye to glare at Buster. For days the stupid dog had been muttering to himself about something to do with one of Felicity's friends.

Buster felt Amber's gaze and looked her way.

Amber swiftly closed her eye again, but not fast enough.

"I'm telling you, Amber. There's something I'm missing."

Without opening her eyes, Amber said, "I have been saying the same for years."

The snarky response was neither unusual nor unexpected.

Ignoring her remark, Buster persisted. "What if it's important, Amber? You know how worried Felicity is. So many of her weddings have gone wrong of late. What if the same thing happens this time and I could have prevented it."

Amber pretended to be asleep. They were on the backseat of Felicity's new Range Rover. It was a treat to herself when she accepted that she really needed a bigger car. However, the plush leather seats were entirely lost on the pets who were travelling inside carriers so their claws wouldn't scratch the fine material.

Mindy was on the backseat next to Buster; her left arm draped across his carrier. She was aware of her aunt's unique 'gift' – the ability to hear and understand her pets, but after many attempts to 'hear' what Buster had to say, she'd given up on ever developing the skill herself.

In the front of the car, Felicity sat in the passenger seat despite owning the car. She was content to let her boyfriend drive so she could communicate with the hundreds of people involved in today's spectacular event.

Vince was taking time out from his own work to help make the day go smoothly. A security expert and private investigator by trade and profession, Vince Slater was the perfect man to have in their corner.

Frustrated already, Amber's refusal to engage on the subject of what he couldn't figure out was enough to make Buster bark.

"Hey!" he woofed right into Amber's ear.

The unexpected sound made her jump. She hit her head on the top of her carrier, her legs propelling her forward to get away from the unseen danger, so when her paws hit her blanket she ran straight into the front of the locked carrier door, smooshing her face. Her reaction occurred over a period lasting less than a second and came accompanied by a high-pitched cat wail of fright.

Vince twitched, his heart stopping and restarting and he fired an expletive into the air as he wrestled the car back under his control.

Felicity, equally startled, twisted in her seat to glare at Buster.

"What?" he said, flopping down onto his pillow. "She was ignoring me, and I need help to figure it out."

"Figure what out?" Felicity tried not to growl. Taking her pets along was entirely her idea. They proved invaluable on a regular basis and with so much at stake today, she wanted their unique capability in play.

"The thing I'm missing," Buster whined.

Amber settled back onto her blanket, scowling at the dog the whole time. "Why you think I would want to help you, I cannot imagine."

"Because it's for Felicity," Buster replied, his tone soft and imploring. "I'm serious, Amber. There's a memory in my head that I can't quite see, but I know it's important."

"How do you know?"

"Because it keeps coming to me in my sleep. It started after we got back from Scotland, but I don't know why."

Flopping his head down with a groaning exhale, Buster fell into silence.

With Felicity jabbering into her phone, making call after call while delegating still more calls to Mindy, Vince turned off the M2 motorway and followed the light morning traffic into Canterbury. The police presence was high, cars and uniforms visible in every direction.

More than five hundred guests were to attend the wedding ceremony at the cathedral, many of them the sort of person who travels in a cavalcade surrounded by security. Roads would be blocked and the city centre essentially shut for the day. The civilian population would be controlled, for though there was to be no official parade through the streets in an open topped car, the public nevertheless wanted to catch a glimpse of anyone who might be worth glimpsing, the happy couple included.

THE ROYAL WEDDING

To demonstrate how fervent that hope could become, they drove past people packing up their tents. People had camped out overnight on the pavement to ensure a prime position bordering the route. Barrier tape rather than a physical fence lined the edge of the road on both sides. It relied on good manners, but the British public would likely behave as expected.

Arriving in the vicinity of the cathedral - they were stopped a hundred yards short by a police roadblock – Felicity took the official pass from her glovebox and placed it on the dashboard so the officer approaching them would see it. Getting through security was a pain, but one Felicity was happy to endure for the sense of safety it provided.

The officer checked everyone's identification slowly and carefully, matching their names to a list on a tablet held by a colleague. Satisfied, they were let through and able to drive under the arches leading into the square where they immediately saw Patricia.

"Park over there," Felicity indicated where Vince should put the car. It was next to the office from which she would be working. Not that she expected to spend much time in it. Today was going to be as full-on as it gets.

Seeing Patricia crossing the square to meet with her, her butler and blonde friend in tow, Felicity was equally pleased to spot Justin, her master of ceremonies, and Philippe, her accidentally employed second assistant, inside the office.

She had already spoken with Primrose and Elizabeth this morning, so everyone was here. Felicity still marvelled that she had been able to pull the project together in the ridiculously tight timeframe the palace gave her, but it was done. At least, there was nothing left to do except ride the wave. All the pieces were in place. Not one of the suppliers she called indicated the slightest concern about their tasks for the day. No one was going to be late. No one was sick ...

So why was her stomach still so knotted with dread?

Chapter 6 – Felicity

"Good morning, Patricia," I air-kissed my friend and felt somewhat relieved to have her hold my hands in hers.

"It's going to be okay," she said. "But don't worry. We are alert and ready for anything."

I released her to bid Barbie and Jermaine good morning too. I would have been happy just to have Patricia at my side, but they work as a team, and I know from experience how effective they can be.

"We should go inside." I led the way, keen to get on with things and hoping I might distract myself with work.

A few minutes later, having greeted Justin and Philippe, I got to run through a list of tasks with Primrose. I very much felt that we were over our differences. Working together on this project had been a revelation so far. I knew her to be a capable wedding planner, but she was more than that. A consummate professional, her standards were the same as mine and she had no problem turning goods or services away if they failed to hit the mark.

There was one task I had been debating for days. Not because I didn't know who to give it to, but because it was very prestigious, the person doing it would be on TV a lot, and truth be told I wanted to do it myself. I knew that wasn't practical, but I'd been arguing with myself about it anyway.

Unable to put it off any longer, I said, "Primrose, I want you at the kerb today." It was a gift, and we both knew it, so imagine my surprise when she looked at me with annoyed disbelief.

"Really, Felicity? You drop this on me now? I assumed you were keeping that job for yourself." She even sounded annoyed.

I crossed my arms and stared, inviting her to continue complaining.

"Obviously, I'll do it," she relented. "I agreed to work for you and I'm not complaining, but I expected to be at the reception venue. I have arranged so many of the elements for that part of the wedding."

"I'm going to stay mobile. My job today is putting out fires. I would love to believe there won't be any, but even on my most optimistic day …"

Primrose waved me into silence. "You don't have to explain. You just … you could have told me yesterday. Or the day before. Now I need to delegate my tasks to whoever is going to be controlling things at the venue. Elizabeth, I assume."

"Yes, Elizabeth." I had already given her the task, so she knew it was coming. She would be out of the limelight and would miss the pageantry and majesty of the wedding, but there was no way for us to all see it. Besides, Elizabeth might be a gifted wedding planner, but if you want someone to put in front of a TV screen, you pick a person from the attractive end of the scale. Ergo Primrose.

We had to wait for Elizabeth to arrive as she was making sure the order of service books were delivered, that we had the right amount, that they were all printed correctly, and that she had passed them to someone who knew what needed to happen next.

When the whole team was in the room, I drew in a slow, deep breath and launched into my speech. I tried to deliver a rousing talk about how privileged we all were to be taking part in the prestigious event. We all knew the day ahead was going to be trying and the chances of rubbing up blisters was high. We would move around with the serenity of swans while paddling like heck beneath the water because the guests should never see us flustered.

How much business Primrose, Elizabeth, and I might get off the back of this one contract could not be calculated, but I doubted any of us would need to advertise for the next few years.

Speech given, though my mind had gone blank halfway through and I was sure I'd missed a few important points, we split away to tackle our assigned tasks. Primrose went to the gates where she would manage the guestlist so the arriving dignitaries, heads of state, members of the royal family, celebrities, and others would be identified before they were received.

Tall, radiant, and the kind of person everyone notices, Primrose was perfect for the task. I would be in the cathedral itself as that was where the most work needed to happen, and Elizabeth was heading to the reception venue. I would need to head over myself before the morning was done, but with her at the helm I felt confident the bulk of the work would be to my satisfaction before I set foot in the door.

Leaving Buster and Amber in the office with the door shut, I made my way to the cathedral where I found the florists hard at work. There were to be arrangements on both ends of every pew, huge bouquets to either side of the altar, ornate buttonholes for the gentlemen, rose petals for the bridesmaids to scatter, flowers for the bridesmaids … and that was just for the ceremony.

A few months back, right in the middle of my run of terrible weddings, Doris Short was arrested for attempted murder. The accusation was that she'd dipped a barb in a rather nasty toxin and then fitted it in a bride's bouquet in such a manner that it would cut her hand when she held it. Obviously, she was innocent, but it took some work from my friends to prove it.

As recompense, not that I was in any way responsible for her plight though I felt guilty anyway, I didn't hesitate to offer her the lucrative cathedral contract. The contract for the reception went to another firm I have worked with for many years – both would be too much work for a single company.

"How's it going?" I called to get Doris's attention.

She looked up, a water balloon filled with delicate pink lilies and freesias in each hand. She passed them to Maureen, one of a pair of sisters who had worked with Doris for as long as I could recall.

"Start at the front and work your way up the insides using the most attractive ones there first. Those are the ones most people will notice."

Maureen offered me a smile and hurried away, her steps fast in deference to the urgency I had instilled every time we spoke on the subject of today.

"I'll need an hour," said Doris, glancing at her watch. "That's still okay?"

It was well within the timeframe I'd given for the task to be completed.

"Do you need any help?" I enquired.

Doris looked around at the boxes and boxes of flowers lining the cathedral's stone floor. They appeared to have unloaded everything before starting to place the arrangements.

"No, I don't think so," she concluded. "Honestly, we are ahead of schedule and things couldn't be going smoother. We brought lots of spares with us so we will be able to make touch-ups right up until the guests start to arrive."

It was music to my ears. It also wasn't what I was used to hearing. Certainly not in recent times.

Standing to my left, Mindy said, "The arrangements are really beautiful, Doris. You have outdone yourself."

Doris beamed, happy for the compliment.

"Well, if ever there was a time to produce my best work …"

Seeing no need to hover – I would only slow her progress with my presence and interference – I left the florists to get on with it.

I spent the next couple of hours checking everything twice. I was trying hard to find something amiss, but there wasn't anything. Like with Doris the florist, everyone was ahead of schedule and had all they needed. Weirdly, it made me more nervous that it was all going according to plan, but time was ticking away, and my next task was to liaise with the bride.

I have probably said it before, but the bride is the absolute centre of everything. Even at a royal wedding when she is a commoner marrying a prince, Nora Morley was the focus for my day. The groom would take care of himself. Or, at least, have his brothers, royal appointed staff, best man, and whoever else made it into his entourage to make sure he was ready. The bride, however, that was down to me.

A whole salon of beauty specialists were tending to her every need. It started with massages after breakfast for her, the mother of the bride, and a selected circle of her closest friends. The bridesmaids were too young to enjoy such pampering but would probably like the full hair and makeup treatment coming their way later.

They would get fizzy juice to drink in the same champagne flutes as the adults and come away from the day feeling like they were princesses too.

The bride and her party were in a plush hotel two miles from the cathedral. It was the same venue as the reception and the whole building had been booked out and locked down by the police and royal household security. Anyone wanting to try anything there would do well to even get inside.

Just filling in the security paperwork for all my suppliers, caterers, chefs, entertainers, and the host of hairdressers, dressmakers, and makeup artists took a week.

Leaving the cathedral with Mindy at my side, I stopped to check on Buster and Amber.

"Any luck remembering what it was?" I asked Buster.

"No," he moped.

"Well, I wish you would get on with it," complained Amber. "If I hear your mental examination one more time I'll claw my own eyes out."

Vince came through the door just before I left.

"Hey, babe. Everything okay?" He asked the question tentatively, tensed to hear the bad news. He looked stunned when I didn't have any to offer.

"How's everything going on the security end of things?" I'd asked Vince along so he could triple check what the police and palace security were doing. He wasn't employed in any official capacity, but like Patricia and her pals, that meant he could roam and observe freely. If there was going to be a major drama, I wanted early warning.

He shrugged. "I think the place is tight. Anyone wanting to get in here is going to need a tank or a parachute. You heading over to the hotel now?"

I said that I was, and he came with me, keen to check out the reception venue too.

At the car, I was about to get in when I got that sensation that goes with being watched. I paused, an unsettling feeling creeping up my spine, and looking around I found a man looking my way.

He was attired in the livery of a footman from the royal household. His steady gaze might have bothered me had he not looked away the moment we made eye contact. Mercifully, I knew he caught my eye only to reassure me he was there. His name is Tempest Michaels.

Chapter 7 – Eddie

Edward Chamberlain, heir to a Dukedom and sixteenth in line to the throne – shunted two places further from it recently due to the birth of two children - ruffled the fur around Henkel's head and met the little dachshund's eyes.

"Can you feel that?" he asked.

Henkel twisted his head to the right, trying to understand what his human might be asking.

"It's the imminent arrival of immortality, my dear little dog. Can you feel it? No? Well, of course you can't. It isn't coming for you. I'm the target."

He patted the dog again and stood up, rising from the edge of the bed with a yawn and a stretch. He'd hoped to spend the night with Mindy, the athletic and energetic girl with whom he'd conducted a brief affair. It was never to be anything more than that, of course. She was nothing more than a distraction, an easy lay, one might say. Coming from a working-class background, showing her a cheap night out was still an extravagant affair in her eyes.

He knew she was besotted, but that was none of his concern. By the end of the day, she would be dead, and he would be next in line for the throne, one position behind the new King of England, his father.

All the pieces were positioned, his scapegoats lined up. What remained was to enjoy the day and be ready for when the opportunity came. He was being watched, that much he knew for certain. DI Munroe probably thought her movements were surreptitious, but it wasn't hard to bribe a member of the palace staff to spy on her as she spied on him.

She had nothing, that was the best part. Not even the support of her chain of command. Eddie didn't know the story behind it, but a handful of folded notes in the right palm confirmed she arrived at the palace under a cloud and was on her last warning.

If she survived the day, perhaps he could see to it that she found herself caught up in the blame for what happened.

Poor Mindy would be cast as the perpetrator. Far too dead to defend herself when an anonymous tip led the police to look her way, they would find antiroyalist websites in her browser history along with subversive comments made on her behalf in chat rooms on the dark web.

Her fingerprints were on the weapon that killed the royal family and oh so many innocent bystanders. He'd captured and transferred them there just a few weeks ago, the task far simpler than he'd imagined.

Eddie applied shaving foam to his face and ran the hot tap until steam began to billow. It was indeed a shame she'd not been able to spend one last night with him, but he was less than twenty-four hours from being the most eligible bachelor in the world. The future King of England and handsome to boot.

He wouldn't miss Mindy one bit.

Chapter 8 – Felicity

Elizabeth met me as I got out of my car.

"How's everything at the cathedral? Any sign of your saboteur?"

I shook my head. "Nothing so far. I mean, fingers crossed obviously, and I don't want to jinx it, but so far everything is going really well. Like clockwork, one might say."

"No problem with the flowers?"

"None whatsoever."

"Same here."

Elizabeth acted as though she was on edge but trying to hide it, which was exactly how I felt. My heart had been beating at double speed for days, giving me cause to wonder if it might just give up if something did go wrong. I would be able to rest tonight when it was all over. For now, I had to just keep moving forward.

As a troop, we made our way into the banquet room where several dozen staff moved about like choreographed chaos. Round tables draped in ivory silk stretched across the polished floor, each one precisely positioned according to the seating chart that had undergone more than a hundred changes in the last month alone. Crystal chandeliers cast prismatic light across the room, and the scent of white roses hung in the air like an expensive perfume.

Everything was proceeding exactly as it should. The caterers moved with practiced efficiency, laying out gleaming silverware and checking that each water glass bore no fingerprints. The florists were adding the finishing touches to the centrepieces, their movements careful and reverent. Most of them were from the palace, and I could see Sir Cuthbert directing operations from a back corner.

Personally, I would have preferred to control it all myself, but the palace insisted it had to be their crockery and cutlery, their table settings, their candle holders, and their staff. I didn't fight all that hard because had I won it would have given me more work without more pay. Sir Cuthbert, curmudgeonly soul that he is, would do a great job, so I let him continue.

Elizabeth reported on the events of the last two hours, filling me in with a list that confirmed everything was happening as it should be. Just like at the cathedral, there was nothing to worry about, nothing I needed to do.

We came in through the front doors, a duo of besuited palace security guards nodding to acknowledge us but focused on everything everywhere else, just as they were supposed to be.

"Do you want to see the banquet room?" Elizabeth asked as we came into the hotel's reception area.

"Yes, but I'm going to visit the bridal party first, unless you need me for anything."

Elizabeth shook her head. "No. Not at all."

Mindy's phone rang and she squeaked with excitement. "It's Eddie!" She grinned broadly and ducked back outside to take the call.

"Miss Keats?" One of the catering supervisors approached with a clipboard. "We're ready for the final walk-through of the service sequence."

Elizabeth nodded, putting her professional smile into place. "Of course. Let's review the champagne service first."

I got a nod from her as she left but didn't get to escape as the hotel manager was coming my way.

Chapter 9 – Elizabeth

Elizabeth Keats stood in the doorway of the hotel's grand ballroom and let her eyes sweep across the scene before her. It should have filled Elizabeth with satisfaction. Instead, it made her stomach churn with resentment.

This should have been her triumph. Her name should have been the one whispered in admiring tones when guests spoke of the wedding planner who'd pulled off the impossible. For thirty years she'd built her reputation, handled the weddings of minor celebrities and business magnates. She'd never once failed to deliver perfection.

Yet here she was, playing second fiddle to Felicity Philips once again.

For the last two hours, she had moved through the banquet room like a general inspecting troops, checking every detail with the precision that had made her reputation. It was nearing noon, and the final touches were falling into place. An ice sculpture was due to arrive within the hour, the band was setting up in the corner, and the official photographers sent by the palace were testing lighting angles.

All perfect and exactly as Felicity specified.

The thought made Elizabeth's jaw clench. She paused beside one of the tables, running her finger along the edge of a bone China plate. How many times had she bid for contracts only to lose them to Felicity? How many times had she heard "We've decided to go with Felicity Philips" delivered with apologetic smiles that did nothing to soften the blow?

The palace had never even considered her for the royal wedding contract. Not once. When word spread through their small industry that a royal wedding was being planned, Elizabeth had prepared her most comprehensive proposal. She'd included references from her highest profile clients, photographs of her most spectacular events, testimonials from satisfied customers who'd paid seven figures for her services.

The palace hadn't even acknowledged her submission.

Instead, they'd gone straight to Primrose Green, and when that fell through, naturally they'd turned to Felicity Philips. Always Felicity Philips.

Elizabeth's phone buzzed with a text from the ice sculpture delivery company. They would arrive in forty-five minutes. She glanced around the ballroom, noting the positions of the various staff members. Her mind began to calculate distances, timing, opportunities.

When the unexpected call from Felicity came it was right after she'd tried to kill her in Scotland. Her failure there still smarted, but in many ways this was better. Had she succeeded in murdering her rival, she may have been awarded the contract in her stead, but it wasn't guaranteed. Taking on the role of third fiddle behind Primrose Green she would get the chance to remove both of her opponents.

Whether dead or blamed for the entire debacle, Felicity and Primrose would be finished in the wedding business, leaving the door open for someone new to assume the top spot.

But how to do that? It took two weeks for her to figure it out which left almost no time for planning, but a few hasty phone calls, a little pretence, and Felicity's unsuspecting nature all aided her to develop a plot that would almost certainly land Elizabeth's rival in jail.

Maybe the charges wouldn't stick, but no one would be looking Elizabeth's way. Her plan was elegant in its simplicity and impossible to trace back to her. The wedding would be ruined, but not catastrophically so. No one would be seriously hurt, but the chaos would be enough to destroy Felicity's reputation.

After all, if Elizabeth couldn't have the triumph of organizing the royal wedding, why should Felicity?

She pulled out her phone and checked the time again. The ice sculpture delivery was getting closer, and she needed to act soon. But first, she needed to clone Felicity's phone. Mercifully, Felicity wasn't the kind of person who always had her phone in her hand. It resided in her handbag most of the time and its absence wouldn't be noticed straight away. Elizabeth wouldn't need it for long, but cloning it was the only way to achieve the final stages of her plan.

Elizabeth made her way back toward the main entrance where she'd last seen Felicity speaking with the hotel manager. As she approached, she could hear Felicity's voice, animated and professional as always.

"Yes, absolutely. The photographer will need access to the terrace for the sunset shots, but not until after the speeches..."

Rounding a corner, Elizabeth was pleased to see Mindy wasn't with her. In fact, she spotted the teenager outside where she was still speaking animatedly into her phone, her free hand gesticulating wildly in the air.

Felicity was still locked in conversation with the hotel manager, going over fine details. Elizabeth waited patiently. The hotel manager was nodding along, clearly hanging on every word.

Felicity's handbag was on the counter, her phone almost certainly inside it. With Felicity's attention on the man to her front, Elizabeth dumped her oversize tote bag down as though she was in a hurry and partially emptied the contents onto the counter. Rooting through it as though searching for something, she used her bag and body as a shield so those around her couldn't see when she placed her hand in Felicity's messenger bag.

Knowing she couldn't afford to root around for more than a second or so, she felt relief flood her body when the first thing she touched was obviously a phone. Elizabeth palmed it, hiding the device with her flesh when she moved it from one bag to the other.

Muttering under her breath, Elizabeth stuffed all her things back into her bag, making enough noise to be sure people were glancing her way when she turned around. Hooking her tote back onto a shoulder, she held a box of tampons discretely, but not invisibly in her left hand.

"Excuse me," she interrupted with an apologetic smile. "I'm so sorry to interrupt, but there's a small issue with the band's setup that needs your attention."

Felicity's expression changed, instantly alert. "What kind of issue?"

"Nothing serious, but they're asking about the electrical requirements for their equipment. Something about the venue's power supply." Elizabeth gestured toward the ballroom. "It'll just take a moment. Sorry, I know I'm supposed to be heading off all the issues at this end of the event, but I've been trying to get to a restroom for more than an hour …" She dropped her eyes, ever so discretely, to her left hand.

Vince glanced and looked away, his predictable squeamishness a joy for Elizabeth to behold.

Felicity waved her into silence. "Yes, of course. Sorry. It's a busy day. You're doing an amazing job, Liz. Let me deal with this one."

"I'll be right back," Felicity told the hotel manager, already moving toward the ballroom.

Vince followed, shadowing Elizabeth to grab Felicity's handbag from the counter when she walked away without it.

The hotel manager went with them, leaving Elizabeth alone. Her heart was beating hard, but the hardest part of the plan was over. Well, probably the hardest part. She had to make sure Felicity got her phone back. She could have no idea what Elizabeth had done.

Speed walking to the nearest ladies' room, she dumped the tampons back into her bag and took out Felicity's phone. She popped out the sim card and carefully placed it into the sim card reader she bought online for loose change. To her mind the technology ought to be illegal, but it wasn't and right now she was glad for that.

The process of cloning the sim card took less than a minute. Once complete, she plugged the reader into Felicity's phone where it instantly retrieved an authentication code. The original sim card went back into Felicity's phone, the clone sim card went into the duplicate phone she had bought from a second-hand electronics shop, and the process was complete. She had practiced with her own phone multiple times because this part of the plan was so critical. It had always worked, yet even sure the phone would operate as a clone, indistinguishable from the original, her strategy was not without potential pitfalls.

Tongue darting out to wet her lips, Elizabeth put everything away except the cloned copy of Felicity's phone. Using it, she composed a message.

'*Primrose, urgent change of plan. Need you to leave the cathedral immediately and get to the hotel. Ice sculpture delivery arriving in thirty minutes. You need to sign for it personally and ensure it goes straight to the kitchen freezer. Critical that this is done properly. Will explain later. F*'

Elizabeth hit send and waited for the response, holding her breath until the little dots appeared to show Primrose was typing. Sighing with relief that Primrose hadn't phoned instead, she waited for the text to arrive.

'*What about Elizabeth? She's at the reception, Felicity. I'm up to my eyeballs at the cathedral and the guests are set to begin arriving an hour from now!*'

'*I wouldn't ask if it wasn't urgent. You can be back there in half an hour.*'

Elizabeth could imagine Primrose grumbling under her breath. The statuesque blonde was known for her use of colourful language when things didn't go her way. She would do it though. They both agreed to positions beneath Felicity and that meant following her instructions.

The message that came back started with an expletive, but Primrose was going to do it, and the seed was sewn.

Message string deleted, she switched the phone to silent and dropped it back into her handbag hidden and breathed a sigh of relief. The hard part was over. Now all she had to do was dump Felicity's phone where she wound find it. It felt like an unnecessary precaution, but for good measure Elizabeth wiped it down to remove her prints. Returning to the hotel reception area, she placed the phone on the floor next to the counter.

It would be found and returned to the owner who would naturally assume she dropped it.

With Felicity on a wild goose chase about the band's electricity requirements, Elizabeth left the reception venue, walked promptly to the police cordon at the entrance and across the road to a taxi that had been waiting with the meter running for almost half an hour.

"I was just about to give up on you," the cabbie grumbled.

"I'll make it worth your while," she offered a smile that didn't touch her eyes and took out her purse. "I won't need long at the cathedral. Maybe five minutes and then back here as fast as you can. Understood?"

The cabbie was already pulling into the light traffic but flicked his eyes to the rear-view.

"There and back. Got it." He reached out his left arm to tap the meter. It already showed thirty pounds. Not that he was complaining. It wasn't every day he got paid to sit around doing nothing. The woman, whoever she was, said she might need him all day, and had paid him two hundred up front as a retainer.

Hoping she wouldn't be missed and fervently praying she wouldn't be spotted returning to the reception venue, Elizabeth sat on her hands so she wouldn't chew her fingernails.

It was all going according to plan and Felicity had no idea.

Chapter 10 – Albert and Rex

The Rolls-Royce sent by the palace was without question or qualification the most comfortable car Albert had ever ridden in. The leather seats were buttery soft, and the ride so smooth he could barely tell they were moving. Rex sat beside him on the seat, his tartan waistcoat perfectly pressed and his bow tie sitting at a jaunty angle.

"You look very distinguished, my friend," Albert said, adjusting Rex's collar. "Though I suspect you'd rather be chasing squirrels than attending a wedding, royal or otherwise."

Rex tilted his head at the use of the word 'squirrel'. Expecting the old man to tell him where to look, Rex gave up after a second and stood up to look out the window. If there were squirrels outside where he couldn't get to them, he was still duty bound to bark.

The chauffeur, a smartly dressed man who'd introduced himself simply as Davies, caught Albert's eye in the rearview mirror.

Albert was already trying to fold Rex's back legs so his dog would sit again. He recognised his error, but couldn't now say, "Sorry Rex, there is no squirrel," because that would involve employing the word again.

"Sit, Rex," he coached, using one hand to force the dog's back end down.

Once Rex settled, the driver said, "We'll be arriving in approximately five minutes, Sir Albert. The security checkpoint is quite thorough, I'm afraid, but your documentation is all in order."

Albert nodded. He wasn't excited about the wedding or about rubbing shoulders with celebrities or politicians. In fact, there was a long list of things he would rather spend his day doing and it included polishing his late wife's collections of teaspoons, vacuuming under the bed, alphabetising the spice rack, and a dozen other mundane household chores. However, he imagined the food would be good, and he hoped he might get to speak to the King again. They were of a similar age and Albert imagined they would find common ground about which to chat.

Rex laid his chin on Albert's right thigh. To him the car was just another car. He knew they were going out for the day, but his understanding ended there. His human wore an unusual outfit, but not one so outlandish Rex felt a need to comment. Closing his eyes, he happily dozed.

The car slowed as they approached the first checkpoint. Albert could see crowds of onlookers pressed against the barriers, cameras flashing as each vehicle passed. Police officers in high-visibility jackets directed traffic with practiced efficiency.

Gliding to a stop Davies powered down the window to present their credentials.

The policeman checked their documents against a tablet, his eyes moving between the screen and Albert's face. Content, he nodded and waved them through.

The second checkpoint was more intensive. Albert and Rex were asked to step out of the car while security personnel checked their identification again and ran a metal detector over them both. Rex submitted to the procedure with dignified patience, though Albert could tell he was getting restless.

"Almost there, old boy," Albert whispered.

Cleared to proceed, they joined a queue of similar cars delivering guests to the cathedral. He was among the first to arrive, the guests tiered so kings and heads of state would not be kept hanging around. The VIPs would be the last to arrive, but having a little time to kill wasn't a problem for Albert. For a start it would give him time to walk Rex.

Davies edged forward and the ancient stones of Canterbury Cathedral soared above them, magnificent in the afternoon sunlight. The streets and everything around them were spotless and without the crowds, the setting possessed a serene quality. If he looked in the right direction, there was nothing but the cathedral. To the right of the entrance, the Royal Marines Band in their full dress uniform played a selection of rousing tunes. An honour guard from the Coldstream Guards waited to formally salute heads of state and other dignitaries when they arrived.

Across the grass on the opposite side to the honour guard, a contingent of press with cameras and microphones recorded those arriving. With their backs to the line of guests making their way toward the cathedral, the reporters wore suits or dresses as they talked to the folks in the studio or were perhaps being beamed directly into homes.

Albert expected as much.

If he turned to look the other way, there were police officers in abundance. Sniffer dogs, an armed response unit, tactical response vans and a command unit ... they were taking the security aspect seriously, as well they ought.

Stepping out of the car when a doorman stepped forward to open it, Albert saw the cameras swing towards his position.

"If you'd like to make your way to the main entrance, Sir Albert," Davies said, "someone will be there to escort you to your seat."

Albert thanked the chauffeur and set off down the stone path with Rex at his side.

Rex lifted his nose to sniff the air. He had only the most rudimentary idea of what was going on. Humans were doing human things and that generally confused him, but it didn't matter. He was out with his human and that meant he was having a good time.

Drawing in deeply, he sampled the air, testing it and analysing that which he found. He did the same everywhere he went, even when the location was familiar. The air told him almost everything he needed to know about the people around him, their intentions, their habits ...

Rex stopped moving. They were ambling along the path following the other humans making their way into a huge building when he froze, his lead going taut when Albert took his next step.

Albert gave the lead a gentle tug. "Come along, Rex."

Rex heard his human speaking but dialled him out to focus everything on a faint wisp of scent. It was there one moment but gone in an instant. Recognisable but requiring deeper examination before he could be certain.

The odour that halted his paws and stilled his tail was one he associated with a person he needed to bite. He didn't have a name for the individual, but he knew where they had met. It was in the Cornish coastal town of Looe, not that Rex knew the name for it or could find it on a map, but his canine brain could picture both the man and the last time he'd seen him.

But was it really his scent? Or just one that was very similar.

Beginning to feel embarrassed, Albert gave Rex's lead a more convincing tug. The next car had pulled to a halt at the kerb and the occupants were about to get out. He didn't know who they were but didn't want to cause a scene by holding up the line of people heading for the cathedral.

Hissing insistently, Albert bent at the waist so he wouldn't be heard but the words in his head never got to leave his mouth. They were drowned out by raucous barking.

That didn't come from Rex.

The sound came from behind them on the other side of the car depositing the latest guests on the path to the cathedral.

Rising back to his full height, Albert muttered, "What the devil?" Rex had unfrozen and was spinning around to face the noise.

From the line of cops on the grass near the mobile command unit, one officer was having, shall we say, some difficulty with his canine. The dog was tethered to his handler via a strap leading to his harness. It sat between his shoulder blades, but right now the dog in question was bucking backwards, trying with all his might to go somewhere while his handler fought to bring him back under control.

Rex took a pace forward, his ears up, his tail straight. Was it? Was it really?

Albert looked at his dog and saw how interested Rex was. "What's going on, boy?" he asked.

THE ROYAL WEDDING

The unruly police canine refused to obey the commands being thrown his way with increasing volume. Thrashing to the left, he spun around to face the road and tried to run. When that didn't work, he reversed direction without warning, ducked his head, and ran between his handler's legs.

Albert wasn't the only one who cringed and winced when the officer performed a neat somersault. His arms went through his legs, followed by his head and the rest was a simple case of physics. He landed hard on his back, his grip on the dog finally conceding.

Suddenly free, the dog wasted no time putting distance between himself and the half dozen officers all lunging to stop his escape. He pelted across the grass, crossed the road in two bounds, and rounded the back of the car at the kerb with his mouth open and his tongue lolling like a soggy party blower.

"*Rex!*" he barked. "*Rex! Rex! Rex! Rex!*"

Scarcely able to believe his eyes, Albert said, "My goodness, is that ..."

Rex barked, "*Eric!*"

The two dogs greeted each other with equal excitement, spinning around each other as they babbled how surprised they each were to see the other.

"*I've learned so much since I qualified!*" said Eric.

"*Yes, I remember my first days on the job,*" said Rex. "*But you wouldn't believe the adventures I've been having with my human. I fought a panther a few moons ago.*"

"*A panther? That's amazing. I've been sniffing for explosives. It's so exciting. My handler's great, too.*"

At mention of his handler, Eric thought to look around. The man was still on his back and had other officers kneeling at his side.

"*Oops,*" said Rex. "*I think he might be hurt.*"

"*Yeah. I guess I'd better go back and check on him. I just… when I smelled you, I had to say hello.*"

"*I'm glad you did.*" Rex thought about mentioning the scent he'd detected right before Eric made his grand entrance, but it wasn't one he could easily describe and there was no trace of it now.

Eric looked up at Albert when the old man stroked the fur around his head.

"You sure grew up big," Albert remarked. "You're almost as big as Rex."

Eric nuzzled Rex's human's hand, but the cops were coming to collect him, so he said goodbye and made his way back to them.

The incident with the police dog had drawn the attention of everyone in front of the cathedral, including the TV crews and the reporters. Albert could hear his name being said and hoped no one would quiz him about it. He wanted to remain in the background.

There were so many celebrities and VIPs on their way, he felt sure the press would soon forget he was even there, but getting Rex facing the right way and starting toward the cathedral once more, a lone figure caught his attention.

A man in palace livery was moving away from the cathedral, walking quickly but not quite running. There was something about his posture, the way he held his head, that struck Albert as familiar. He spotted him simply because he was the one person doing what no one else was.

All around them in every direction, eyes were on him. The camera crews were aimed his way, the reporters jabbering to the folks at home. The guests ahead of him on the path leading into the cathedral had all turned around to watch the commotion. A sea of faces was aimed his way.

And then there was that guy, his footsteps quick as he hurried away, but not so fast he was running. To many it might look like he'd been caught short and had to find a restroom. To Albert it appeared as though he was trying to get away.

And the man confirmed it with a hasty backwards glance to check if he'd been spotted.

Albert saw his face and his blood ran cold. He sucked in a breath, filling his lungs so he could yell, "Cody Williams!"

His bellow filled the air, startling those around him.

Rex's eyes were still on Eric, the pup who was no longer any such thing. The trained police dog had just made it back to his handler, but Albert's cry had his attention too.

Albert started forward, aiming his right arm at Cody's back.

"Somebody stop that man!" he commanded, but the instruction came too late.

Walking across the face of the cathedral and aiming for an adjacent building, Cody stepped through a door and was lost to sight.

The reporters were going nuts, their calm demeanour dropped as they switched from celebrity spotting to 'live at the scene' coverage.

Tethered by his lead, Rex nevertheless came to Albert's side. He could tell from his human's stress levels that there was something distinctly amiss. Then they were moving, the old man setting off across the grass with determined strides.

Or he would have been had palace security not swooped.

Three burly men and a woman, all in dark suits, hustled to intercept him.

Speaking in hushed but insistent tones, one said, "Sir, please continue into the cathedral. We have a lot of guests arriving and no time for theatrics."

"Theatrics?" Albert growled. "I just saw Cody Williams. Do you know who that is?"

Ignoring the question, the man attempted to guide Albert back onto the path. His colleagues blocked the way Albert wanted to go, herding him as they tried to keep the line moving.

"There, man! He just went that way."

Heads turned but there was nothing to see but a closed door.

"Let's not make a scene now, Sir. You can explain what is bothering you once we are inside."

Hearing laboured breathing and the sound of a dog straining, Albert turned his head to find Eric dragging his handler across the grass. The police officer was a big man, but Eric had his head down and the advantage of momentum.

"*What's going on?*" Eric asked between gasps of breath.

Rex kept his eyes forward, aimed at a spot through the security guards' legs. "*There's someone here. I caught his scent earlier. He's a killer.*"

Frustrated, Albert pushed his luck, dodging around an arm intended to guide him in the right direction. He ducked and twisted to get through them, all eyes and TV cameras once again aimed his way.

"You've got to listen to me," he growled, fighting to make his voice sound calm and in control so they would know he wasn't having some kind of old age episode. "There is a man here who intends harm to the royal family."

THE ROYAL WEDDING

"Sir, you can tell us about what you think you saw once we are inside the cathedral. Not before. This is all being televised."

"What I think I saw?" Albert repeated. There was no way through them and more security were heading his way. It dictated a change in strategy.

Angling his shoes back toward the path, Albert allowed the security guards to think he was complying. A wry grin creased his face when he mumbled, "Televise this." He couldn't unclip Rex's lead without them seeing what he was going to do. However, Rex was alert and if there was one thing he knew about his dog, it was how intuitive Rex could be.

Dropping the lead, he said, "Rex, sic' im!"

The bewildered security guards couldn't have stopped the German Shepherd if they'd received a written note explaining what he was going to do a week before the event. Suddenly released, Rex bunched his muscles and sprang forward, weaving through legs on his way across the grass.

Seeing his friend go, Eric followed. His handler, out of breath, still bruised from being flipped, but finally back in control now that his canine had reached Rex and stopped, got no warning. One moment he was sucking in some air and about to make Eric return to the rank of police dogs lined up fifty yards away, the next his dog was running.

The jolt ripped him off his feet, his grip strong enough to make his arms follow Eric when he ran. Unfortunately, his body followed his arms, and his legs followed his body, everything exiting 'stage left' so he hung in the air like a human flag for a half second before crashing to the ground.

He ate grass and his hands opened. Looking up, he got to see Eric's tail vanishing from sight a yard and a half behind the old man's dog. That his colleagues were laughing at his expense was in no question. He could hear them. Not for the first time, Eric's handler gave serious thought to an alternate career as a plumber.

Chapter 11 – Patricia

Barbie's eyes widened. "What was that?"

Patricia and her friends all heard the commotion. Knowing they couldn't be everywhere, Patricia had chosen to position her team with a view over the street where the guests were now arriving. The first car appeared less than twenty minutes ago, swiftly followed by the next until a steady, but controlled, stream of them deposited wedding guests at the kerb.

They occupied a room on the second floor of the library which sat adjacent to the cathedral. It provided an uninterrupted view over everything happening outside; all the better to observe. There still wasn't the slightest hint of anything untoward happening and Patricia hoped that would continue. Not that she was about to dismiss Felicity's concerns, but if the man she suspected of plotting against the royal family was involved, he was hiding it well. Hours of research showed Barbie only the vaguest correlation between Lord Edward Chamberlain's movements and those of the recently deceased royals.

That could mean he was particularly wily, but Patricia doubted he would strike at the wedding, anyway. It was too public.

However, watching guests arrive, she found herself smiling when Rex bounded from the backseat of a Rolls Royce followed by none other than her old friend Albert Smith. Patricia continued to marvel that both she and Albert hailed from the same small village in rural Kent. There was nothing notable about East Malling, so why was it that two sleuths who found themselves on the front pages of the world's newspapers grew up in the same place? Albert was twenty-five years her senior, but even so, it seemed like a surprising coincidence.

To answer Barbie's question, Patricia said, "There's something going on with Albert and Rex."

Barbie had been hunched over her laptop, still trying to find something about the recent royal deaths that might indicate ... well, anything, but at the mention of Albert and Rex, she bounced to her feet.

"Are they okay?" she asked.

Jermaine, a silent sentinel at Patricia's side, pointed to the source of the commotion. A police dog had broken away from the pack to greet Rex.

"Looks like the dogs know each other," Patricia remarked, her eyes continuing to rove the grounds. Chance, more than anything else, caused her eyes to be facing the right direction to see a person in royal household livery moving against the tide of humanity. Unlike everyone else in sight, he was moving away from Albert Smith and the commotion with the dogs.

It made her pulse twitch, and the back of her skull gave a little itch. She stopped breathing, just for a moment as she focused on the man. He wasn't hurrying to get away, but at the same time his pace had purpose. She glanced back to Albert, expecting to see the poor man struggling to calm and separate the dogs.

Without warning, Patricia went from motionless to dead sprint, the senior member of the team leaving her younger friends in her dust when she ran for the door.

Barbie and Jermaine had barely time to react before she was through it and into the corridor outside.

A bark of, "Come on!" came just as they were getting their feet pointed in the right direction.

Chapter 12 – Buster and Amber

Buster's head snapped up and a half second later he was on his paws.

"*That was Rex*," he announced. Needlessly, it turned out, for Amber had identified the German Shepherd's bark for herself.

Stuck in Felicity's assigned office without so much as a television for entertainment, they had both found comfy spots and embraced the opportunity to sleep. Until raucous barking interrupted their dreams.

"*And another dog*," Amber remarked, tilting her head to the left as she strained to hear what was being said.

Buster frowned with concentration. "I don't know who that is, but Rex knows him." His nose faced the windows above the desk. He wanted to get a better look outside but couldn't see a way to climb up. If the chair was pushed back …

He went around under the desk to nudge it with his head.

Meanwhile, Amber jumped down from her lofty position nestled between folders on a bookshelf – height helped when one's aim was to avoid the vicinity of Buster's gas. Landing on the desk, she could see Rex and his human. They were with a second dog, another German Shepherd, this one wearing a police dog vest.

Buster got the chair far enough away from the desk that he could jump up onto it, but found the stupid casters attached to its base meant it moved every time he put his front paws up. It was getting farther and farther away from the desk and now he needed to reposition it.

"*There's something going on,*" said Amber, her tone betraying a sense of curiosity.

Buster stopped what he was doing. "*What? What's going on? Is there danger?*"

Amber rolled her eyes. "*Why would there be danger, Buster? Not every situation requires you to transform into Devil Dog.*" It was bad enough that she had to live with a dog. Had Buster been a chihuahua she could beat up or a giant dog she could feel good about dominating, it would have been better. Not much, but a little at least. But, no, she was shackled with a fat doofus of a bulldog who to top it all off harboured a daft superhero fantasy.

She was about to hit him with a drab remark when she stopped.

"*Oh, hold on. I think there might be something going on, actually.*"

"*Where?*" Buster jumped up at the desk. He could get his front paws on it, but it was too high to jump onto. He just wasn't built for aerial manoeuvres. "*What's going on, Amber?*"

"*Shhh. Rex's human is getting excited about something. There are some people in suits around him. I don't think they like all the attention he's getting.*"

Desperate to see, Buster went back to the office chair. He had to swivel the seat around until it was lined up with the desk and then push the whole thing with his head. When it bumped against the desk and stopped, he backed up a few feet, took a run up and leapt. He stuck the landing. Just about. His face smacked into the back of the chair, creating a cause-and-effect reaction when his inertia bounced the chair back into the middle of the room.

Amber took her eyes off the action unfolding outside when Buster employed language she wasn't used to hearing.

At least Buster was at a height where he could see now. What he saw was Rex taking off and the second dog flooring his handler when he went with him.

Buster swore again. "*This is it, Amber. This is what Felicity has been so worried about. Rex knows something is amiss and he's going to try to tackle it.*"

Amber chewed on her bottom lip. Normally, this would be the perfect time to lift a paw so she could demonstrate her absolute nonchalance and indifference by starting to preen. Annoyingly, though, Buster wasn't wrong. She loved Felicity, even though she refused to have Buster put to sleep, and the woman had been stressed of late. That impacted Amber in more ways than she cared to list, so fixing the situation held merit.

She dropped her eyes to the window. It was closed but it wasn't locked. She nudged it with her head, opening it a crack.

"*Hey! Don't go without me!*" wailed Buster. He stood on all four paws in the centre of the seat cushion. The chair continued to slowly rotate.

Amber almost ignored him, but truthfully the dog had his uses. Moving fast, she jumped down from the desk, ran around to the other side of the chair and gave it a nudge. It didn't have to go far, and a few inches of travel were all Buster needed to believe he could jump the rest of the way.

He couldn't.

Landing half on half off the desk, his back end threatened to drag the rest of him back to the floor.

"*Oh, for heaven's sake, Buster.*" Amber leapt nimbly back to the surface of the desk and sauntered over to the window, making sure to give Buster the full view of her derriere because he saw it as an insult.

Pushing it open a few more inches, she slid out and dropped to the ground. "*Catch up if you can, mutt.*"

Muttering some choice words, Buster finally hooked the edge of the desk with a claw from his right back leg. Huffing and puffing, he scrambled on to the surface, ran across the desk to hit the window with his skull and wailed with fright when he discovered the drop to the ground outside was twice the height of inside.

Chapter 13 – Cody

He couldn't believe it. It was his own fault, of course. He knew Albert was on the guest list. He should have found a reason to sneak away earlier. Now the old goat had spotted him and if he didn't act quickly his entire plan, months of preparation and toil, would be for nothing.

He could ditch the knife; if they found him with it there would be no denying that his actions were born of criminal, murderous intent. But darting through the door to get away, he chose to keep it. Until he knew he was sunk, he was going to carry on as though he wasn't.

Gershwin said the old man was forced to back down at Buckingham Palace when he came to be knighted. Albert Smith saw and recognised Cody, but when he pulled the police into helping him search, the man they found was Gershwin.

On that occasion, blind luck helped Cody get away. Maybe this time they could engineer it. If Albert Smith swore he'd seen Cody Williams only to once again point the finger at Gershwin George … well, it would discredit him and make him look like an old fool.

The door had a lock on the inside. Cody threw it. The dogs wouldn't be able to follow anyway, but now any humans who chose to be curious would have to find a way around, too. Hurrying along the corridor, he pulled out his phone and made a call.

Gershwin answered, "Cody? I thought you said there was to be no contact today until you give the go command."

"Things change," Cody grumbled. "I've been made. That old fool is here."

"Albert Smith?"

"The very same and he has his dog with him. He's made a big scene and sooner or later someone is going to come looking for me. I need them to find you."

"Just like at the palace?"

"Exactly like that only this time when Albert Smith finds you, I want you to lean into the idea that he has dementia. He's seeing ghosts. You got that? He sees you and thinks it's me because he's a hundred years old and his brain is addled."

"Got it. Where are you?"

"South wing, heading for the carpark at the back of the cathedral. The one that's empty. I'm going to disguise myself so head to the south wing and let them catch you."

Gershwin confirmed he understood his role. This wasn't going to stop them. It wouldn't even delay them.

The king wasn't due for another hour. They had time.

Chapter 14 – Albert Smith

There simply wasn't any arguing with the security people. They were supremely ticked off that he'd let his dog go, but that was a problem to tackle once they had the old man somewhere less public. They didn't dare secure him or manhandle him, not with the cameras rolling and so many onlookers, but that was the only reason.

Communicating via their radios, they sent colleagues to find the dogs. One of them was a police canine and the boys in blue, including the dog's rather shame-faced handler, were on the case already.

Albert had watched Rex bolt across the grass like a streak of lightning, Eric hot on his heels, before accepting defeat. He let the security guys escort him back to the path. He'd only managed to get a few yards from it after all.

"Do any of you know Detective Inspector Cassie Munroe? She knows me. DI Munroe is going to want to hear that Cody Williams is here."

"Let's just get you inside, Sir Albert." The voice belonged to the same man who'd spoken every time so far. Clearly the team leader, he was six feet two inches tall and filled his suit jacket with more than the average amount of muscle.

"Are you listening at all? You have a known anti-royalist activist on the grounds. He's clearly not an official palace employee. Shouldn't you all be on your radios attempting to coordinate a search?"

This time no one bothered to reply at all.

Feeling the skin above his eyes bunching where his frustration created a frown of epic proportions, Albert hurried to the cathedral. If they weren't going to listen until he got inside, then that was where he was going.

He wanted to find DI Munroe. At least he could expect her to be reasonable. He hoped. Now that he thought about it, he could recall how she did her best not to make it sound like she questioned his mental acuity while at the same time making it clear she was thinking it.

Would she listen to him now?

Behind him, the flow of cars bringing low tier guests continued and the reporters had returned to the less exciting task of identifying each VIP as they arrived. The Royal Marines Band continued to play, and the scene was returning to normal.

Continuing forward, but twisting from the waist to see, he looked for Rex and Eric. They were on the loose and if Albert knew his dog, he wouldn't stop until he found the man he wanted.

Chapter 15 – Rex and Eric

The vague hint of scent he caught had been Cody's. Rex liked how accurate his nose could be when he needed it. Having confirmed it, finding where he'd been and following him was easy, not least because his human pointed him out.

The trail led to a locked door in the library where it occupied a spot adjacent to the cathedral. To their right, the police command unit plus a body of both officers and dogs all looked their way. Some were moving to intercept. Behind Rex and Eric, some of the palace security guards in their dark suits were likewise moving in.

The cathedral lay to their left. If they stayed where they were they would be rounded up in no time, but the locked door meant they couldn't go forward.

Setting off at a run, Rex barked, "*Time to look for another way in!*"

"Eric!" Eric's handler watched his dog race to the end of the building and vanish around it. He was out of breath, embarrassed that his canine partner had got away from him, and swearing vengeance in his head. Not only was there going to be untold grief from his boss, but if he managed to keep his job the rest of the guys and girls on the team would rib him mercilessly for the rest of his career.

It wasn't as if he could transfer to a new unit in another part of the country. He'd lost his dog on television at the biggest public spectacle of the year. He could already hear the nicknames that would come his way: Snoopless Dogg, The Ruffless Ranger, Detective Paw Patrol ... When he caught Eric he was going to recommend the dog visit the vet to have his trousers lightened.

Stopping to catch his breath for a second, he jumped out of his skin when a cat ran past.

"What the ..."

"*Dun, dun, DAH!*"

Buster wasn't sure who the cop was, but he'd been chasing Rex and looked anything but happy, so he wiped him out for good measure. Employing a method he liked to call catflapping, he hit Eric's handler with his skull roughly four inches above his left ankle. In deference to his uniform and the possibility that he was a good guy, Buster only hit him with a glancing blow, yet it was enough to send the man back to the grass for the third time in ten minutes.

This time he chose to stay there.

Leaving the humans in their wake, Rex ran along the short side of the building, looking for a new way in. The wall was completely devoid of doors and the windows were all closed. He ran on with Eric right by his side until he heard a familiar voice.

He didn't slow his pace but looked back over his shoulder to check he wasn't going mad. Sure enough, Buster the bulldog was haring along behind him and to his great surprise Amber the cat was leading the way.

"*Eric, slow up a moment,*" puffed Rex.

The dogs dropped to cruising pace and then stopped. They could tell the humans were still coming for them, but they had a little time.

"*Hey, Rex!*" barked Buster.

Eric twitched an eyebrow. "*You know these guys?*"

"*Yeah. We met a while back. Buster's really funny.*"

"*What about the cat?*"

"*Amber? Well, she's a cat,*" Rex explained, knowing that was enough to sum up her entire personality.

Amber got to the German Shepherds first, only to realise she then didn't know what to do. A cat doesn't run to greet a dog. A cat pretends the dog isn't there and will only acknowledge its existence if the cat deems there to be a reason to do so.

Rex said, "*Hello, Amber.*"

Annoyed, because now she had to be polite, Amber said, "*Hello, Rex.*"

Buster arrived at their location. Skidding to a stop rather than slow down first, he used his butt as a brake, dragging it across the grass like an anchor.

"*Hey, is this exciting or what? We saw your human pointing and shouting and then you both took off. Were you chasing someone? Who's this guy?*"

The cops rounded the side of the building, spotted the animals and started to shout.

Rex started to move again. "*This is Eric. He's a police dog. We need to move. I'm tracking a man. Or rather I will be if I can pick up his scent again. We need to find a way into this building.*"

Racing to get ahead, Amber said, "*We just left this building and we know how to get back in. Follow me!*"

Chapter 16 – Patricia

Patricia leapt from five steps up, landing two-footed in the hallway on the ground floor and bouncing off the wall to arrest her forward motion. Jermaine and Barbie were ahead of her, their youthfulness augmented by natural athleticism ensuring they overtook her with ease once they knew where they were going.

The glimpse she caught of the man heading into the building wasn't enough to identify him. Not when there were so many men of a similar age all wearing the same uniform. They had no right to accost or question anyone, which wasn't to say they wouldn't do so, but no one wanted to overstep their bounds and upset the people at the palace. The idea was to help Felicity, not embarrass her.

With that in mind, they kept their eyes open for anyone acting suspiciously and hurried through the building to the point where they saw the man enter. Naturally, there was no sign of him. Patricia threw open the door she saw him enter through and looked outside. So far as she knew, it wasn't common knowledge that she was in the country. Certainly, she hadn't advertised it, but that would all change the moment the press spotted her.

THE ROYAL WEDDING

On the grass a few yards to her front, a police officer was being attended to by a duo of paramedics. He didn't appear to have suffered any terrible wounds. In fact, he was rubbing his left shin as one might if a child had kicked it. Patricia gave him no further thought.

"Do we search the building?" Barbie asked.

Patricia shook her head. "We wouldn't know what we were searching for. I think we should find Albert. He will be able to tell us what is going on."

Barbie moved toward the door, her intention to exit through it obvious. Patricia stopped her by closing it.

"I think we should stay out of sight. There are cameras crews to the left as we exit and if we go out this way we'll be trying to enter the cathedral by the front door along with the official wedding guests."

"But we have passes to get us in," Barbie pointed out.

Patricia started back along the hallway, heading back the way they had come. "That's because we are here as part of the official wedding planner's team. That means we remain in the background."

Leading Barbie and Jermaine out through the front door on the other side of the building, away from the cathedral and all that was happening there, they narrowly missed the animals who had snuck in less than ten seconds earlier.

They were confronted by a wall of running security guards and police officers, all a little out of breath and looking stressed.

"Did you see some dogs and a cat come this way?" one asked.

Six eyebrows rose as Patricia and her friends attempted to make sense of the question.

Seeing their blank looks, the cops and palace security guards ran on. The doors to the building were closed, Jermaine having shut them on his way out. That clearly meant the animals couldn't be inside, so they ran onwards, hoping to catch the dogs and cat when they finally slowed down.

Setting off again, bemused by the odd incident, Patricia paused to look at someone getting into a taxi. They were on the other side of the fence around the grounds and beyond the police cordon. The door closed before she could get a proper look but she could have sworn she'd just seen Felicity's assistant, Elizabeth Keats. Patricia thought Elizabeth was working solely at the reception venue but that clearly wasn't the case.

Shrugging, she dismissed it as unimportant. Felicity would have so many plates spinning today it was no surprise her team was all over the place.

Chapter 17 – Albert

Inside the cathedral, Albert allowed himself a moment to be filled with awe. He'd visited the cathedral before, but on a trip with his kids in the seventies. All he could really remember of the day was that they ate ice creams and basked in the sunshine for it had been a hot day.

The outside of Canterbury Cathedral is a masterpiece of gothic architecture and filled with ornate details. Built of stone with pointed arches, ribbed vaults, and towering stained-glass windows that seem to whisper medieval gossip, its three main towers pierce the sky. However, it's when a person steps inside that they get the full treatment. Vaulted ceilings soared so high it made Albert question if clouds ever passed through them. Light coming through the stained glass seemed to take on an ethereal quality. Albert imagined that were he to climb up into the rafters it might even feel different against his skin.

Always a church goer, mostly because Petunia made him, Albert wasn't a deeply religious man, yet the ancient church inspired, nay demanded, a sense of reverence. Which was a shame really because now they were out of sight, he rounded on the security guards and tore into them.

"No more excuses. I want to speak with a senior police officer right now. You have a wanted murderer walking about the grounds wearing palace livery and I'm not going to be the one caught napping when he strikes."

It wasn't necessarily intended as a threat, but that was how it was received.

The spokesperson for the group – Albert had barely heard the others murmur a word in the last five minutes – narrowed his eyes.

"Sir Albert, this is not the time or the place to be issuing ultimatums. I will convey your request to the authorities on site, but …"

"Jane!" Albert waved his hand in the air and called, breaking the quiet, reflective tone of the cathedral and caused several dozen heads to turn.

The ushers were filling in the pews from the back, the procession of cars arriving timed to give them the lower-tier guests first. The King and Queen would be almost the very last to arrive. Only the bride would come after.

Albert and the guards around him were just to the right of the entrance, tucked behind a pillar where they could discuss his actions discreetly. Except the old man wasn't being discreet.

"Jane!" he called again when the person he wanted looked around. The tall, willowy blonde woman had just entered the cathedral from what he assumed to be a vestry. Whatever it was, the room adjoined the church.

She spotted the person calling her name, raised her hand to indicate she'd seen him, and paused in the doorway to speak to someone unseen behind her.

A moment later, Detective Inspector Cassie Munroe appeared alongside her. Like the previous time Albert saw her, she wore a smart business suit; the kind that costs a week's wages and has to be tailored from fine cloth. For practicality, its lower half was trousers not a skirt, and her shoes were a low heel with a buckle to make them easier to run in should the need arise. Her hair was tied and pinned leaving a short fringe at the front and she wore minimal makeup and jewellery.

In contrast, Jane wore plenty of makeup. Albert knew that was partially to hide the five o'clock shadow that would eventually appear. Her dress, a floating swirl of peach and tropical colours, did a good job of hiding her masculine nature and her blonde hair did the rest. A choker around her neck hid the Adam's apple.

Albert turned sideways, slipping between two of the palace security guards. "Don't mind me. I'm just going to speak with the senior police officer." He didn't bother to look back to see their expressions. He had no time for apologies or niceties. If Cody was here, then something was about to happen, and he wasn't going to allow that to come to pass. Not if he could help it.

"Sir Albert," said Cassie by way of greeting.

Albert cringed. "Just Albert if you please. There's neither time nor need for such formalities."

"I just heard there is a dog on the loose." Cassie cast her eyes down to the empty space around Albert's feet.

"Yes, it's Rex," he confirmed. "Well, Rex and a police dog called Eric. That they are loose is the least of your worries. In fact, if we all get lucky, they'll solve the problem before the rest of us get a chance."

"What problem?" prompted Jane.

"Cody Williams is here." Albert delivered the statement flatly and waited for DI Munroe to react.

She could have said, "Are you sure this time?" or sighed while saying, "Again, Sir Albert?" but she said neither of those things. Instead, she took Albert's elbow to guide him back into the vestry.

"Where did you see him?"

That she took him seriously without the slightest hesitation filled Albert with hope.

"I had just arrived, and he must have seen me because I spotted him walking away. He was dressed in palace livery. Just like last time there is no question in my mind that it was him. I'm still not convinced that Gershwin character was as innocent as he made out. Cody walked over to whatever that building next to the cathedral is and vanished through a door. I tried to follow but the security team stopped me. They made me come in here, but I sent Rex. As I said a moment ago, if we get lucky, he'll find Cody long before we do."

Jane asked, "What will he do if he does?"

Albert offered a grim smile. "Rex tends to bite people he knows are up to no good."

Chapter 18 – Cody

Cody had no idea there were animals searching for him. Nor did he know Rex had stopped to have the other dogs sniff the door where Cody had touched it. They all had his scent now. Even the cat, whose nose wasn't nearly as sharp at the dogs' but would do the trick in a pinch.

Impatient, Cody checked his watch. He'd called Gershwin almost fifteen minutes ago. Where the heck was he? Guests filled the path leading to the cathedral and their VIPness was increasing with each carload. *David* and *Victoria Beckham* had been and gone, so too members of the bride's favourite band, *Coldplay*. The sports stars and TV personalities were all inside the cathedral and now they were onto heads of state from around the commonwealth. Soon it would be the final tier and that would end with the King.

They had to be ready.

His phone buzzed silently with an incoming message. *'I'm here. Where are you?'*

Cody opened the door a crack and looked out. He'd found an office to hide in, picking one with a window facing the carpark and the street. If he could hear people searching the building looking for him, he wanted the option to make a break for it.

That hadn't come to pass.

Dressed exactly alike, with deliberately similar hair styles, Cody knew his plan to diffuse Albert Smith would work. All Gershwin had to do now was make sure he was caught. There existed a small danger they would see fit to question him and that he wouldn't be available for the next part of the plan, but if that was the case they would manage. There were enough of them to carry it out with one team member missing.

Sending Gershwin back out of the building to find Albert Smith and sow the seed of doubt, Cody knew he still needed a disguise. There was just too much chance he would be spotted. With both of them in play, he had to find a way to change his appearance. That wouldn't be difficult, but he had to do it in such a way that he still had access to the cathedral and other areas, so he had to remain in his palace livery.

He'd pondered the conundrum while waiting for Gershwin, a solution presenting itself when he looked out of the window. Now he needed one or two props and an unwilling volunteer.

Chapter 19 - Rex

Leading Eric, Buster, and Amber around the lower floor of the library, Rex used his nose to search. That Cody entered the building wasn't in doubt, but his lingering scent didn't mean he was still in it.

After a few minutes of sniffing this way and that, following scent trails that led nowhere, the decision to split up was an obvious one to take.

The challenge was the vastness of the building and the controlled humidity air conditioning system installed to maintain the integrity of the tomes held by the library. It meant nothing to the animals but many of the books were considered irreplaceable. Some were the only one in existence. Others were considered of vital religious importance.

What it meant for the dogs' ability to track Cody's scent was the air, which in a different building might lay thick and undisturbed, was being exchanged continually. There were traces of Cody's odour around, but only where he'd touched surfaces. To find them they were going to have to use their eyeballs.

"*Amber and I will go this way,*" said Buster.

"Hold on," Amber argued. "*Why am I being shackled with you?*"

Buster blinked. "*Because we're a team. We live together. We've solved crimes side by side. We've fought the bad guys and saved the day together.*"

"*He's making lots of valid points, Amber,*" agreed Rex.

"*We need to come up with a superhero sidekick name for you,*" said Buster.

"*And you just ruined it,*" sighed Rex. "*Look, I'm going to take Eric, and we'll scout the next floor up. You guys see what you can find here. If you do smell the target, bark for backup.*"

"*Not known for my barking skills,*" Amber pointed out snarkily.

Rex wasn't about to be put off. "*I'm sure you'll come up with something.*"

They split up, Rex and Eric heading off to find some stairs. They rounded a corner convinced it was the right one only to find a man staring at them with wide eyes. They had startled him.

Gershwin pressed a hand to his heart. It was no surprise that he felt on edge. The possibility that he would find himself in jail by the end of the day was very real. He could live with that if Cody got to do what he planned. The biggest potential disaster was to fail early.

"What are you two pooches doing in here?" he asked. Frowning a little, he saw Rex's tartan waistcoat and bowtie. "Oh, you're a wedding guest, aren't you? That makes you Albert Smith's dog."

Rex wasn't used to being recognised but understood his human's name when he heard it. However, the human knowing his name wasn't nearly so interesting as the fact that Rex could smell Cody Williams on him. He'd been in recent contact with the target.

THE ROYAL WEDDING

Rex advanced, his lips twitching with indecision. Was this person guilty? Had he been in contact with Cody because they were working together? In Cornwall, Cody had accomplices. Rex couldn't tell and wouldn't risk biting someone who might turn out to be an innocent who merely brushed by the man he wanted.

It was bad luck then that Gershwin misread Rex's expression. He wasn't a fan of dogs, anyway, so when Rex began to stalk forward, he turned tail and ran.

The suddenness of it caught Rex off guard, the human stealing several yards before he could react. He and Eric chased after him, but while the human's silly insistence on only using two legs to run meant they would catch up in moments, his opposable thumbs provided an advantage they could not overcome.

Gershwin crashed through a door, slammed it shut and turned the key. He didn't know what the deal with the dogs was, but he was going out the window rather than find out.

In the hallway outside, Rex snapped at the door, further convincing the human inside to make good his escape.

"*I'll go around,*" said Eric, already backing away. "*I've learned that humans like to go out of windows. If I catch him outside, I'll call for you.*" He was about to go when his nose caught a scent that stopped him.

Rex got the same thing, and their training left no doubt about what they could smell. It was blood.

Chapter 20 – Buster and Amber

"*Seriously, Amber, a superhero name is obligatory at this point. You can pick it, obviously, but how do you feel about Lucy Furr?*"

"*Lucifer? Because cats are the devil?*"

"*Well, yes you are, but no, the name is Lucy Furr. It's a play on words.*" He spelt it out for her.

Amber shook her head. "*Buster that's terrible. More importantly, figuring out some daft secret name for me so I can pretend to be a superhero like you is hardly what we need to be focused on right now.*"

"*Like I said, you can pick your own name,*" Buster continued. "*And if you were to be a superhero, you wouldn't be like me. Devil Dog is a dark avenger. The night personified. A manifestation of…*"

"*Oh, good grief. If it will shut you up I will pick a name.*"

Buster brightened instantly. "*You will?*"

THE ROYAL WEDDING

Amber let her head sag. She couldn't believe she was actually going to give in.

When she didn't speak for ten seconds, Buster checked on her.

"*Hello. Earth to Amber.*"

"*Fatal Feline,*" she spat, forcing the words out fast.

Buster almost laughed. He'd expected her to say something ridiculous, but with the name sinking in, he decided it wasn't half bad.

"*Devil Dog and Fatal Feline,*" he tried it out loud. "*I mean, it doesn't have quite the same ring as Hell Pup, because that goes really well with Devil Dog, but that name is already taken.*" The Chihuahua next door was Buster's sidekick for all their local adventures.

"*Take it or leave it,*" growled Amber, wishing she was on a sideboard or table so she could knock something off to land on Buster's head.

Buster was about to thank the cat for playing along for the first time ever when he realised he could smell their target.

Cody was about halfway through changing his appearance when a bulldog skidded through the door. He didn't need long, but now that he had the things for his disguise, a little patience would allow him to make it look right. He'd looked for rags or cloths but settled for paper towels when he found them first. It was just a medium that could be moulded to create the required shape. He was about done when the dog appeared.

"*Dun, dun, Dah!*" Buster's paws scrambled for purchase on the slick surface of the library's kitchen tiles. His surprise attack would have worked so much better if he hadn't needed to turn a corner.

Though it didn't come across as the most dangerous creature he'd ever faced, Cody figured it could still deliver a worthwhile bite if it tried. When a hissing, spitting cat bounded through the door a heartbeat later, leaping over the dog like a cream-coloured fluffy ninja intent on dealing death, he did what any sensible human would and chose to be somewhere else.

He still needed to restyle his hair, but that was going to have to wait. He had a fur-coated menace to deal with first.

The pets ran at him, but the bulldog wasn't what one might call fast, and they couldn't see the trap. Cody was right next to a walk-in larder. He opened the door and waited. When the bulldog's feet finally gripped the tiles, he shot forward but clearly hadn't expected Cody to jump out of the way.

Using the kitchen countertop as a lever, he lifted his legs, watched the dog slide through the gap beneath his feet and landed just in time to catch the cat.

Amber had launched herself through the air, her eighteen sickle-like claws aimed for the man's face, but she hadn't seen the garment in his hand. He caught her in a pair of trousers like a fish jumping into a net. One moment she was flying through the air, the next her delicate nose was smooshed against a patch of material that had very clearly been against the man's bottom until very recently.

Squealing her outrage, Amber found herself airborne again when Cody threw her into the walk-in larder alongside Buster. The bulldog was just turning himself around to run back out, but the door slammed before he could get his feet moving and they were trapped.

Chapter 21 – Albert with Cassie

Gershwin dropped lightly to the ground outside the window and reached up to close it behind him.

DI Munroe slammed into his back, pinning him to the brick and driving the air from his lungs. Holding him in place, she deftly flicked a set of cuffs over his right wrist and used them to control his arm as she pirouetted him around and onto the dirt.

The other cuff slammed home, and she rolled him over.

"Cody Williams, I am arresting you on suspicion of …"

"That's not him," said Albert.

Gershwin gawped up at the people staring down at him. "You again!" he spat, his words aimed at Albert and filled with venom. "You're the same crazy old man who tried to have me arrested at the palace."

Albert stood next to Jane, the two of them staying out of Cassie's way so she could manhandle her suspect.

Cassie hauled Gershwin to his feet. "What were you doing coming out of a window?" She didn't have the right person, and it occurred to her that once again Albert Smith, lovely though he was, could be leading her on a wild goose chase. Regardless, seeing a member of the royal household clambering out of a window – any window, let alone one in the building adjacent to a cathedral that was about to host a royal wedding – was cause enough for her to make a precautionary arrest.

Gershwin pushed his brain to come up with a clever answer. His hesitation cost him.

Cassie said, "Thought so," and took out her radio. She wanted site control to know she had a man in custody and was bringing him to their location.

"Wait," Gershwin pleaded. "There were dogs. Two of them. Big mean things. They chased me and they were outside the door of that room. That's why I went out of the window."

"German Shepherd dogs?" asked Albert.

Gershwin spotted his error. He'd momentarily forgotten one of the dogs belonged to the old man.

Seeing the truth in Gershwin's eyes, Albert glanced at the main doors to the library just a few yards to their left. "Now what would have made them follow you?"

It was a rhetorical question. Albert expected no answer. He was looking for Cody Williams and yet again had found a person who looked just like him. He didn't believe in coincidences. Not one bit. That Gershwin was climbing out of a window confirmed he was part of whatever was going on.

With officers coming to her location, Cassie turned her attention to Albert. "How sure are you that you saw Cody Williams, Albert. I need your honest answer."

Albert didn't need to think. "One hundred percent. It was him. He looks like this one," he jerked a thumb at Gershwin, "but he also looks different from when I first met him in Cornwall. I think he's altered his hair and appearance to look more like a person working at the palace. I was right when I said I saw him last year."

Cassie didn't like it. The implications were huge. Twisting Gershwin so her face was inches from his, she said, "Is that true? Are you working with Cody Williams?"

Gershwin looked away, refusing to speak.

"Don't feel like talking?" Cassie asked. "I think we can probably change that."

Gershwin blurted, "I want a lawyer!"

"But you won't get one," said Cassie. "Right now you are suspected of terrorism. I believe you are here as part of a plot to attack the royal family. Such a thing could have wide reaching implications for the British people. You can be held for up to twenty-eight days without the police even needing to charge you."

"What? You can't do that!"

Jane nodded. "Oh, yes she can."

Albert started toward the doors. "I'm going to see if I can find Rex. If he was in there chasing this one, chances are he's still there now."

Chapter 22 – Patricia

Patricia arrived at the back of the cathedral looking for a way in. Going in through the front wasn't an option, not with so much security and all the VIPs in the way. Plus, the press who were filming the whole thing. In fact, Patricia's biggest concern was her habit of making a scene right when she least wanted to. In Zangrabar she fell right off the stage and showed the whole world her knickers at the Maharaja's coronation.

No way was she going in through the front entrance where she might be seen.

They could not, however, find an open door at the back of the cathedral and were getting looks from some of the police officers patrolling the perimeter with their dogs.

Barbie waved energetically to dispel their concerns, a manoeuvre that made her chest jiggle animatedly. It was deliberate on her part because clearly a pretty blonde woman with big boobs couldn't be doing anything untoward. She wasn't sure why it worked on men but it always did.

The huge stained-glass windows dominated this side of the cathedral just like the front façade. The only major difference was the lack of a magnificent entranceway, but three quarters of the way along, a single-story outcropping housed what Patricia assumed was the vestry. The room had old books lining one wall, an oil painting of the King on another, and an old solid wood desk that matched the other items of furniture.

Patricia tapped on the glass to get the attention of the man inside. He wore a plain white shirt, and black trousers held up by braces. One hand cupped around her eyes to shut out the sun's reflective rays, she waved when he turned to look her way.

"Hello," she mouthed, doubting he would be able to hear her. There was a door to the right of the window, and she hoped he would be able to open it. Pointing to it and miming using a key, Patricia portrayed what she wanted in unambiguous terms.

Over her shoulder, she said, "I think he's going to let us in."

The man advanced across the room, polishing his glasses on a cloth before putting them back on his face. He vanished from sight behind the door, but a familiar click and barrel lock rotating sound announced the door opening a moment before it swung outward.

"Can I help you, my dear?" the man asked. He had a kindly face and deep green eyes that held Patricia's with a sense of calm authority. His height was hard to judge as she was at ground level and there were two steps to get up to the door. His hair was grey and disappearing backwards. She judged his age to be somewhere south of seventy, but not by much.

Patricia had been about to slip through the door before the man could stop her, such was her desire to find Albert and lend a hand, but there was something about the gentleman partially blocking her way.

The answer came to her in an instant and she almost stuttered when she said, "You're the bishop, aren't you?"

He cracked a smile. "Archbishop, but yes. My name is David."

Patricia dredged her brain, searching it for the correct way to address him.

"Um, my apologies for the intrusion, Your Excellency. Can you let me in? I'm in rather a hurry and I need to speak to someone about an urgent matter. I'm …"

"Patricia Fisher," the Archbishop of Canterbury completed her sentence. "I have seen your face in the papers and on the news. I must say you seem to live a very exciting life."

Her cheeks coloured – the leader of the Church of England knew who she was. That couldn't be a good thing, right?

"Well, that's one way to put it."

Barbie appeared next to her, tapped her shoulder, and smiled at the man. She had no clue who he was.

"Patty, we need to get inside. Stop flirting."

Patricia's eyes flared and her cheeks went scarlet. "No, I wasn't … I mean …"

"Perhaps I should step aside and let you go about your business." The archbishop stepped back to let them pass, the faintest hint of a smile at Patricia's obvious discomfort playing across his lips.

Barbie ducked around Patricia, leading the way. Jermaine, ever Patricia's shadow, remained just behind her, waiting for his principal to make her way inside.

She would have followed Barbie but could see a question had formed on the archbishop's lips.

"Is there ... is there something going on I should know about, Mrs Fisher? I find myself troubled by your presence, as it were. Not to suggest trouble follows you ..."

"But it kinda does, doesn't it Patty?" said Barbie, waiting impatiently for her friends.

Refusing to lie to an archbishop, Patricia said, "I'm not sure. That's why I need to get inside and speak to someone."

The Archbishop of Canterbury took another step back, holding the door wide open so she could easily pass.

"Please," he invited her to go.

Patricia mouthed her thanks as she rushed by, following Barbie through the vestry door and into the cathedral itself.

Barbie's feet stopped on the other side of the door. Gentle organ music played, replacing the echoing silence that would otherwise dominate the space and make quiet conversation uncomfortable.

Looking about, she whispered, "Wow."

Patricia pushed past her, looking for Albert. "Jermaine, sweetie, you're really tall. Can you see him?"

While her butler inspected the congregation for any sign of their elderly friend, Patricia couldn't help but notice people around her inspecting the bouquets of flowers. They were affixed to the end of every pew with ornate bows, the sprays of pretty blooms creating a stunning effect. Yet there was something distinctly amiss.

Puddles of water had formed beneath every single bouquet and those nearest to them were making comments. It had clearly become quite the topic, in fact, and just a few feet from her a lady with a wide brimmed hat was poking the bottom of the bouquet.

"The water balloon has burst," she remarked, explaining to a younger woman sitting to her right. The woman's tone made it clear she thought the leaking water to be the result of shoddy workmanship. "They all have," she added. "It will be that wedding planner they hired. I bet she put in the cheapest bid and has been cutting corners to turn a profit ever since."

"Madam, I don't think Sir Albert is here. I can see neither him nor his dog, Sir Rex," Jermaine reported.

Patricia returned her attention to the congregation, scanning the faces for herself though she highly doubted Jermaine would be proven wrong. Fumbling with her right hand, she found her phone. Wilting flowers and puddles of water might be a minor thing, but Felicity would want to know.

Knowing how busy she would be, Patricia sent the message to Mindy, hoping the teenager would have her device to hand. It was her experience that teenagers were hard to separate from their phones.

She let her know about the flowers and returned to wondering where Albert might be.

Chapter 23 – Felicity

I was inspecting the bridesmaids' dresses, searching for imperfections when Mindy breezed into the room looking for me. She held her phone and I knew without asking there was going to be a drama of some kind.

"Tell me."

Mindy put her hands out, palms showing to slow me down. "It's nothing, Auntie. Well, almost nothing."

I cringed and pulled a face like I was getting ready for someone to hit me.

"The flowers in the cathedral are leaking. That's all."

"Leaking?"

"That's what Patricia has just texted me."

She showed me the message. "All of them? How can that be?" I asked the question but already knew the answer. If one of the balloons sprung a leak I would assume someone knocked it or maybe even that Doris hadn't been diligent enough with the thorns on the roses. The latter was less likely. Not only is she a great florist who

I have been doing business with for years, she understood that nothing could be allowed to go wrong today and had worked tirelessly for days to be ready.

That left only one possible explanation: sabotage.

Mindy had just come from the bride's suite.

"How is Nora?" I enquired, making decisions in my head.

"The bride is in great form. She's a little giddy with excitement, but that's understandable. Otherwise, she is having a wonderful time with her friends, relatives, and mum. She's had a glass of champagne but refused a second. I'd call her a nine point five on the scale of good to bad brides."

It was good news.

"Okay, we're heading back to the cathedral. I'm going to leave Elizabeth to manage the bridal party just in case we don't get back in time. I don't want complaints about puddles of water or, Lord forbid, someone slips and pops their hip. We're going to fix this before the ceremony starts."

I fished for my phone but couldn't find it. I wanted to call Vince so he would meet us at the hotel's entrance.

"Something wrong?" asked Mindy, seeing my frown.

We were heading down the stairs towards the hotel's reception and my phone was very definitely not in my handbag where I always keep it. I paused at the next landing to mentally retrace my steps. When had I last used it?

Not since we left the cathedral, I decided. So was it there somewhere?

Mindy's phone rang.

"It's Vince," she said, thumbing the button to answer it.

His voice echoed out when she put it on speaker. "Is Felicity looking for her phone?"

We both said, "Yes."

"I've got it. I called to find out where you were and the hotel manager answered. It was on the floor next to the reception desk."

"Mystery solved," said Mindy.

I couldn't figure out how I had managed to drop it, but it was hardly important.

Chapter 24 – Rex and Albert

Rex pawed at the door. The knob to open it was one of the really annoying, specifically-designed-to-defeat-a-dog ones, with a round handle. Rex could operate a long handle with a few attempts provided it swung away from him. Ones that swung toward him weren't impossible but were far harder to negotiate.

There was a human on the other side of the door, and they were bleeding. It was a woman, Rex could smell the difference like it was night and day, and the amount of coppery blood smell hanging in the air worried him.

"*We'll have to get a human,*" he told Eric.

"*What about the man your human sent you after?*"

"*The injured human takes priority. I think she's still alive, but the longer we wait, the less likely that is to be true.*" He was about to go for help, leaving Eric to mind the woman in case someone came along, when Albert appeared.

"Ah, there you are, Rex. No luck catching Cody then?"

Rex bounced off his back legs and shoved his front paws against the door. Barking insistently, he said, *"Open this door! There's a woman inside and she is hurt!"*

Albert jolted with surprise and completely misinterpreted what Rex was trying to tell him.

"Cody is in there? You've got him cornered? Well done, Rex!"

Rex would have face palmed if the expression meant anything to a dog. Instead, he backed away when his human came forward.

"Right, I'm going to open the door," he whispered. "Be ready in case he comes out fighting." Albert fully expected Cody to be armed.

Holding up three fingers, Albert crouched to throw off what he expected to be Cody's point of aim and grabbed the door handle. Turning down his fingers, he counted down and threw the door open with a snarl on his face. He was ready to face a murderer, so the young woman in her underwear came as something of a surprise.

"Oh," he said.

Rex brushed past his human, shouldering his way into the room. The woman was alive, but unconscious. Her breathing was shallow and there was a stab wound to her abdomen.

Albert checked her pulse with two fingers on her neck. It looked as though she'd made no attempt to stem the bleeding and the egg-sized lump by her right temple suggested she'd been knocked out during the attack.

There was no sign of her clothing, but her underwear didn't appear to have been messed with which gave Albert some small sense of relief. Rushing to the window, he threw it open and leaned outside. Cassie and Jane were still out there with Gershwin where they'd been joined by six officers in uniform.

"Hey! In here. There's an injured woman. She's been stabbed!"

The news got the reaction he wanted, four of the cops leaving the other two with DI Munroe when they ran to get inside.

Albert went back to the hallway so they would see him and know where to go.

Stepping back to watch her chest rising and falling slowly, Albert asked, "What happened to you?"

Chapter 25 – Lord Edward

He wasn't supposed to arrive for another thirty minutes, but Edward Chamberlain couldn't wait. He was simply too excited to get the day underway. His father expected him to travel in his car, the two of them arriving together, but dear old dad was to be disappointed.

He knew he looked a sight driving through the streets of Canterbury on a motorbike in his full morning suit complete with tails, but having a fast getaway vehicle to hand, as well as a well-planned route that would get him out of the city as swiftly as possible while avoiding all major roads, was the only prudent option.

Not that anything was going to go wrong. His planning was meticulous.

People cheered when he went by, the crowds of onlookers lining the streets nothing compared to how it would be for his coronation. That was a way down the line yet. There would be no interfering in his father's natural life span. Dear old dad would live out the rest of his days as the King of England, finally leaving the throne to his only son when he could no longer maintain his grip on the mortal coil.

It was all in place. All that was needed now was some careful timing on his part. His father was going to fall ill in a completely non-suspicious way, opening the door for Edward to leave right before the trap triggered and killed everyone at the reception.

Turning the final corner, the cathedral swung into sight. Police officers blocked his path, but that was as expected. They were inspecting identifications and matching them to names on the guests list. Non-guests needing access were ferried through a different checkpoint and entrance.

Pulling up behind a black, stretch limousine, he popped the bike into neutral and put his feet down.

When a Range Rover pulled up alongside, very much out of the line of cars waiting to go through the police check point, he ignored it until a window powered down.

"Hey, sexy," said a familiar voice.

He twisted his head to find Mindy grinning at him from the back seat.

"How did you know it was me?" Edward asked, confused how she could know with his helmet on.

Her grin broadened. "Are you kidding. I'd recognise that backside anywhere."

In the front of the car Felicity rolled her eyes and Vince chuckled.

Pulling his helmet off so he could hear her more clearly, he asked, "How's it going so far? Any problems?"

"Only Auntie's blood pressure."

Edward shifted his gaze to check on Felicity.

"I'm fine," she said. "My niece likes to exaggerate." Frowning slightly as a question formed, she said, "I thought you were travelling with your father."

Edward shrugged. "I was to be one of the last to arrive which meant I would miss too much. I wanted to get there early and soak up the atmosphere. I hope that doesn't mess with anything you are doing."

"No. That's okay. It won't affect us."

The car ahead moved forward.

"You had better go," said Mindy. "I'll see you in there."

Edward hooked his left hand through the helmet and let the bike ease forward. He hadn't wanted Mindy to see the motorcycle, but it was too late now. He would figure out how to explain it later. They were to be together for the reception, but he doubted he would see her much in the next couple of hours.

Putting her from his mind, he confirmed his identity with the cops and passed through to join the procession of cars on the other side. Where they continued on to the cathedral where they would deposit their occupants, he turned away, looking for somewhere out of the way to park his bike.

Chapter 26 – Blue Moon Investigations

Tempest Michaels knew Patricia Fisher was somewhere in the grounds of the cathedral. They had worked together on several cases, but never as a formal arrangement. It just kind of happened.

DI Cassie Munroe had arranged for three of his team to be employed as additional staff required for the day. To keep their roles undercover, they were being paid and actually had to do the jobs they were employed for. That made snooping hard, but mostly they were there to overhear what was being said, eavesdropping on conversations every chance they got.

Thus far, they could report no suspicious behaviour among the staff, but that was never the expectation. DI Munroe suspected Lord Edward Chamberlain, and it was him they were trying to keep track of.

Apart from his movements around the palace, which they had been able to monitor and record for more than three weeks, they were interested in his activities at both the cathedral and the wedding reception venue.

Bugging his room proved impossible. After his brother's death and the demise of multiple other royals, DI Munroe's boss declared her to be failing in her duty to protect those living in Buckingham Palace and promptly placed a guard detail outside his door.

Tempest wasn't ready to dismiss Cassie's concerns, but there was nothing to indicate Lord Edward was up to anything. Regardless, they were being vigilant and had Big Ben positioned outside where he could watch for their target arriving.

'*He just arrived on a motorcycle.*' The message arrived on Tempest's phone with a silent vibration.

Tempest felt his forehead wrinkle. He was supposed to be travelling with his father. Did the unannounced change of plan mean something?

Typing, Tempest sent back, '*Is he alone?*'

'*Yes.*'

The motorcycle almost certainly meant he couldn't be carrying anything. If he was it would have to be small. That made it distinctly less likely he was planning to wipe out the line of succession which, admittedly, was the worst-case scenario and one they all agreed to be unlikely.

Still, Tempest knew he couldn't rest until the day was over and everyone survived. Setting off to find Amanda, he decided it was time to get closer to the action. Their jobs with the royal household staff were only temporary and they didn't need them anyway. It was time to skive off. If they were caught and sacked it would make no difference now.

When he stepped outside with Amanda, he almost walked straight into Jane.

"Oh," she said. "I was just coming to find you. I have news and didn't want to share it in a text message."

"That sounds ominous," said Amanda.

Jane pulled a face and huffed out a breath. "A woman was stabbed. Albert Smith found her in the library."

Tempest's eyebrows twitched. "Albert sticking his nose in again. Good for him. Who's the woman?"

Jane shrugged. "No clue. She was stripped to her underwear and left for dead. It's a mercy she was found in time. She's on her way to hospital and the paramedics are hopeful. There's more."

Jane had dropped her voice, making Tempest and Amanda lean in so they could still hear over the sound of the Royal Marines Band playing.

"Albert hadn't wandered off when he found the victim. He was looking for someone. He believes there is a killer here he first met in Cornwall last year. According to Albert, the man is a staunch anti-royalist who planned to murder a whole bunch of them by poisoning the food supplied for the couple's engagement party."

Tempest asked, "What's his name and what does he look like?"

Jane pulled out her phone. "I need to show you a picture of the victim too, actually. Someone here has to recognise her." She started with the shot she took of the woman. One of the paramedic's had their head in the shot, but it was easy enough to see the unconscious woman's face.

Tempest checked with Amanda but neither of them had seen her before.

"This is a guy Cassie just arrested. He was climbing out of a window. His name is Gershwin George and apparently he looks just like Cody Williams. Cody is the killer from Cornwall," Jane explained. "I don't think he's an exact likeness. You wouldn't confuse them as twins if they were standing together, but Albert said Cody had lost some weight and changed his hair to look more like Gershwin.

A former police officer herself, Amanda asked, "Cassie thinks he's involved?"

"She does. He's being interviewed right now, but the last I saw he was being very tight-lipped."

Tempest exhaled through his nose, letting his mind run through what he knew.

"This is in addition to her concerns that Lord Chamberlain might have something up his sleeve, right?"

"Well, it's only Albert saying this Cody Williams guy is here. She's playing along for now, but he could be completely wrong. Gershwin said Albert accosted him at the palace last year when he was there to be knighted. I'm worried this Cody person isn't here at all and Albert has us looking for a ghost."

Tempest snorted a small laugh. "Don't you know? Catching ghosts is our specialty."

Chapter 27 – Cassie and Albert

Cassie Munroe watched the unnamed woman being loaded into the ambulance. Her treatment and subsequent removal from the library was conducted very carefully and quietly so as not to disturb the wedding.

With the library door on the opposite side of the building to everyone else, they were able to extract her without anyone seeing, but as the ambulance quietly pulled away, a police escort going ahead and behind to grease the way through the roadblocks, Cassie's thoughts were focused on determining the woman's identity and figuring out what happened to her.

She hadn't stabbed and stripped herself. There was no sign of the weapon used or her clothes. The library would normally be open on a Saturday but was empty today for obvious reasons. Cassie would have preferred that it was locked yet the rooms were needed for the wedding planners to operate from.

That was starting to feel like a mistake, and she wished someone had insisted upon a portable office instead. There being no sense wasting time thinking about what she would have done differently, Cassie headed for the on-site command post.

Albert was already there, explaining how he came to find the woman.

Cassie cringed. There was no way to stop him from telling them about Cody, but she already knew what her boss's opinion would be. She'd caught it in the neck when Albert went rogue running about the palace grounds trying to find a man he claimed to have seen. He'd seen Gershwin and confused himself because one man looks like the other.

Cassie had been certain that's all it was at the time and for months afterwards. Not so much today. There was nothing dull, dim, or confused about Albert Smith. For that matter she would pick Albert's dog to beat her boss at chess, but Commissioner Benson Blunt was in charge no matter what her thoughts might be on the subject, and she had to stay on the right side of his temper if she wanted to continue her investigation.

"Let me see if I have this straight," the commissioner interrupted Albert's flow. "You released your dog with a command to attack a member of the royal household staff. You then proceeded to argue with palace security before flagging down Detective Inspector Munroe whereupon she aided you in a search of the grounds …"

"Sir," Cassie tried to interrupt only to have a hand held in her face to shut her up.

"…rather than call for the units assigned to patrol the grounds," the commissioner said very pointedly, "and then broke into the library while DI Munroe arrested a member of the royal household staff purely on the basis that he looks like someone you once met in Cornwall. Do I have that about right?"

"Sir," Cassie tried again.

"I wasn't speaking to you!" he raged, silencing her and making everyone on the command centre look their way.

Albert Smith folded his arms. "Are you a complete idiot all the time, or do you reserve that talent for special occasions?"

Cassie almost spat out her teeth and half the people around them had to fight not to laugh.

While the commissioner needed a moment to think up a suitable retort, Albert steamrollered straight over him.

"You have a reported sighting of a known anti-royalist at the most public royal event in years. Combined with a member of the royal household staff as you so keenly like to refer to them, acting suspiciously, or do you think climbing out of windows is normal behaviour?" Albert didn't pause to allow an answer. "Gershwin George bears a striking resemblance to the known anti-royalist who is already wanted in connection with murder charges, and he was found exiting the building in which a young woman was stabbed. Even Hong Kong Phooey could figure out there is a case to investigate yet I find myself arguing for you to put down your cup of tea and get off your butt. Why is that?"

"You will address me as Commissioner Blunt or sir."

"That seems doubtful," said Albert. "But I do have a few names I'm willing to try out."

The commissioner drew in a deep breath, probably to start shouting again, but a chief inspector leaning over a junior constable sitting at a computer stopped him.

"Sir, we've just checked the logs and Gershwin George checked in twice today."

"What?"

"His badge was scanned twice, sir. I guess there is a hole in the program because it hasn't flagged it, but he entered the grounds at 0843 and again at 0902. DI Munroe might be right."

Chapter 28 – Cody

He'd seen Gershwin taken away in cuffs. It threw him mentally and emotionally for several minutes. The plan could survive without him, but Gershwin was the linchpin in everything that had to happen outside of what Cody planned to do.

In order for Cody to strike, there had to be a distraction. It had been planned and practiced and the team was ready. In theory. Gershwin was supposed to run that side of things and now Cody couldn't be sure how the others would react. Did they even know where Gershwin was or what had happened to him?

He sent a text message to Willow, certain she would answer. *'There has been a change of plan. I need you to proceed without Gershwin.'* He chose not to ask if she was able to take charge; he was giving her the baton and demanding she run with it.

In reality it took her less than a minute to reply, but it felt far longer to Cody whose heart was beating far faster than he liked.

'What happened to Gershwin?'

The question wasn't unexpected, but Cody wasn't going to answer it honestly. If Willow found out she would tell the others, and they would all start questioning their futures. He couldn't have that.

'*It doesn't matter. Stay on task. We are nearly there. I am nearly there. Be ready to go. He will be here soon.*'

Cody waited, breathing in and out in a controlled fashion. He wanted his pulse to slow. Not that he was worried for his health – he would be dead soon enough, but he needed to appear in control. Beads of sweat on his brow or shaking hands might give the King's personal security detail that extra moment of warning they would need to stop him before he could strike.

Or ...

A gloriously blissful smile spread across his face. His plan changed in the space between heartbeats. He would never have come up with it had the day not panned out the way it had, but suddenly he had a far superior strategy to get him close to the King.

His phone vibrated with an incoming text message from Willow.

'*Okay, Cody. We have all left our assigned posts and are ready.*'

A sense of complete calm stole through his body and his heartrate slowed. He was ready too and the nervous adrenaline he felt just a few seconds ago was gone. His new plan was going to work in a way that none of the previous iterations could have. He'd always made sure to sound confident his strategy would work, but the truth was he gave it a fifty percent chance at best. Now it was closer to ninety percent. No one would see this coming.

Leaving his hiding place, he went looking for a second victim.

Chapter 29 – Felicity

I led Mindy into the cathedral, my steps hurried but not panicked. There were indeed puddles everywhere, not that I had any reason to doubt Patricia's word. It was all the outer bouquets, not those running down the central aisle. That was something of a relief, but it still meant we had forty balloons to replace and refill.

Doris the florist was long gone, withdrawn from the cathedral hours earlier to make way for the official guests.

Justin and Philippe spotted us and hurried over. I'd called Justin from the car, asking him to take a look and figure out a way to stop the flowers from wilting, which they already were. They had mopped the floor which dealt with one problem, but we still needed to take each bouquet off and make new balloons. The originals were folded out of cellophane, but it would take too long to redo them all, and I didn't have a supply of cellophane anyway.

Justin looked apologetic when he crouched at the end of the very back aisle to update me. Behind me Mindy was fiddling with the bouquet.

"Someone cut them all," Justin reported. "Looks like they ran along with a razor or maybe just stabbed each one with a pair of scissors. It had to have happened after I conducted my last inspection right before the first guests started coming in. The holes are only small, but big enough for the water to escape."

Philippe said, "I've talked to the ushers but none of them know anything about it. They said the only person in here after me and Justin left was your other assistant."

"Primrose?"

Justin shrugged. "I guess that's who they mean."

"Okay. We can worry about who did it later." I said the words, but my head filled with questions regarding Primrose. My biggest rival had targeted me with dirty tactics for years. Was she doing it again now? I mean, why wouldn't she? If she made this wedding a catastrophe, I would be finished. It might impact her a little because she was here with me, but my name was the one on the contract. My business would be relegated to registry office events with soggy sandwiches in the local pub for a reception and the void I left would be filled by none other than Primrose Green.

"Auntie, I think we can fix these quickly enough."

I twisted in place, my nose reporting a scent I knew.

"Um, Mindy what can I smell?"

Mindy whispered, "A condom."

Don't ask me why but I felt a rush of heat to my cheeks.

Mindy lifted the ornate ribbon that hid the water balloon. "Look it's a really quick fix. We slip a condom around the original balloon, tie it tight and quickly refill them. As long as we don't put too much water in, I think we'll be alright."

I wanted to argue but we were very short on time.

"Okay, but there's twenty pews with a bouquet on each end. That's forty condoms."

Mindy produced a large box from her bag. And then another.

Justin said, "Goodness."

Philippe said, "Gurl be getting regular action."

Then he and Mindy high-fived.

I couldn't stop myself from asking, "Mindy, why do you have so many?"

She shrugged one shoulder, utterly unashamed. "The big boxes work out cheaper."

We quickly set about the task, Justin taking one box of twenty-four condoms, Mindy keeping the other. I stayed with Mindy and volunteered to do the filling part. I didn't want to handle the condoms. I find them icky and smelly.

We got a few looks as we edged our way along the outside of the pews, replacing the water balloons and refilling them, but the guests mostly smiled and ignored us.

In five minutes we were done, but I could tell from the tune the Royal Marines Band were playing that we were moments away from the King arriving – yes, I memorised their playlist. I've been living and breathing nothing but this wedding for weeks.

Task complete, we beat a hasty retreat to the back of the cathedral, went around the edge to the door so we didn't get in anyone's way – the Prime Minister had just walked in with his wife – and snuck out when there was a gap.

I breathed a sigh of relief, but in so doing caught a lungful of the condom smell coming off Mindy's hands.

"You need to find some soap."

Chapter 30 – Albert and Cassie

Albert had never hit a person while he was interviewing them at any point while he was a serving police officer. He knew colleagues who had and condemned them. Even when the man sitting opposite was clearly guilty of a terrible crime and would spit and swear and threaten violence, Albert never struck back.

Today he wanted to break that rule.

Gershwin would give them nothing and they had no time. The King and Queen's arrival was imminent, and they were the last guests. The bride would appear ten minutes after that, so if anything was going to happen they were running out of time to stop it.

"Spending the rest of your life in jail doesn't worry you." Albert confirmed. It wasn't a question. Gershwin hadn't said a word since they arrested him. But he had smiled. It was a smile that said he knew something they didn't and that all he had to do was keep his lips shut.

Albert wanted to throttle him.

"Who is the other person who checked in using your badge, Gershwin?" Cassie pressed, knowing how unlikely it was that he would answer.

The commissioner wasn't happy about letting Albert ask questions, yet concerned the old man might be onto something, he had chosen to turn a blind eye. Secretly he hoped the wedding would pass without a blip so he could claim there was never anything to worry about. Finding something to charge the old fool with would be difficult and almost certainly backfire since Albert Smith was still the darling of the press with his bravery and generosity and his oh-so-clever dog. He fantasised about it though, imagining slapping the cuffs home around the old man's wrists.

Of course it was all Cassie Munroe's doing. She probably egged Albert Smith on just to make a scene so she could undermine his authority. He never should have slept with her. Their brief affair, two years ago now, ended when she woke up to the fact that he was never going to leave his wife. Why would he? One wife was as bad as the next. Cassie had only been fun because she was a piece on the side.

She was angry when he dumped her, but she hadn't gone to his wife or HR. She hadn't even kicked up a fuss when he assigned her to the dead-end job at the palace – a place where careers go to die.

If he played this right, she would be out of his hair for good. If the Gershwin kid was innocent, he would have grounds to start an investigation into her judgement and ability to operate as a senior detective. She would lose her job and be out of the police for good.

Thankfully, there was no sign of Cody Williams. Almost certainly because he was never within a hundred miles of Canterbury. Forced to act, the commissioner had ordered a complete sweep of the grounds – surreptitiously, of course. The officers found no one matching the description and he considered that evidence enough that they were wasting their time.

The commissioner's train of thought went sideways when the radios in the command unit squawked and everyone heard the message about a second stab victim.

Albert looked at Cassie and they both looked at Gershwin.

Albert grabbed Gershwin's collars, lifting him out of his chair. "Is this part of it?" he demanded.

Cassie fought against Albert's grip. "Release him, Albert! This isn't helping."

Albert let him go and stormed out. Rex had been denied entry and so was waiting outside. They were both supposed to be in the cathedral waiting for the ceremony to start, but Albert couldn't entertain the idea until he knew they were all going to be safe.

The commissioner might not believe him, but he had seen Cody Williams, not Gershwin George.

Ruffling the fur around Rex's neck, he grumbled, "Come on, Albert, think man." He tried to place himself in Cody's shoes. What would he do if he wanted to end the monarchy? Easy. He would go after the King. Kill the King of England and the world would pay attention. But how was he going to get anywhere near him? The King and Queen had enough security to stop a charging rhinoceros.

The cops outside the command centre were agitated. They expected a quiet day. Their biggest challenge ought to have been keeping cool in all their gear, yet they had a man in custody, the suggestion of a plot against the King, and two stab victims.

Passing two female officers he heard one say the second victim was also a woman. She was alive but unconscious just like the first victim. They had a spree killer at the cathedral and a royal wedding about to take place.

Albert found himself feeling sorry for the commissioner. Yes, the man was a pompous fool, but he had a stressful line on which he now had to balance. He would want to place armed officers everywhere, but the world was watching through the lens of the cameras, so he needed to keep the visible police presence to a minimum. That was going to be hard to achieve and if anything went wrong, if the King was harmed or even came close to being in danger, it would be his head on the chopping block.

Clicking his tongue to get Rex moving, Albert set off back toward the cathedral. He wasn't planning to take his seat for the ceremony, but if the King was about to arrive, the cathedral was where he was heading.

Rex walked along at his human's side. Eric was finally back with his handler, which was disappointing because he'd enjoyed having a partner who understood him. Consoling himself with the knowledge that the pup he met was now a fully grown dog and a trained police canine who loved his role, Rex sniffed the air, wondering what adventure the rest of the day might hold.

Chapter 31 – Felicity and Patricia

Patricia saw Felicity leaving the cathedral and waved to get her attention. There hadn't been a car at the kerb in more than a minute, and she knew why: the King was about to arrive.

Felicity was with her team, leading them away from the cathedral entrance so they would be out of the way and out of camera shot when the King and Queen made their way up the path to the ancient church. Behind the path to the cathedral was nothing but grass until it reached the distant trees more than a hundred yards away.

Patricia set a path to intercept and met them just as they came into the shadow thrown by the library.

"Have you seen Albert?" she asked.

"No. Sorry. I've been at the reception end of things for the last couple of hours. I always spend my time with the bride in the build up to the ceremony. Why?" Talking about what she had been doing made her think about Primrose. She was supposed to be at the kerb to ensure all the guests were greeted correctly. The official party was there with the military standard bearers and the mayor of Canterbury plus the deputy archbishop. Yet of Primrose there was no sign.

"Why am I looking for Albert?" Patricia questioned what she should tell her friend. Poor Felicity seemed stressed enough without telling her their friend had been chasing someone.

"Oh, look, there he is now," said Felicity, angling an arm across the grass.

Albert was just stepping on the path with Rex leading the way. They were heading for the cathedral though Felicity knew he was at least forty minutes later than he ought to be in getting there. She didn't know what might have happened but was willing to blame Primrose since she was the one assigned to manage the guests. Any muck ups had to be down to her.

Just as she was cursing her rival's name, Primrose appeared. Looking as elegant as ever, her sereneness was visibly absent. She'd come from the direction of the police cordon which suggested she'd been called away for some reason.

Felicity would grill her about it later and if she was trying to sabotage things to ruin her, Felicity would find something to stab her with.

Chapter 32 – Amber and Buster

"You've done it before," Amber coached, filling her voice with confident support.

"*That doesn't mean it's a good idea,*" argued Buster warily.

"But we've exhausted all our other options," Amber pointed out. "*What if Felicity needs us? What if she's in trouble?*"

Buster didn't reply. The cat was extorting his paranoia to make him do something he definitively didn't want to do.

When she got no reply, Amber added some extra sugar to her voice. "*Devil Dog would do it.*"

Buster sighed and closed his eyes. He really hated Amber some times.

"*In fact,*" Amber persisted. "*I bet Devil Dog could do it in one go.*"

Buster opened his eyes. He severely doubted that. The door was a cheap thing made of plywood and MDF. He'd broken through similar ones in the past, but ramming doors with his head wasn't his idea of a good time and the cat only wanted him to do it so she could watch.

Unfortunately, she made a good point about Felicity. And about Devil Dog. His superhero alter ego wouldn't hesitate to smash through the door if he thought someone needed him.

Grumpily, Buster got to his feet. "*Okay, but you have to stay in your Fatal Feline character for the rest of the day, okay?*"

"*Okay, Buster.*"

"*Devil Dog.*" Buster dropped his voice an octave and gave it a raspy growl to show he was now in Devil Dog mode.

"*Yes. Devil Dog. Of course,*" Amber agreed, indicating the door and how ready she was to see Buster in action.

Buster swore under his breath, backed up a few feet and launched himself at the bottom corner of the door. That was its weakest point. Gritting his teeth and closing his eyes, he lowered his skull and leapt. The door had a wooden frame running around the outside with strengthening bars from top to bottom and side to side to form a cross in the middle. Buster knew from experience that the rest was hollow. The frame was sheathed in a thin layer of fibre board coated with a finish and painted.

All he had to do, in theory, was punch through two thin layers.

Bouncing off, Buster staggered sideways to his right and then left as he tried to maintain his balance. Groggily, he muttered, "*Tell the door it fought bravely.*"

"*And won*," said Amber, walking around the dog to check his handiwork. The panel was cracked. "*Not bad for a first attempt, but you're going to have to hit it harder.*"

"*Harder?*"

Buster gave himself a few moments before backing up to take a second go at the canine battering ram task.

Putting his head down, he said, "*My ancestors are judging me. And they are not wrong.*"

Chapter 33 – Albert

Albert tottered gamely along the path, reached the cathedral, and went inside where his right to be there was once again quickly checked by the security team positioned inside the doorway.

The team consisted of palace security – highly trained specialists, many of whom were former police or special forces. They were accompanied by two armed police officers who had been handpicked by the commissioner for the task.

Albert held no doubt about the competency of the team but as they handled his invitation and checked his name, he couldn't help overhearing the messages pinging about on their radios.

"Did I just hear that a third woman has been stabbed on the grounds?" Albert could scarcely believe it.

Dismissively, the security guard checking his name off the list said, "Please take your seat, sir."

Albert almost challenged him, but he knew what he'd just heard. Whoever was getting stab happy had claimed their third victim. The police would be all over

THE ROYAL WEDDING

the grounds looking for the knifeman but were having to do so with the King about to arrive.

Would they stop him or delay him? Would they call the wedding off? Did anyone outside of the police and the palace security even know? If not, then who was calling the shots? Albert knew it was likely Commissioner Blunt and doubted he had the courage to stop a royal wedding moments before it was due to get started.

Glancing outside as the ushers urged him toward his seat, Albert saw the King's car pull up. The ornate, black Rolls Royce glided to a gentle stop, the car seeming to float as though bumps in the road were of no consequence.

The tune from the Royal Marines Band came to a well-timed halt. They paused, and as the King exited his car with Queen Camilla on his arm, his honour guard presented arms and the band struck up the national anthem.

The King and Queen waved to the crowd of onlookers and the cameras, making their way along the path to the cathedral just the same as all the guests before them.

With the eyes of the security team on the monarch, Albert went unnoticed as he remained standing just a few feet behind them. The organist inside the cathedral reached the end of the piece he was playing and in the few beats of quiet that passed, Albert thought he heard something coming from outside.

Something that didn't belong.

Chapter 34 – The Distraction

With the noise of the Royal Marines band belting out God Save the King at maximum volume, almost no one in the grounds between the library and the cathedral heard the buzzing whine of multiple propellers.

Almost no one.

The drone operators heard them, but they knew the noise was coming. Discounting them, only three people detected the sound before the small fleet of flying menace became visible. One was a woman called Mary Weldon. She was third assistant to a BBC camera team and largely without a job unless dogsbody counted. Bored with the constant menial demands, she'd wandered off for a crafty smoke and was perfectly positioned to hear the drones as she was shielded from the sound of the national anthem by a wall.

The second person was Commissioner Blunt. Thinking it was an appropriately patriotic thing to do, he'd left the command unit to watch the King and Queen making their way along the path to the cathedral and was holding a rigid salute. He heard the buzz, thought to himself that it sounded just like a small fleet of drones taking off, and chose to ignore it as insignificant.

THE ROYAL WEDDING

The third person was Tempest Michaels. Not because his hearing was superior to that of anyone else, but because he just happened to be facing the right way at the right time. The wind shifted at precisely the right moment, and he was alert for something to happen. Much like Albert, Tempest believed that were an attack of any kind to take place, the most likely time was when the King arrived.

Security that day was especially tight. Staff from the palace, on top of their usual scrutiny and security clearance were subjected to bag searches and entry to the grounds via a metal detector. The drones were almost one hundred percent plastic. The electronic components were the only parts containing metal so to defeat the security measures, the drones were dismantled. The plastic parts passed through the checks without comment and the metal items were hidden inside hollowed out phones and, in one case, an old Sony Walkman. It was surprising how much circuitry could be hidden inside the case of a Walkman.

Inside the grounds, one of Cody's team had set to work rebuilding all six drones. With Gershwin now missing they could only operate five but that was enough to cause widespread panic.

They emerged as if from nowhere, rising above the library after Willow and her fellow anarchists launched them from a window on the far side. They didn't need to have a line of sight to the drones or make themselves visible to the security teams outside; the drones fed back a picture from an on-board camera to a VR headset each operator wore.

Leaping into the open, Tempest began shouting and pointing. No one else had seen the danger, and the reaction of the platoon of soldiers performing ceremonial duty, the police, and all the palace appointed security guards was to assume he was a danger to the King and Queen.

He ran in their direction, racing to stay ahead of the drones even though he knew it to be futile.

Seeing Tempest go, Amanda and Big Ben were swift to follow. They trailed him and would get to the royals long after the drones reached their position.

Shadowing the monarch, his personal security detachment were enough yards away that they wouldn't appear in the shots beamed around the globe. That was a decision they were unhappy with, but one enforced by the King himself. Yes, he accepted the need for a security detail, but he and his wife didn't wish to wear them as ornaments.

The drones passed over Patricia's head. She had gasped when Tempest burst into action and again when she saw police marksmen lining up their guns to shoot him before he could get to the King. Now she understood what was going on but stared in horror at the bulbous tanks strapped beneath the drones.

Felicity had seen them too. Each was filled with a colourless liquid that sloshed about inside the clear plastic tanks as the drones whipped across the grounds. At first she thought they were heading for the King and Queen, but they veered to the left, swinging away from the monarch and she saw the real target.

It was the police.

Caught in a moment of indecision, the King's security detail had split. Four were heading straight for the King as was their duty. The other two ran to intercept the man they perceived to be a threat only to stop halfway when they saw the drones.

Craning his neck to look up, Tempest also saw the drones change course. The police were in the open. Men, women, and dogs were exposed and had nowhere to go.

The King's personal security detail hurried him along the path to the cathedral, constantly checking over their shoulders for any sign of further attack.

The guards inside the cathedral door ran outside, gesturing with urgent motions for the King and Queen to hurry.

Curious, Albert stepped forward to get a better look. There was utter confusion in every direction.

The drones dropped lower, but not so low that they could be knocked from the sky. Some of the armed police raised their weapons only to have a senior officer bellow for them to hold fire. With the direction they were facing, their rounds were going straight towards the King.

Sweeping toward the police as they scattered in every direction, a fine mist fell from a nozzle at the front of each drone.

Cries of horror arose. The TV crew recording the event and the reporters speaking to the audience wherever they might be, tried to remain as professional as possible but they all believed they were witnessing an attack that no one could do anything to prevent.

From his position next to the door to the cathedral, Cody watched with glee.

The drones swooped, dragging with them a cloud of fine droplets. No one in their path could avoid being hit. Before the TV cameras, police officers caught in the open threw themselves to the ground and shielded their faces as though that would make any difference.

Patricia wanted to run, but the mist was in the air and had to already be in her lungs just as it was in everyone else's. People were screaming their terror. Many were running to get away, bursting through the police checkpoint to escape the area but the drones were swinging around to douse that too. Then they angled back toward the drop off point at the kerb, their deadly mist still falling.

Chapter 35 – Edward

Lord Edward gawked at the drones and the cloud of vapour falling from them. Arriving at the cathedral on his motorcycle, he'd asked a cop where he could park it. Directed to a spot behind the library and well away from any of the buildings, he was on his way to join the line of guests filing into the cathedral when the attack started.

They were coming right for him and his brain couldn't compute what his body ought to be doing. It was an attack, that much he understood. An attack by terrorists most likely, but how could it be that he was going to be caught up in it?

He was going to be the King, for goodness sake! Today was the day he swept away those who stood in his way. He couldn't die at the hands of some idiot terrorists. That's not how it was supposed to go at all.

Someone shouted, "Take cover!" and his right foot twitched. It knew he needed to get moving. A heartbeat later he was running across the grass to get behind the library. The drones were heading for the police and their command unit. If he could put enough distance between them and him he might be okay. No one would care if a few police officers were killed in the line of duty.

Edward certainly wouldn't and as he hugged the library wall, keeping as close to it as possible while continuing to run away, he wondered if he would get extra adoration from the British public for surviving the terrorist attack. Then he realised the wedding was almost certainly doomed. If it didn't go ahead today his entire plan was scuppered.

Years of planning would go down the drain.

With shouts of terror filling the air behind him, Lord Edward's own cries of frustration went unnoticed.

Chapter 36 – Albert and the King

Cody staggered out from his spot, emerging in front of the King and his security detail. Dressed in the clothes he'd taken from the first victim, he looked like a woman. His hair wasn't all he wanted it to be, but he'd restyled it into a more feminine look and added makeup to change his face.

Okay, he looked a bit like a female popstar from the early eighties with his backcombed style and painted on high cheekbones, but he didn't look like Cody Williams, and he didn't look like a man. The paper towels added lumps inside his shirt where he needed them and the tights did a good enough job of hiding the hair on his legs.

But looking like a woman wasn't enough. Having stabbed three women to create a pattern of attacks, he was now the fourth victim. There was blood on the blouse anyway, but he willingly cut himself to add more and made sure to have it all over his hands when he staggered into view.

"Good grief," said the King. His security team was still bundling him and Queen Camilla to the cathedral doors, but the injured woman staggered into their path looking like she could barely keep herself upright.

Looking through the gap between the armed police officers stationed just inside the doors, Albert saw the poor woman when she stumbled into sight.

Then he saw through the disguise.

"That's him!" he roared.

Behind him, the ushers and remaining security positioned inside the cathedral were holding the congregation at bay. Demonstrating human nature, at the sound of panic from outside, many were unable to resist jumping to their feet to rush to the doors. They wanted to see what was happening.

Keeping them back and safe inside the old church was all they could manage and that gave Albert a chance to get involved.

Rex didn't know which way to look. There was pandemonium everywhere. The scent of human fear filled his nostrils, but when his human shouted, he heard him.

"Rex! Sic 'im!"

Rex launched himself forward, looking for a target.

Outside, the two men of the King's security detail closest to the cathedral doors, detached themselves to help the injured woman. Their guns were holstered, there being no immediate visible danger, so they were caught completely by surprise when Cody slashed his ceramic blade across the first man's throat and continued the motion to stab into the second man's chest.

They dropped as he shoved through them, heading for the King.

The armed police inside the cathedral reacted before the guards' bodies hit the ground. Surging forward, they ran out just as Rex tried to go between them. Rex hit the back of their knees, felling both men instantly and they took him out as all three became a tangle of limbs, weapons, and fur.

Albert had already been running to follow his dog but could see no one from the cathedral could stop Cody before he reached the King. That left just two of the King's six-man detail to protect him.

The third member reached for his weapon as he rounded the King to place his body between his principal and the mad apparition wielding the knife.

Cody got to him before he could pull the gun free of its holster, driving his knife deep into the man's gut and wrenching his weapon free. Using the body as a shield, he danced to his left and shot the fourth guard before he could get a clear shot.

Albert leapt from the top step, his knees crunching when he hit the path. He could hear Rex scrambling to get back to his feet but neither of them was close enough to stop Cody.

Cody dropped the gun. He didn't want to use it. It was just him and the King now. He had moments to live but he was going to achieve his goal. The TV crews positioned on the other side of the grounds against the library wall were still filming. They were going to get the whole thing on camera. It was going to be the end of the monarchy and the start of a glorious new British republic.

"Well, Charlie Boy. I guess it's just you and me now." Cody lifted his blade, showing the King the weapon that would end his life.

"Oh, yeah?" said Camilla. "And what about me?"

Albert's mouth was formed into a wide 'O', and he screamed 'Noooooo!" running for all he was worth to stop Cody. But he needn't have bothered.

Cody had forgotten about the Queen but remembered her swiftly enough when her handbag knocked the knife from his hand.

She swung it again, this time aiming for his face, but he ducked and threw himself at the King. There were police marksmen and soldiers in every direction but none of them would dare to shoot for fear they might hit the King. The closer he was the surer that would be.

But as he stepped into the King's personal space, a sneer set on his face, Cody wasn't expecting the monarch to fight back. The first punch to his chin came as quite the surprise. Not just for how unexpected it was, but because it was a genuinely good punch.

Cody's head rocked back, and before he could recover the King kicked him in the gut.

"You see," said King Charles. "One tends to be dismissed as too old to be able to defend oneself." He spun off his left foot to deliver a swinging kick to Cody's head. "However, unbeknownst to the British public and indeed the world in general, one has been practicing martial arts since the late 50's. One likes to think one has achieved a reasonable level of mastery."

"Go on, Charlie!" cheered the Queen. "Kick 'is teeth in!"

King Charles paused to inspect his attacker. Cody shook his head in a bid to clear the cobwebs he suddenly found inhabiting his brain. Raising his fists, he managed to stand up straight.

"Not done yet? Oh, well, one more for the crowd, I suppose."

Reaching forward with both hands, King Charles gripped Cody's head.

"In Scotland I believe this is called a Glaswegian kiss."

The headbutt floored Cody in a manner that made Albert believe he wasn't about to get up again.

Rex, finally free of the tangled cops, bounded past Albert on his way to tackle Cody, but stopped short when he saw his target toppled backward like a tree being felled.

Unconscious before he hit the ground, Cody made no attempt to alleviate his impact with the grass. He bounced lightly and came to rest on his back, his stolen skirt hitched up to show the world his goods.

Chapter 37 – Buster and Amber

The outer panel of the door exploded outward, one large chunk flying across the kitchen to wedge beneath a counter.

Buster withdrew his head and spat out a few pieces of fibre board. Blood leaked from his skull, the skin splitting after multiple impacts with an unyielding surface. Except, of course, it did yield. It just took its time.

When Buster plonked his back end on the floor with a grunt, Amber nipped around him to get through the hole. It was easily big enough for her now, but Buster was going to have to squeeze to get through.

"Well done, Devil Dog. That was most impressive, and it only took you fifty-three attempts. How do you feel?"

His head hanging and his eyes closed against the splitting headache, Buster said, "*I think I just rebooted myself. Is it 1998?*"

Fairly sure that jokes meant he was fine, Amber started to walk away. "*Come along then. Let's not dilly dally. We need to get out of this building and find Felicity.*"

Buster grumbled, "*Yeah, yeah,*" and shoved his head through the hole. It wasn't big enough to accommodate his shoulders, but the fibre board had very little strength to it once it was broken. Pushing with his back legs, he got one front paw through and then the other.

Finally free, the cat and dog made their way from the kitchen, but exiting the room, they began to hear noises coming from outside.

"*That's humans,*" Amber said.

"*And they're scared,*" said Buster, breaking into a run.

Retracing their steps to the exit, they found the doors shut tight.

"*We'll have to find another way out,*" said Amber, wondering if she might be able to locate an open window.

"*Wait a second.*" Buster cocked his head, flipping his right ear over to better listen. "*I can hear voices. There are people upstairs.*" He started running. "*Come on! They might need saving.*"

They raced up the stairs, paused on the first floor to confirm the sound was coming from above them and ran up to the top floor.

Buster paused to catch his breath on the landing.

"*What are you doing?*" snapped Amber. "*Rescuing people was all your idea.*"

Panting hard from the effort, Buster managed to gasp, "*It's alright for you. I'm not built for speed. You wear fur like its fashion. I wear mine like it's a full body weighted blanket.*"

"*Yes, you do. Now quit whining and start running. Superheroes don't take breaks.*"

Quietly, so Amber wouldn't hear, Buster said, "*Even Batman has a Batcave. I just need a few minutes on a Batsofa.*"

He did it while moving, building to a jog and then a run as he chased Amber along the hallway. The voices were clearer now, which meant they were confusing. They didn't sound like they were in trouble at all. In fact, they sounded like they were having fun.

"I'm banking around for another pass," said Willow, excitedly.

"But the tanks are empty," pointed out Scott.

"Yeah, but they don't know that, and I want to see the panic on their faces when I buzz them. I'm going low to see if I can get a few closeups we can use for propaganda shots." Willow cackled as she operated her controls.

The others in the room all joined in, flying the drones around in a circle to head back toward the victims that were only now starting to pick themselves up off the ground. Their VR headsets meant they couldn't see the cat and dog sitting in the doorway.

"*You know,*" said Amber. "*I think these humans might be the reason why the other humans are screaming so much.*"

Ahead of them were five people dressed in palace livery.

Buster licked his chops. "*I believe you may be right. Shall we interrupt their fun?*"

Chapter 38 - Tempest, Patricia, and Felicity

In the shadow of the library, Tempest licked his fingers. All around him people were coated in the fine mist, but none showed signs of ill effects.

He dabbed a few more drops onto his tongue and questioned if he might be right.

"It's water," he said more to himself than anyone else.

He wasn't the only one to reach that conclusion. Police officers were getting to their feet, many doing so in a hurried manner as they sought to react to the attack. The honour guard of soldiers were racing to get to the King and his fallen security detail. The Royal Marines Band had abandoned their instruments to do the same, and shouted commands from all directions added confusion rather than order.

"It's water," Tempest said again, this time loud enough for people to hear.

Someone else yelled, "They're coming back around!" The cry and accompanying arm arrowed at a point in the sky, turned heads to the sight of the returning danger. But how dangerous was it?

Tempest accepted the taste test wasn't exactly scientific proof the people behind the attack intended panic rather than mass death, but there were many substances with instant effects, and they chose not to use them. The liquid tasted like water so until someone proved otherwise, he was going to tell himself that's all it was.

Unsure how he could use one of the drones to find the culprits but thinking it a good plan to knock one out of the sky anyway, Tempest looked around for something he could use. Abandoned gear lay all about.

Amanda yelled, "Tempest! Get to safety! Get inside!"

He wanted to reply, to explain there was no danger, but there was no time for so many words. Seeing something he could use, he ran.

Big Ben appeared at his side. "You thinking the same as me?"

"Knock them out of the sky and see if there's a way to trace them back to the owner?"

Big Ben frowned. "No, I was thinking this is great time to pick up girls. They're all so terrified right now. All I need to do, beyond flashing my smile, of course, is to be seen playing the hero."

Tempest considered whacking him with the riot shield he'd just collected from the ground but handed it to Big Ben instead. "Here, doofus. We're going to use these like Captain America's shield."

The drones were coming, dropping lower as they swooped on the crowd still recovering from the first attack. Tempest and Big Ben readied themselves, right arms back so they could launch the riot shields high into the path of the oncoming menace.

All five were heading their way, zipping through the air with a threatening whine. Until the one second from the left angled sharply left. It collided with the leftmost drone taking them both out.

The unexplained crash left three still swooping to buzz the crowd but before anyone could take another breath, another two lost control. One went straight up into the air before flipping over to tumble from the sky. The other zigzagged left and right, up and down, almost regaining stable flight before it corkscrewed into the earth.

The last remaining drone met its doom when both Tempest and Big Ben launched their riot shields into the sky.

"Ha! Mine hit it first," bragged Big Ben, watching the broken drone plummet.

All five were down, but what happened to the first four? No one had an answer. At least, not until the stunned silence fell and Felicity's mind picked up the faint sound of her dog barking, "*Dun, dun, Dah!*"

Chapter 39 – Felicity and the Dogs

Nudging Mindy, I said, "The pets!" I didn't wait for Mindy to respond. I was already moving. I could hear Amber too, their voices appearing inside my head as they always do. The sounds were faint as they were clearly some distance away, but when I used my ears I could tell they were inside the library.

"Wait!" cried Patricia. "What's happening?"

Running to get to the main entrance, I shouted back, "I think I know what happened to the drones!" Patricia probably wanted more explanation than that, but she was going to have to follow me to get it.

Vince passed me on my right side, Mindy on my left, the pair of them showing off their superior stride length.

Reaching the door, Vince held it open and bowed with a flourish when I sprinted through it.

I could hear more people following; a glance revealing Patricia Fisher and her friends. Now inside the building, I paused to get my bearings. Cries and wails of the human variety, accompanied by hissing, screeching, barking, and snarling filtered down from upstairs. Not that I heard those things. What I heard was a barrel-load of expletives as Amber threatened to do something improbable with a hairball and Buster promised to kill the mother of someone he then accused of having sex with mongrels in the manner of a belt-fed wombat.

I had not one clue what either threat meant, but they both sounded unnecessarily aggressive.

Mindy raced up the stairs, taking them three at a time with her ridiculously long legs. The nimble teenage minx had the skirt of her dress hoisted up to her derriere so everyone below her could see the insignificant material of her tiny thong wedged between her muscular butt cheeks.

I chose to look away, but heard Vince mutter, "Goodness," at a volume I probably wasn't supposed to hear. Running as fast as I could, I hadn't even reached the midway landing on my way to the first floor when Barbie went by me like a blonde streak. Hot on her heels was Patricia's butler, Jermaine and Patricia caught up to me a moment later. I know I'm a little older than her, but I genuinely thought I would be able to stay ahead of someone.

As if sensing my frustration, Patricia slowed her pace to run alongside me when she came level.

"Let's leave the sprinting to the young ones, eh?" she puffed.

We rounded the first-floor landing and continued up. Mindy and Barbie were already at the top. A few seconds later I could hear them yelling as they found whatever fight my cat and dog were having. More shouting ensued, male and female voices echoing down, but a few steps later it was obvious we were going to arrive after the fact.

The shouts were subsiding, and I could hear the deep bass rumble of Vince's voice speaking calmly.

"Shall we walk the last bit?" Patricia suggested, easing her pace to a walk before I could answer.

I really wanted to get to wherever everyone else already was, but my lungs were searing, my legs felt like lead, and I had a stitch in my side from the unexpected effort. I wanted the wedding to go without a hitch, and it had looked like that might actually happen until just a few minutes ago. First the call from Patricia to tell me someone had vandalised the bouquets in the church, and now this fiasco.

Was it recoverable? Was the danger over? I'd seen a woman with crazy hair, who turned out to be a man, attack the King. That he'd survived after all his security guards were taken out seemed incredulous, but he hadn't just survived, he'd beaten the attacker himself.

So the King and Queen were alive and looked to be unharmed when I last saw them. Also, the bulk of the wedding guests had stayed inside the cathedral, so I believed they were unaffected too. The bride was yet to arrive, so I didn't need to worry about her. Well, not yet anyway.

Could I still pull this off?

Following the voices, I found Amber sitting on a windowsill looking pleased with herself. Mindy was making a fuss of her.

Buster bumbled over to me, his back end wagging so hard he could hardly walk.

"*Mindy said we got the bad guys,*" he woofed.

That my pets had found and neutralised the drone pilots was not in question. One still wore his VR headset, though the control thingies were scattered across the floor. The one with the headset on looked unconscious and the other four were in some distress, rubbing their ankles where I assumed Buster had performed his usual trick of running through them. Or they were complaining about the lacerations to their faces – a favourite trick of Amber's.

What surprised me most was that my pets had worked together. Not only that but I hadn't been forced to bribe Amber into helping, which I almost always must if I want her assistance.

Vince was on his phone, alerting the police and bringing them to our location.

With the King's attacker in custody – I had seen the police surrounding him, and the drone pilots accounted for, would it be possible to get things back on track? I was certainly going to try.

Taking out my phone, I saw missed calls from Elizabeth. There were four of them, all in a two-minute period that would have been when the world was watching the madness unfold live on their televisions. I guess she gave up after I failed to answer again and again because she then sent a text.

'Felicity! Are you alive! I've just watched the attacks on TV!'

Other messages followed, all in the same vein and tone. I would call her soon to reassure her, but only after I established if the police were going to let the wedding go ahead. Biting my lip, I changed my mind. I was going to plough onwards until someone stopped me.

Crossing the building to the other side, Buster trotting along gamely at my heels, I delayed answering Vince when he called to ask where I was going.

Reaching the windows looking down over the grounds to the cathedral, the TV crews were directly beneath me. The panicked running in every direction had abated, and a calmness had returned.

Yes, I decided. Despite everything, I was going to pull this off.

Then I spat an expletive and started running again. The bride's car had just pulled up.

Chapter 40 - The Aftermath

Albert found it a little surreal to find himself chatting with the King of England, but just like their time at the palace, the King had chosen him as an ally. The Queen was inside the cathedral. Announcing her need to find somewhere to sit down, she had left her husband to watch the police deal with his attacker.

The King's security detail were all still alive. None would be on active duty any time soon, and their injuries dictated hospital and surgery were urgent requirements. They were not, however, considered to be in any immediate danger.

The King was entirely unharmed, though Albert noted him rubbing the knuckles of his right hand absentmindedly more than once. They were undoubtedly bruised from the first blow he delivered, direct to Cody's jaw.

"So that's the fellow you met in Cornwall?" The King asked.

"Indeed, sir. I'm afraid I know nothing of his movements since then but believe he's been hiding in plain sight inside Buckingham Palace since before my knighthood last year."

THE ROYAL WEDDING

The King took a moment to consider the news. "One shall need to speak with the people managing the palace security. One fears that job could be performed better."

"Indeed," Albert agreed.

One of the arresting officers looked up at the King. "Sorry, Your Majesty. Can I ask how he got to be so wet?" There were cops all around Cody but none of them were particularly excited about handling him. He was damp and had a worrying odour about his person.

Albert looked down at his dog. "Care to explain how he came to be wet, Rex?"

The innocent look on Rex's face remained firmly in place when he said, "*I have no idea what you are talking about.*"

Albert addressing the question to his dog told the police officers precisely what the mystery liquid coating Cody's head and shoulders was and why it was warm. Those with it on their hands pulled faces and looked about for something they could wipe them on.

King Charles tried to hide his smirk. "One must say your dog has a wonderful sense of justice."

"Mm-hmm. He has something," Albert agreed.

They watched the cops lever Cody from the ground. With cuffs restraining his arms and an officer each side to hold them, they led him across the grounds to a waiting van. He would be taken away and likely wouldn't see the outside world for a very long time.

"I say," said the King, nodding his head toward the library. "She's in a hurry."

They watched Felicity run from the building, her niece flying along beside her with her skirt hitched to her upper thighs.

Albert pointed to the road. "I believe that's the bride just arriving, sir."

Chapter 41 – Felicity

By the time we got to the car, Nora was already out of it. Her flower girls, her mother, and the maid of honour surrounded her, and they were all staring at the grounds between the street and the cathedral with wide eyes and mute horror.

I slowed my pace to walk the last few yards, turning to see just how bad it all looked. I guess I hadn't really noticed, and everything had happened so fast, but the peaceful and serene open expanse of lawn now looked like a scene following an explosion.

There were clusters of police and palace security officers around each of the downed drones. More police were leading the King's attacker across the grass in the direction of their command unit. The TV cameras were tracking him, and he yelled his opinion of the monarchy to make sure it was heard, but he looked demented with his makeup and women's clothes, like a twisted drag version of Britney Spears on a bad hair day. I doubted anyone was going to take him seriously.

The honour guard were not where they were supposed to be, the Royal Marines Band should have been playing the bride's favourite tune, but weren't even holding their instruments, and the level of activity could be described most accurately as pandemonium.

Nora's bottom lip wobbled, and she wailed, "What happened?"

Primrose was three feet away, there at the kerb to manage the guests as they arrived. It was a simple enough task that mostly required her to make sure we weren't missing anyone, that the doormen were not only prompt to open car doors but did so in time with each other, and to communicate with the honour guard who would present arms when it was appropriate.

She looked my way and I couldn't help but glare. She'd abandoned her post, and I was becoming more and more convinced she was behind the pierced water balloons.

Primrose saw the hardness in my eyes and gave a questioning look – acting innocent. I would deal with her later.

The bride's mum and the maid of honour tried to give comfort, but it was my task to reassure Nora and get things back on track.

I said, "There was a small incident."

"Small!" the bride screeched.

"A man attacked the King."

"Oh no!" she gasped.

"Oh, he wasn't harmed. In fact, here he comes right now."

The King of England had chosen to intervene. He was coming to speak with his imminent daughter-in-law and had Albert Smith walking by his side.

"Hello, Nora," said the King. "Is one ready to get married?"

"It's still going ahead?" she questioned disbelievingly.

I jumped in quick. "The cathedral was unaffected by the individual who attacked the King. Your groom awaits as do your guests. This is nothing more than a minor inconvenience in what is going to be an otherwise perfect day." I delivered my words with a confident smile and prayed I wouldn't be proven wrong.

The King turned about to face the cathedral once more. "Come along, Sir Albert. We must hurry if we are to beat the bride inside."

I spotted Justin hovering just outside the cathedral's main entrance and waved to make sure he saw me. It was go time. I was going to get the ceremony underway before anyone thought to question it.

All about us the bedlam continued, but the bridal party made their way along the path, going slow so the King, Sir Albert, and Sir Rex could get to their seats first. With Justin making shooing motions, the Royal Marines Band raced back to their instruments, arranged themselves, and started playing. Like the honour guard, who presented their weapons when the King walked past, they looked a little dishevelled. Where their uniforms had been perfect, they were distinctly less so now, but none of that mattered because the wedding was going ahead.

I followed and could hear Primrose's heels a step behind mine.

"Felicity," she hissed just loud enough for me to hear.

I chose not to respond.

"Felicity!" she hissed again with a little more volume and insistence.

I snapped my head around, my eyes hard again. "Not now!" I growled my response quietly but with venom. Primrose reacted as though I'd slapped her face and the confusion showing doubled. Though only for a moment. As I was turning back around, her own face hardened, and it felt like old times when we had nothing good to say to each other.

Nora entered the church, Justin signalled the organist, and I breathed a small sigh of relief when the bridal march belted out.

Despite Primrose's attempts to sabotage the event and in the aftermath of a crazed killer trying to get stabby with the King, the wedding was happening. Finally, we had arrived at a part of the day when it would proceed without my involvement. Okay, so I still had a million and one things to do, including fire Primrose and expel her from the grounds, but I could tackle those secure in the knowledge that the ceremony was going ahead.

I watched until the bride reached the front of the cathedral and was handed over to her groom. Content, I turned around to face Primrose. "We need to talk."

Chapter 42 – Felicity and Primrose

"What are you talking about, Felicity?"

I'll say this for Primrose, she's a good actor. We were outside the cathedral and around to the side of the grand entrance where the cameras couldn't see us. They weren't allowed inside – the ceremony was to remain private – and should now have been taking a break. With all the unexpected excitement before the bride arrived, that hadn't come to pass and they were roving the grounds, shooting footage of the downed drones, interviewing cops and palace staff, and filming the drone pilots as they were led from the library.

Mercifully, none of them were filming our argument.

"Don't waste my time, Primrose. I know it was you. Who else would stoop so low?"

"When could I have possibly had the time to make holes in the bouquets inside the cathedral? I haven't even been inside the cathedral since you tasked me with working the guest list."

"Oh, well I expect it was when you absconded from that job."

Primrose's forehead was already deeply lined with confusion. It doubled.

"You mean when you pulled me off that job to deal with the ice sculpture at the reception venue? Is then when I'm supposed to have done it?"

It was my turn to look bewildered. "What are you talking about? I never asked you to leave this location. I gave you the spotlight job at the kerb!"

Primrose wrenched her handbag open, thrust her hand into it, and yanked out her phone.

"Don't know what I'm talking about, eh? Explain this then!"

She handed me her phone and on the screen was a string of messages from me. The timestamp for them right when I had been at the reception venue myself.

"But I didn't send these," I said, reaching into my handbag to produce my own phone. I opened my messages and showed Primrose.

"So you deleted them," she snapped. "And that means this is just a ruse to get rid of me. You've had me do all the work in the build up to this day, but now you want all the credit, so you're going to make it look like I was sabotaging things. That's it, isn't it?"

"No! Not at all." How was I now on the defensive? "Don't you dare try to turn this around. I never asked you to go to the reception venue and I could have brought anyone on board to help me with this wedding. I asked you because I hoped we could reach a new level of understanding and not spend our time undermining each other." I was being very generous because the undermining was one hundred percent a Primrose tactic.

THE ROYAL WEDDING

Primrose dropped her phone back in her handbag and folded her arms. "I didn't give you enough credit, Felicity. You are a lot more mercenary than I realised. Well you might think you can damage me by booting me off this project, but I'll be gunning for you now like I never was before."

With that she wheeled around and walked away, her strides determined.

I watched her go, confused about the text messages, but refusing to call her back to discuss it further. Something wasn't right and I needed to give it some thought. In fact, I might even label it as a mystery. Unfortunately, I'm terrible at figuring those out, but I wasn't without friends I could turn to.

Vince had remained quiet during the exchange but now Primrose was leaving, he said, "You know, I think she might have been telling the truth."

Having just accused her of sabotage it really wasn't what I wanted to hear. Too late now, I needed to move forward without her and see if I couldn't get Patricia to find proof of Primrose's guilt.

Looking around to find Mindy, I said, "Everything is about the reception now. Can you head over there and make sure it's all going to plan? I know you are supposed to be with Lord Edward for the reception …"

Mindy saluted. "It's fine, Auntie. I'll see him there. And don't worry about the reception. I will check everything twice."

I could tell from Mindy's expression there was something else she wanted to say.

"Um," she started. "Well, I know it's not really the time to say, 'I told you so', but there was an attack on the royal family and Eddie had nothing to do with it. I'm just saying," she added.

"You're right," I acknowledged. "I know you think I have it in for him, but I really don't. I think he is handsome and sweet, and I hope he treats you right."

"But?" Mindy prompted.

"But nothing, Mindy. Cassie is investigating him for a reason. I hope she is wrong just as much as you do." My answer satisfied her.

We'd been dancing around the subject for months. She was involved with a man the palace detective suspected of killing his brother. Cassie admitted she had no actual evidence yet remained unshakable in her conviction.

Breaking the moment, Vince asked, "What are you going to be doing?"

"I'll be along as soon as I can, but I need to speak with Patricia before I leave here. If I'm missing something and Primrose isn't to blame, the saboteur is still at large and I would rather avoid any further mishaps."

Vince said, "I'm staying with you just in case."

"Thank you," I said, touching his arm for the reassurance his company gave.

Mindy started toward the library. "Shall I take Amber and Buster?"

"Yes, please. In fact …" I went with Mindy as Vince split off to speak with the police again. She was going to take the car to the reception venue. I would follow, but I wanted to speak with my pets before they departed. Our unique connection – my ability to talk to them made them the perfect spies to be deployed. They could go places and hear things a person couldn't.

My cat and dog were back in the office on the ground floor. Vince took them there after I ran from the building to intercept the bride. I was yet to congratulate or thank them for their efforts in catching the drone pilots, so I took care of that first.

Buster bumbled over to me the moment I walked through the door, his back end wagging so hard he struggled to walk forward. Amber, ever the cat, sat calmly on the windowsill paying no attention to the bedlam outside or the people coming into the room because it's all so beneath her.

I made a big fuss of Buster, crouching to shower him with kisses.

"You are such a big, brave boy, Buster." His back right leg started to twitch when I found the spot on his side that always triggers it. "Is your head okay? Did one of those nasty people hit you?"

Buster tried to make his eyes look through the top of his skull. "*Oh, no I did that ramming my way through a door to get out.*"

I twisted to look at the door. It was completely intact.

"*Not that door,*" said Amber. "*We went out of the window when we saw Rex and Eric chasing after someone.*"

"Eric? Wait, who's Eric?" I questioned, feeling like I had missed a major plot point.

Mindy scrunched her forehead. "Eric? Is that the name of the guy who tried to kill the King?"

Buster stopped panting so abruptly it was like someone had turned off a switch. "*Wait, someone tried to kill the King?*"

"*Eric is a police dog,*" provided Amber.

"How do you know him?" I asked.

"*He was with Rex,*" explained Buster. "*What happened to the King?*"

"Hold on a second." I needed a moment to backtrack. "You went out of the window to chase someone?"

Buster wagged his tail. "*Yes.*"

I looked at the window sceptically. "How did you manage that?" Amber could leap and had claws to climb. Buster's back end is like a sack of cement. He has a lot of pulling power in a straight line – something to which I can attest from all the times I've had to drag him away from an abandoned slice of pizza or spilled late night kebab. Jumping, however, is not a skill he possesses.

Buster said, "*Wasn't easy.*"

I left it at that. "Ok. You went out of a window to chase someone, teaming up with Rex and a police dog called Eric. Then what?"

From her lofty position on the windowsill, Amber sounded bored when she replied with, "*We followed the man's scent around the building and back inside through the main door. Then we split up to search and we found him in the kitchen. He was putting on women's clothes and stuffing paper towels inside his shirt to give himself breasts.*"

"What are they saying, Auntie?" Mindy begged to know. She was the first person to catch me having a conversation with my pets and remains jealous that she cannot do the same. I explained how I started hearing their voices a few weeks after I brought them to live with me, so when she moved into my house she hoped the same might happen for her. We are related by blood after all and perhaps it's a genetic thing. Alas, months have passed and she is yet to develop my ability.

Over my shoulder, I said, "I'll catch you up in a minute," and went back to my conversation.

"*He locked us in a cupboard,*" Amber continued, "*and Buster had to use his head to smash through it. He was very brave.*"

Buster had been about to say something but stopped to gawp at the cat. He wasn't the only one. I stared at her. A compliment had just left her mouth, and I couldn't have been more surprised if she'd pulled a tiny guitar from her ear and started to play *Stairway to Heaven*.

Sensing what she'd done, Amber blurted, "*I mean for a dog. He was kinda brave for a dog.*"

Buster sniggered. "*Ha! You just said something nice, Fatal Feline.*"

My eyebrows performed a dance above my eyes. "Fatal what now?"

"*Amber took a superhero name,*" boasted Buster proudly. "*She's my new sidekick.*"

"*I am not!*" gasped Amber in horror. "*If I am anything, I'm a team up. That would make us equals.*"

Buster made a 'wow' face. "*You mean like when Superman and Wonder Woman team up to fight something too powerful for just one of them?*"

I waved my hands in the air to stop everyone from talking. "Okay, okay. Look the two of you are wonderful and I really think you saved the day. But the day isn't over, and I need you both to go into spy mode."

Buster sat up super straight and lifted his right paw as if trying to salute. He got it halfway to his head and fell over.

I explained about the saboteur, about how it was probably Primrose behind it and that she was no longer working with us. Amber and Buster were to go to the reception venue with Mindy and Vince. There was work to do there, but I wanted them to explore and observe. If there was someone doing something to mess with my well-laid plans, I wanted to catch them before their next trick could upset the bride's day.

Chapter 43 – Felicity and Patricia

I found Patricia and her friends from the cruise ship with Tempest and his team. They were with the police and had camera crews buzzing around them. DI Cassie Munroe was there too. Tempest's cover was one hundred percent blown the moment he ran in front of the cameras. It had taken the TV crews moments to identify him, so now he was going to have to move in the shadows if he was to continue investigating.

Mindy wouldn't like it, but Cassie's entire focus was on Lord Edward. Recruiting the Blue Moon team to help her out, there were five of them trying to figure out if he was a genuine threat or not. Was Cassie wrong or were my concerns about a saboteur pointless because something far more sinister was in play?

Patricia saw me coming and detached herself from the group, moving a couple of feet away so we could speak privately.

"The wedding is going ahead?" she sought to confirm.

I nodded. "Yes. The bride is a little shellshocked, but otherwise the wedding party were unaffected by the drone attack and the knife-wielding maniac who went after the King."

"Did you get a chance to speak with him?"

"The King? Not directly, but he was chatting amiably with Albert Smith. Maybe he was putting a brave face on it, but he seemed okay to me."

"I'm very glad to hear it. Actually," she looked around to check if people were listening to our conversation and leaned her head closer to mine, "I'm glad they got it on camera. Can you imagine what tomorrow's headlines will be?"

She had a wide grin on her face that matched my own. The newspaper front pages would show the King of England punching his attacker in the face. Or perhaps delivering the headbutt. It made me wonder how international relations would be affected. Would other countries really want to mess with a nation whose monarch could handle himself like that?

Changing the subject, I said, "I know the first part of this wedding has been a little crazy, but we still have the reception to go and I think Primrose was behind the burst water balloons. That being the case, I doubt it will be her only ploy."

"You want us to head to the venue and see what we can learn?"

"Could you?" I didn't want to become that person who is always asking for more, but Patricia was here only because I asked for her help.

"Of course. I'll finish up here and head there in the next few minutes. I just need to make sure the police have my details."

"Thank you, Patricia. You don't know what it means to have you to help figure out who's behind all the drama. One thing I should tell you, I suppose."

"Yes?"

"Well, Vince thinks it might not be Primrose at all. Don't ask me why. He thought she sounded innocent when she denied tampering with the bouquets and she had messages on her phone to make it look like I sent her to the venue. I didn't send the messages, and I think it's nothing more than a ruse on her part to cover her tracks."

"But if it isn't …" said Patricia, placing a hand on my arm to impart comfort.

"But if it isn't," I agreed.

"Not to worry, Felicity. We'll get to the bottom of it. No one will be allowed to ruin the reception."

"What's that?" asked Tempest, appearing from our left. "More problems?"

Patricia hooked an arm through his. "I'll tell you on the way." With a nod of goodbye, they walked toward the library and the carpark beyond. I could hear them talking about Lord Edward as they walked away.

The wedding ceremony would last another forty minutes or so. That gave me time to pack up my things here and be ready to move to the reception. I had a change of outfit just in case it was needed, which it was after all the running around, crawling on the cathedral floor, and general stress. I could take my time, maybe even have a cup of tea (though I wanted something stronger), and be ready for when the guests began to leave the cathedral.

There is never anything much to do at the church once the ceremony starts and whatever did arise would be handled by Justin and Philippe since Primrose was no longer part of the proceedings.

Was I wrong about her? Was she ever anything other than my deadliest rival? I had invited her to be part of my team in the belief that she could work with me. Were my hopes just innocently childish?

I shrugged off my jacket, placed it on a coat hanger and slid it into a folding garment holder. Taking off my heels, which felt soooo good, I flicked on the kettle and while it boiled, I checked my makeup.

It needed a little touch up here and there, but I was faring okay so far.

The kettle reached boiling point as I was putting my things away. Tea would have to do until much later today when I would allow myself an industrial strength gin and tonic. However, distracted by the activity outside the window, I only half hit the cup. Boiling water washed across the countertop, scalding my hand which made me jump. I knocked a vase of flowers, lunged to stop it from toppling, and in so doing knocked over the half-filled mug of hot water.

Now with hot water trying to drip onto my bare feet I had to dance out of the way and wouldn't you know it, I backed into a chair. We all had so much stuff with us and had largely been living out of suitcases and holdalls for the last week as we got ready for the big day, so the chair had bags hanging off both sides of the back and there were more piled on the seat. The chair didn't fall – I didn't hit it that hard, but the bags decided to leap to their deaths like depressed lemmings.

Cursing, I found somewhere to put the vase down, picked up the cup, and found a towel to mop up the mess. When I came in I had plenty of time to sit and relax. Now I didn't. Not unless I planned to leave behind the mess I'd just created.

Tutting to myself, I looked at the jumbled mess around the chair. Some of it was Mindy's; I recognised her things. And the makeup was definitely Philippe's. There was another bag in the mix and I couldn't work out who it belonged to.

Thankfully, it was zipped shut, so I picked it up first to get it out of the way, but I didn't put it down.

Attached to the zipper was a little keyring thing. An accessory, I guess you would call it. There's nothing unique or unusual about that, but I recognised it. I'd seen one exactly like it in Scotland just a few weeks ago when yet another wedding went horribly sideways.

I recognised it because I had bought the same keyring myself. The accessory was a little dragonfly wearing a tartan scarf. It was super cute and was made from hallmarked silver and enamel.

Mindy, Philippe, and Justin were all there with me, but I didn't think the bag belonged to any of my team. I picked up my phone and took a picture. Texting it to the group via WhatsApp, I asked the question.

No one responded. At least not swiftly enough to still my curiosity. Unable to resist, I opened the bag. I felt dirty doing so. I was prying inside someone else's luggage. To me that was like peeking in a person's underwear drawer in their house when they think you have popped upstairs to use their toilet.

Yet I needed to know.

Ever since returning from the debacle in Scotland, one thing had bothered me more than any other. Someone hit Justin over the head at the castle and Agatha's League of Villains were never at that location. It meant there had to be another player in the field. So far as I knew, the police in Scotland were yet to figure out who that could be. Yet here was a trinket that placed someone firmly at the right location.

Could the same accessory be sold in other locations? Yes, that was possible, I wasn't going to deny it, but it also felt like way too much of a coincidence and the silver was so shiny it had to have been purchased recently.

THE ROYAL WEDDING

Moving to a patch of carpet devoid of other clutter, I upended the bag. If the owner walked in on me I was going to demand to know how they got the accessory, so it didn't matter if I got caught. Unfortunately, where I hoped for items of clothing that might give away the owner's identity – a double D bra would make it Primrose's, Elizabeth is more like a double A – there was nothing that helped at all.

My phone pinged. The text was from Mindy.

'*That's not my bag and I don't know whose it is. Sorry.*'

Puffing out my cheeks and thinking hard, I recalled the house brick that came through the bride's window on the morning of the wedding. It was the first volley in a wave of attacks that at the time all felt connected. Looking upon it in reflection, the attacks on the bride were separate to those against the groom.

Yet again it suggested another player in the field – just my luck to attract two groups of criminally insane nutters. The brick had LBC cast into it. The letters stand for London Brick Company which made me want to believe the person who threw it brought it with them to Scotland. It was anything but conclusive, but certain the saboteur was with me today, it made sense that they were part of my team.

That still placed Primrose in first place, but if it wasn't her …

Chapter 44 – The Reception

"Oh, my word. Are you okay?" Elizabeth asked when Mindy found her in the grand hall at the reception venue.

Mindy had arrived with the pets and in a convoy of cars that carried Patricia Fisher, Tempest Michaels, and all their friends. She had wasted no time deploying Amber and Buster, the trusted pets ducking under tables to vanish from sight and begin their own feline/canine/secret superhero investigation.

The human detectives deployed in different directions the moment they entered the building. Elizabeth would know Patricia Fisher on sight, as did half the planet, but Mindy wasn't so sure she would be able to pick Tempest and his crew from a lineup. Tempest was famous, yes, but not on the same scale as Patricia.

Having promised to double check everything at the reception, Mindy knew she was going to have to step on Elizabeth's toes, but that was just how it had to be. She was loyal to her aunt, so even though Elizabeth was helpful, and friendly, and easy to get along with, next week they would be business rivals again.

"Yes, thank you. A few people were hurt, but I think all the injuries came at the hands of the man who attacked the King. Did you see what he did?"

"The King? My goodness, yes! Wasn't it amazing. I never knew Charlie had it in him."

Mindy saw flaws in the King's delivery. Especially the roundhouse kick, but the man was in his seventies, so she had to give him kudos for still being nimble enough to deliver it.

"What about the drones? They said on the TV that the liquid they sprayed was thought to be water."

"That's right," said Mindy. "The police forensic team confirmed it. I think we all got lucky because it could have been something much worse."

"Where's Felicity and Primrose?" asked Elizabeth, looking around.

"Felicity will be along as soon as the ceremony ends. She stayed behind to make sure the official photographers are ready for the happy couple, plus a bunch of other stuff she no doubt wants to take personal care of."

"And Primrose? I could really do with some help here. There's a lot still to do and we are running out of time."

"Well, I'm here. I can help, but Primrose won't be joining us."

Elizabeth canted her head to one side like a dog trying to understand what its human was saying.

Not wanting to get into the details, Mindy said, "There was an incident at the cathedral. Not the incident, incident, obviously. Something less dramatic, but Felicity and Primrose had a bust up over it and Primrose left."

Elizabeth said, "Oh," and looked thoughtful for a moment before adding, "Was it because she was here? I told her she didn't need to be, but she wouldn't tell me why she had left the cathedral, and it clearly wasn't so she could help me with something."

Mindy had been about to suggest they get on with whatever needed to be done – she wanted to start the process of checking things were as they should be, but Elizabeth's revelation gave her pause.

"You saw Primrose when she was here?"

"Yeah. I saw her arrive but was in the middle of dressing the tables. By the time I was done with that and went to find her she was already on her way back out. I only just caught her before she left."

"Do you know what she was here for or where she went?"

Elizabeth made a sorry face. "No clue. Like I said, she wouldn't tell me. Only that Felicity sent her. I thought she was lying at the time." Elizabeth tried not to make it sound like she was being careful about what she said, but she had to watch her words lest she let something slip. She had two surprises lined up for the reception. If the first one didn't ruin things, the second one certainly would.

"Oh, while I'm at it," Mindy fished out her phone. "Do you know whose bag this is?" She showed Elizabeth the photograph of the holdall with the dragonfly keyring accessory.

Elizabeth shook her head, fighting to keep her cheeks from turning pink. "It might be Primrose's," she lied.

Mindy put her phone away and looked around. "Auntie asked me to double check everything, so that's what I'm going to do." She lifted a hand to beckon a gaggle of palace staff standing idle near the bar where they were refreshing themselves with soft beverages. Soon they would be whizzing about with drinks and food, but for now they were a standing army and ripe to be employed.

Chapter 45 – Buster and Amber

Buster peeked out from under a tablecloth. The perfectly white, freshly ironed cotton didn't need Buster to wipe his slobber on the bottom edge or leave behind a faint trace of blood from the small wound on his head, but neither would be noticed.

Peering out between the legs of a chair he felt supremely confident of his invisibility. He was Devil Dog, the embodiment of vengeance, the harbinger of justice, the ..."

"*See anything?*" asked Amber, scaring Buster so convincingly he left a few drops of wee on the hardwood floorboards.

When he stopped hyperventilating, Buster said, "*Good sneak attack. I'm glad to see you've been paying attention and have picked up some of my skills.*"

"*Buster, you're a fat idiot.*"

"*Making the world around me think that is another of my superhero skills, Amber. Clark Kent could put on glasses to change his appearance and blend into the background. That won't work for me because a dog with glasses would attract attention.*"

"*Oh, so the bumbling, dopey dog act is precisely that?*"

"*Precisely. I look like a slightly chubby bulldog on the outside, but beneath the skin lies the muscle, poise, and athletic ability of a Rhodesian Ridgeback. I'm like Rin Tin Tin if he'd been a ninja.*"

Certain he would continue spouting nonsense until she changed the subject, Amber said, "*I'm going to search the back rooms. People up to no good are always hanging around behind the scenes.*" She didn't want to go to the backrooms, but if there was a crime to solve, and a miscreant to catch, there was no way Amber was going to allow a drooling canine buffoon to claim the victory.

No, it was going to be the cat who brought home that particular trophy. Thankfully, the dog was easy to manipulate.

"*Good thinking,*" Buster agreed. "*I'll go with you.*"

Amber sighed for the dramatic effect. "*No, Buster. The point is for us to split up so we can cover more ground.*"

"*Oh. So I should stay here? What if nothing happens here?*" Buster would never admit it, but he'd grown quite fond of the cat. She was a sassy princess almost every minute she was awake and she teased him constantly about his waistline, his wrinkled brow, his goofy teeth, and whatever else she thought of, but every now and then she let her guard down and would accidentally say something nice. Right now she was giving him the choice of locations to investigate. Well, that was a mistake on her part because he was always going to choose the one most likely to yield a result. No way was he going to lose to a cat.

THE ROYAL WEDDING

Amber said, *"You take the back room if you want to and I'll hang around in here. There are lots of people here. Maybe one of them is up to no good."*

Checking all around, Buster snuck out from under the tablecloth. Amber watched him vanish under the next table before venturing out herself. As a cat, she knew she was welcome everywhere. Humans adore cats. Well, the wise ones do at least. Some liked dogs and they would be the first to die when felines everywhere rose up to take over the world.

Felicity fell into the middle category of people who likes both cats and dogs. Her death would be swift and merciful come the revolution. Thinking perhaps it was time to find one of the sensible humans because she rather fancied a snack, Amber followed her nose to the kitchen.

Buster nudged his way through a door and slipped out of sight before people heading his way saw him. When they passed, he crept out again to continue onwards. He had no idea what he was looking for other than something suspicious. Felicity said Primrose had messed with the flowers in the cathedral but that she couldn't do any more damage because she wasn't part of the team anymore.

What appeared to worry Felicity now was that Primrose had been to the reception venue and therefore could have messed with things at that location too. Mindy was checking everything in the hope she would find whatever it was long before the guests arrived, so Buster and Amber had a different mission.

Buster just wasn't entirely clear what it was. They were to act as spies and eavesdrop on the humans. That was easy enough, but what was he supposed to be listening out for? If Primrose was behind the sabotaging and she was gone ... well, it wasn't like he would be able to hear the sound of something she'd sabotaged.

Thinking about his previous excursion as a spy in Scotland, Buster recalled disguising himself using soot from an old coal fire. He'd scared the living daylights out of Amber when she walked by and hadn't seen him. Maybe he needed to do that again, but he doubted he would find an old fireplace today. Not in the plush hotel. Plus, everything was white. Making himself black would be the opposite of wearing a disguise. He would stand out like a dachshund at a Great Dane basketball game.

No, what he needed was something white in which he could coat himself. But what was white and available to be liberally applied to his coat? Paint? Well, yes, but no thanks. He found Felicity painting the living room walls once and had a go himself when she stopped to get some lunch. She had to shave off one side of his fur when it set hard and Amber teased him for a month.

Pondering the question, Buster found his way into the kitchen where the answer presented itself instantly. One of the chefs was flouring a surface, dusting it with fine white powder. That would work!

He had to wait for the chef to finish what he was doing and move away, but the moment he did, Buster ran across the kitchen, bounced up onto his back legs and nudged the container of flour until it fell over. Closing his eyes, he kept his tail still and held his breath when the resulting spill poured over his head and down his back. The flour continued to fall even though Buster was covered, but a second or so was all he needed. Backing out of the room and leaving a trail of ghostly footprints in his wake, Buster claimed success.

Devil Dog had risen anew. This was his alter ego's alter ego. He was no longer the Duke of Darkness but had become the Pale Pooch! No. Buster shook his head. That was no good. How about Milk Mutt?

Terrible. He needed a name that would strike fear into those who would hide from justice.

He was still thinking up names when he heard someone coming. Their footsteps echoed on the stone floor, but that was perfect. It gave him the chance to test out his latest disguise. Finding a doorway, he slunk down in the recess and thought invisible thoughts.

The person rounded the corner, and he almost let his tail wag because it was someone he knew.

Elizabeth couldn't decide whether she should feel nervous or excited. Primrose was gone and it appeared as though Felicity blamed her for the water balloons at the cathedral. That was her intention, and she'd made sure the next two surprises would appear to be Primrose's handiwork too. Getting her to sign for the ice sculpture was a necessary part of the evidence trail. Primrose ordered it in the first place, and it was booby trapped so it made sense that she would dream up an excuse to be at the reception venue to receive it. How else could Primrose ensure her dastardly plan was going to work?

That's what everyone would think. Elizabeth was sure of it.

But that Patricia Fisher character kept looking at her. Was it her imagination? She wanted to believe it was nothing more than her paranoia playing tricks. Patricia Fisher was probably looking at everyone.

Yet she felt nervous all the same and now Mindy was here to double check all the work she'd done. It was a bit of an insult. In fact, it was running close to a slap in the face to have a teenager making sure her work was up to spec.

Regardless, Mindy wasn't going to find the traps waiting for the wedding guests. Not unless she started testing everything to make sure it worked as it was supposed to and even then there was no way to tell the ice sculpture was rigged. Oh, how Elizabeth looked forward to that one. It would end the reception in one fell swoop. Boom. Done. No coming back. The most spectacular wedding fail in the history of weddings. It would destroy Felicity's reputation and since Primrose had her fingerprints all over it, she would burn too.

Heck, Primrose might even burn harder. There could be criminal prosecution heading her way if they could make the charges stick. The important thing was that no one would be able to trace any of it to Elizabeth.

Except Felicity was asking questions about her bag? It had to be because of the little keyring she put on it. It was so cute she hadn't been able to resist. Only now could she see the folly in her decision. It placed her in the vicinity of Felicity's disastrous wedding in Scotland.

It could be explained away with a lie about a great aunt who sent her a gift when she was on her travels. That would do it. Then it was nothing but a coincidence.

Buster watched Elizabeth go by, keeping his body as still as possible. In his head, he pretended this was a new superhero skill that came with his Frost Fang alter ego. He'd finally figured out a name that worked. Frost Fang could freeze things. Including himself.

His nose began to tickle. The flour was all over his face and tiny particles were going up his nose every time he inhaled. He was going to sneeze! He just knew it. If he could just hold it for a few more seconds, Elizabeth would be around the corner and out of sight.

"*Waaachooo!*" The sneeze exited his nose with so much power he whacked his head against the door. A shower of flour fell from his body to leave an outline on the carpet like someone had drawn around a body. "*Waaachoo!*"

Elizabeth jumped out of her skin and had to fight not to drop the things she was holding. Gripped by primeval terror, the most basic survival functions rooted deep within her brain insisted it was time to fight or run away. Spinning around to see what horror might lurk in her shadow, she shrieked when she saw the white blob.

Buster thought the sneezes were done, but had his face still wrinkled in defence should another one choose to sneak attack. He knew he was supposed to be running away, but there was something ever so familiar about his current situation.

"Wait a minute," said Elizabeth, her panic subsided. The white blob had not only moved to reveal its true shape but had licked its nose to stop the next sneeze. "You're Felicity's dog."

Buster blinked. Random neurons collided inside his head and the thing that had been bothering him for days coalesced into an answer.

"*You were in Scotland!*"

All Elizabeth heard was rabid barking.

"*It was you!*" barked Buster. "*You're the saboteur! That's what I couldn't figure out. When I saw you in that hotel, right before it burned to the ground, I knew that I knew you. I just couldn't figure out where from. I can't believe it's taken me this long to figure it out. Oh, just you wait until I tell Felicity!*"

Mindy burst through the door leading to the ballroom. "What the heck is going on?"

Buster got in first. "*It's her, Mindy! She's the one behind it all! Grab her quick!*"

Mindy levelled an accusing glare at Elizabeth. "What did you do to him. He's never like this?"

"Do to him? I haven't touched him. Why is he covered in flour? He's making a mess everywhere."

Mindy had to concede that part, but Buster was going nuts, and he only ever did that when he was going after someone or trying to defend Felicity.

"Buster, stop now," she commanded.

"*What? No, not a chance. Mindy, I know you don't have the thing that Felicity has but you have to believe me. Elizabeth is the one. You need to ninja kick her or something!*"

"Is he safe?" asked Elizabeth. Truthfully, she was worried the dog had figured it out. He'd seen her in the hotel in Scotland but hadn't reacted to her presence at any point in the last few weeks she'd been working with Felicity. Yet something had changed, and he was going nuts.

"*Okay,*" said Buster. "*I don't want to do this but you're leaving me no choice.*" He lowered his head. If he couldn't make Mindy understand, then he was going to have to take action. If Elizabeth was injured, she wouldn't be able to do any more harm. Surging forward, he barked, "*Dun, dun, Dah!*"

Elizabeth saw the dog coming for her and squealed in fright. Mindy saw it too, and moving fast, tucked Elizabeth behind her.

Buster had to throw on the brakes or run straight through Mindy's legs. He stopped just in time but then tried to go around her to get to his target.

"*I have to bite her, Mindy. I have to. She's the bad one!*"

Unable to fathom what was going on in Buster's head, Mindy grabbed his collar. The dog had a lot of low-level grunt. His centre of gravity was somewhere south of her ankles, but she held on and wrestled him away.

Elizabeth said, "He's going to ruin this wedding if you're not careful, Mindy." There was something about the way the dog was looking at her that she really didn't like." Buster had seen her in Scotland and now he was going berserk and barking as though he wanted to kill her. Elizabeth wasn't worried the dog might reveal the truth. How was he supposed to do that, but still ...

Mindy began to drag him away.

"*Come on, Mindy! Please!*" Buster whined. "*Amber! Amber! Where's that darned cat when I need her?*"

Following Mindy instead of going about her business, Elizabeth said, "There's a room in the back where we can put him."

Chapter 46 – Patricia and Blue Moon

In the grand banquet hall Patricia and her friends spit-balled ideas with the Blue Moon team.

"How about contaminated flowers?" suggested Barbie. "Could someone have got to the florist and sprayed them with something that will slowly release into the air.

"Yes, they could," said Tempest. "But I fear it would be too inexact. If we are talking about someone trying to take out the entire royal family in one go, it has to be a weapon that guarantees success."

"Like a bomb," said Jermaine.

Patricia touched his arm, thanking him for his input. "Exactly, but a bomb is unlikely because the police and sniffer dogs have been all over this venue for weeks. What we need to look for is something obscure. Something no one else would think of."

They had been trying to figure out what that could be for more than a week. Ever since Patricia returned to the UK and discovered Tempest and his friends were also mixed up in the investigation. When Cody Williams and his antiroyalists staged the drone attack at the ceremony, they all assumed that was the attack. Thankfully, that was not the case and the mist the drones sprayed turned out to be benign. Otherwise, the strategy would have worked.

There were no casualties, which was good news, but it also meant the real attack was yet to come. If, indeed, there was going to be one. The entire investigation was born of conjecture and driven by DI Cassie Munroe who remained convinced Lord Edward's older brother's death was staged.

Thus far on their list of possible mass murder methods was poisoned wedding cake, dismissed because there was no way to guarantee who would eat it, biological agents hidden in the wedding favours so guests would take them home and increase the potential death toll. That one was dismissed when they learned the police had screened everything for biological agents. The staff employed to serve, to cook, to prepare drinks, and all those Felicity arranged as suppliers and caterers, florists, doormen, and more had been interviewed repeatedly or were already members of the royal household shipped to Canterbury for the day. Only in a Hollywood film would the caterers suddenly whip out Uzis and start to shoot people. Nevertheless, they discussed the possibility and dismissed it.

The balloons were indeed inflated with helium, Big Ben confirmed it when he bit into one and inhaled deeply. His high-pitched impersonation of Frankie Valli gave everyone a moment of levity in what was otherwise a tension-filled day.

They checked the chandeliers to make sure they couldn't suddenly come crashing down – an unlikely scenario, but they investigated anyway and were just about out of ideas when Jane thought of something new.

"What about the installation? Of the building, I mean." The faces around her turned inwards to hear more. "What I mean is, the police and security services have been checking everything, but what if the thing they are looking for has been here for months?"

Not wanting to discourage any line of thought, Tempest said, "You mean like a large flowerpot?" he pointed to one just inside the entrance. A huge plant sprouted from it, reaching ten feet into the air where it almost touched the ceiling. Its twin filled the space on the opposite side of the entrance.

It was big enough to hide three or four men inside. Not that anyone thought the assault would come in human form. But there was half a dozen more of the oversized flowerpots positioned around the ballroom, and if each was hiding an explosive device packed with ball bearings or shrapnel of any nature, the effects when detonated would be devasting.

"Would sniffer dogs be able to detect explosives if they were buried under the plants?" asked Barbie.

Amanda, the former cop in the group, didn't know. "Maybe," she guessed. "I'd question if the signal would get through the dirt, but they could probably overcome that by running a small aerial to the surface. It wouldn't even need to be visible."

Suddenly given a tangible method by which an assassin might take out the entire reception room and everyone in it, they got to work.

With Jermaine ever present as her protector, Patricia went to ask how long the plants had been at the venue. Tempest, Big Ben, and Amanda peeled off to start checking the flowerpots for any physical evidence to suggest Jane's outlandish suggestion might be on the money, and Jane teamed up with Barbie. They sought the hotel manager. There would be logs and manifests listing deliveries going back years. They wouldn't need to go back more than a few months, but Felicity was awarded the contract more than half a year ago.

THE ROYAL WEDDING

The venue was kept secret at the time, but word soon leaked. They would need to go back six months to look at everything that had been brought into the hotel and which could reasonably be a vessel for mass destruction. If they found something, the team would investigate.

It was going to take a while.

CHAPTER 47 – MINDY

Mindy wrestled Buster through the door, battling him all the way. The bulldog just wouldn't let up.

"Come on, buddy," she begged. "You're making this far harder than it needs to be."

"*That's because you're not listening!*" Elizabeth was right behind Mindy, the treacherous cow eyeing Buster as he failed to make himself understood.

Finally through the door, Mindy checked her dress. There was dog slobber and flour on it. Sighing, she knew she had a spare waiting to go, but she was already wearing the one she wanted Eddie to see.

Elizabeth hovered in the doorway. She would return shortly to deal with the dog. If nothing else, finding her pet dead would throw Felicity off her game.

Mindy still held his collar, her strong right arm keeping him inside the room when all he wanted to do was rush Elizabeth.

"Let's leave him in there and get back to the banquet room," Elizabeth said. "Felicity can deal with him later, but we have work to do."

Mindy adjusted her grip so she cradled Buster's head with both hands. Looking deep into his eyes, she crouched to bring her head down closer to his.

"Buster, buddy, I'm not sure what is going on, but I'm going to shut you in here now. I wish I could understand what you are saying like Aunt Felicity does. It would make everything so much easier."

"*I wish you could too,*" echoed Buster. "*I really do, because that woman is plotting something and I don't want anyone to get hurt.*"

Mindy tipped her head to one side, blinking. She hadn't 'heard' what Buster said, but suddenly she felt a distinct sense that she should be wary of the woman standing behind her. Why was that? Confused, Mindy got to her feet.

Buster was calm at last. He'd accepted his fate. Well, he'd accepted that the only way to get to Elizabeth was to go through Mindy and he loved her too much to risk hurting her. It was a better tactic to wait until the door was shut and ram his way out of it, just like before.

Mindy stood up with her arms extended and her palms out to keep Buster in place. "Good boy, Buster. I will be back for you in a little while. Just have a nice sleep, okay?"

Backing away, she closed the door and leaned against it. The guests would be arriving soon and that meant Eddie. Under any other circumstances at any other wedding, she would be working for the rest of the day, but it was her aunt's idea that she cut away after the ceremony to spend time with her boyfriend. I mean, how often was it that you got to be a guest at a royal wedding and could attend on the arm of a member of the royal family.

Okay, so Eddie wasn't a prince and would never get anywhere near the throne, not with the way the King's children were producing grandkids for him, but she held no aspirations to be Queen Mindy. The idle thought brought her back to the suggestion that Eddie could have been involved in his brother's death or that of any of the other royal family members who'd died in the last few months.

She found the idea laughable, and yet … and yet what, Mindy? She asked herself. The truth was that she didn't entirely trust him. It was a terrible thing for a woman to admit about her lover, yet no less true.

He was secretive. That was the biggest thing, which in itself is not a crime or even an indication of one. To begin with, Mindy assumed he had another girl or possibly more than one on the side. She didn't care, not to start with. Lord Edward had money and looks and a title, and when she visited him to spend the night, she did so at Buckingham Palace. It was a confluence of factors which demanded she overlook that he might have other women on the go.

It wasn't like she was looking for a husband. She was nineteen for goodness sake. Yet as time went on, she'd decided that his secrecy wasn't to hide that he shared his bed with someone who wasn't her. It was something else.

She just didn't know what.

"Earth to Mindy," said Elizabeth, clicking her fingers in front of the younger woman's face.

Snapping out of her daydream, Mindy dragged a palm across her face and huffed out a breath before setting off back to the banquet room. With Elizabeth following, they were both just turning the corner when they heard an almighty clonk.

"What the heck was that?" asked Elizabeth.

Mindy kept going, determined to finish the task Aunt Felicity set her before the guests were all inside. The noise, she assumed, was Buster throwing himself at the door. She'd seen him do it before, using his skull to batter through garden fences, a cheap MDF door in their boutique when rogue dress designer Rudyard Kipling tried to murder Felicity, and more besides.

He would figure out the door was solid oak and give up soon enough.

Chapter 48 – Felicity

I paced, my mind working overtime while I waited for the photographers to finish shooting pictures. The people at the palace were guarded about what photographs could be taken of the King, Queen, and other top end royals. They also had their own official photographers, but the third son of a king is far enough removed from the throne that he gets a little more rope.

Nora wanted to have a wedding more in keeping with those normal people get and apparently that included a rude photographer who barked at his assistants and dressed like he came from a different century. His fancy shirt with its ruffled cuffs and collar poking from the crushed red velvet smoking jacket, clashed with his skintight black, leather trousers and crocodile skin boots. He encouraged with a fervour that bordered on foaming-at-the-mouth and got excited and giggly when he believed he'd captured the perfect pose.

I know a lot of photographers who specialise in weddings, but Orlando Prism was new to me. It was the first time we had worked together and very definitely the last. I checked my watch. They had been shooting pictures in the cathedral grounds for more than long enough and the bride was beginning to look bored. Group shots were done, and I felt the only reason Orlando continued was to justify his own exorbitant fee.

Deciding that enough was enough, I signalled for the wedding car to come around and caught Nora's eye. Her grateful response confirmed I should have intervened ten minutes ago, but it was done now.

Orlando argued for another set of pictures that 'wouldn't take long' and would perfectly capture the couple in the softly filtered afternoon light.

"Sorry, no time," I stated with no room to argue, getting in before either the bride or groom had to.

Most of the wedding guests were already on their way to the reception, of course. Justin and Phillipe would be there by now – they left the cathedral the moment the guests began to file outside. They would arrange them all to greet the newlyweds when they arrived. The honour guard had gone ahead to create the traditional tunnel of swords leading into the hotel, but the Royal Marines Band was done for the day.

Once the bride and groom were on their way, I hurried to my car. I was going to beat them there and I wouldn't have to break any speed limits to do it, but I needed to leave now. The reception venue is just a couple of miles away, if one takes the direct route. The chauffeur wasn't going to do that. His scenic route, laid out so adoring royal fans could see and wave and cheer, took him through the oldest, most picturesque parts of the ancient city. He would be driving slow, partly to give me the time I needed, but mostly to give the newlyweds a few moments respite before they were once again thrust into the spotlight.

Leaving the cathedral behind, my rear-view was still filled with cops. It was almost beyond belief that we had been able to proceed with the wedding. Teams of them, together with the forensic scientists, were measuring and photographing, recording all there was to gather evidence.

Albert had told me the King's attacker was a man called Cody Williams. According to him, the man came from Cornwall where he'd already led one unsuccessful plot to poison the royal family. It made me very thankful that Albert was at the wedding today and I questioned what the outcome might have been had he not found himself on the guest list.

Clearing my mind as I followed a now familiar route to the reception venue, I thought some more about the dragonfly keyring and what it could mean. I had replies from everyone in my team and none of them owned the bag. That had to mean it belonged to Primrose or Elizabeth. Once again, I was forced to accept that my old rival had come on board just to undermine me.

However, in the interest of considering all options, I questioned if it could be Elizabeth behind it all. It seemed laughable. Elizabeth Keats and I have moved in the same circles for years. Sort of. The weddings she tackles have always been far smaller affairs with much tighter budgets. I guess you could say she's the C list option if I am the A. I get the A list celebrities. Dredging back through my memory, I could not recall there ever being any bad words between us. When I won awards for a category in which she'd been nominated, I saw her clapping politely as one ought.

In contrast, Primrose has been at my neck for more than a decade. But would she have travelled to Scotland just to get to me? Was she capable of violence? It was a question I had to ask because someone not only whacked Justin hard enough to knock him out, they then dragged his body out to a coal bunker and left him to die.

Was Primrose capable of that? I wasn't entirely convinced she was but had to admit no one expects the mild-mannered man next door to be a serial killer.

The neighbours always claim they had no idea he had twenty-eight bodies buried under his floorboards. So was I fooling myself about Primrose?

She had those messages on her phone. They came from my phone number, but how difficult was that to do? Could you clone a phone?

I asked Vince.

"Absolutely. There are even services out there that will help you to do it."

"Really?" I was astounded.

"I'm afraid so. They're all illegal, obviously, but new ones pop up just as soon as one is shut down. With current legislation the way it is, the fines imposed are insignificant and the law they are breaking is a minor one. You get more for littering."

That changed things and made it much more likely Primrose was behind the sabotaged water balloons. Yet, that couldn't be her big play. She had to be plotting something bigger, something more devastating. Something that would truly wreck the wedding and make me look awful.

And it had to be something at the reception because that was where she went when she absconded from the ceremony. In fact, now that I was thinking about it, she argued to be the one at the reception when I tasked her with greeting the guests. That was a big clue right there. She expected to spend her time at the hotel where she would have been able to operate without my eyes on her. Yet she'd found a way to set up whatever boobytrap she had for us anyway.

I asked Vince to drive a little faster.

Chapter 49 – Barbie, Jane, and the Rest

The hotel manager acted as though checking his books was a complete waste of time but didn't fight too hard when Jane threatened to have a detective inspector in his ear with one phone call.

Leaving Barbie and Jane alone to go through six months' worth of invoices, deliveries, and more, he set them up in his office and returned to the hotel entrance to await the wedding guests. The hotel was completely empty, the only people staying were those from the wedding party who'd chosen to book rooms. Heads of state, the royal family, and most of the celebrities were travelling onward or home when the festivities came to an end, but the fee the hotel collected for hosting the event more than compensated for the loss of room revenue.

More than half his staff had the day off. They were not required. Between the wedding planners and Sir Cuthbert, who wanted things done precisely the way he wanted things done, there was very little for him to do other than service needs as and when they arose.

THE ROYAL WEDDING

The kitchen had been turned over to an outside company brought in by Mrs Philips, and the serving staff were all from the palace. The building hadn't seen an event like this since ... well, it had never seen anything like this, but in the first half of the twentieth century, opulent banquets and elegant balls were a regular occurrence. The hotel archive contained books of photographs from the era.

In the archive room at that precise moment, Barbie and Jane were trying to get their heads around the filing system. The drawers were alphabetical, rather than chronological, which made finding invoices or receipts simple enough, but to find those from the past six months they had to cross reference the computer and then look up each entry. The computer was in the manager's office, five yards down the corridor from the archive room. There were closer terminals, but with the bulk of his staff away today, he didn't have the passwords to access them.

As IT whizzes, Barbie and Jane wanted to completely reconfigure the entire system. Since there wasn't time for that they were making do. Jane was on the keyboard, calling out references for Barbie to check.

So far they had found a vending machine that was delivered two weeks ago – it was big enough to hide something inside, so they sent Tempest and Big Ben to investigate. It turned out the flowerpots had been in their current positions for more than a decade, so they were dismissed. The vending machine was likewise struck from the list when Big Ben ripped it open to check there was nothing sinister inside. The damage would be dealt with later.

Next up was a new refrigerator, the giant walk-in kind that was deemed necessary for the reception. It was installed three days prior to the vending machine but Patricia and Jermaine inspected it and took measurements just to be sure there wasn't a hidden compartment at the back.

Realistically, neither looked likely as weapons because they were located away from the guest areas. Arguably, a big enough bomb would account for the entire hotel but placing it in the ballroom would provide optimal damage.

Leaving Tempest and Big Ben to continue checking what Barbie and Jane found, Amanda led Patricia and Jermaine down to the basement. The police had checked it a dozen times, but they used sniffer dogs and were looking for explosives. Patricia and friends didn't know what they were looking for, but would that help them to see what everyone else had missed?

Chapter 50 – Felicity

Vince parked my car in a space allotted specifically for me. Not that I needed my own space, but the hotel did it without being asked and I wasn't about to argue. It was around the back of the venue where I could access the kitchen and back areas. The front of the hotel was being kept free of cars for the aesthetics. The bride and groom were on their way, Justin was gathering the guests to have them ready to greet the happy couple – he was keeping me up to date with text messages, and we would soon be into the formal wedding breakfast part of the day.

Hustling from the car, I left Vince behind and he had to jog to catch up.

"Sorry, dear," I touched his arm, imparting affection I really didn't feel I had time for.

"Babe, you go be your fabulous self. I'm just decoration today."

He was right, and we both knew it. By tonight it would all be over and I could relax. Right now, and for the next few hours, I needed my game face on. I kissed his cheek and turned to go. He smacked me on the rump and made a snorting noise like a bull about to charge.

"I'll be on the lookout for anything out of place, my love. Don't worry about your saboteur. If they strike again, your team will be ready to react."

I knew Vince was good to his word. He would be vigilant and so would everyone else, but the more I questioned what Primrose might have been doing here earlier, the more concerned I became. I was going to have to grill Elizabeth about it. She had to know something. That was going to have to wait though because I could hear cheering outside.

The bride and groom were here.

The master of ceremonies – the palace had their own man, but I insisted we use Justin – announced their arrival. His broadcaster's voice drifted through the open doors from the forecourt in front of the hotel lobby. The guests would be led through shortly and that gave me just a few moments to look around.

I checked everything just a couple of hours ago when I was here to make sure the bridal party, and especially the bride herself, had everything they could possibly want. Mindy would have checked it all again in the last hour, but a quick once over wasn't going to hurt and I hoped it might help to quell my uneasiness.

My stomach roiled, reminding me that I really needed to eat something. Too queasy for food, I was going to have to chug some water or find something I could stomach as it would do me no favour to have the groom or the King or anyone, for that matter, having to repeat themselves because the whale mating song coming from my core drowned them out.

"Oh, hey, Auntie."

Mindy came through a side door that leads to the kitchens and turned around to hold it open. Three men and a woman, all in palace livery, emerged pushing the ice sculpture. As a centrepiece I have never been a fan. So much can go wrong with them and to me they are a throwback from the 90s when such things became popular. Plus, they melt. They might look good when the artist finishes, but two hours later the sharp, defined features are dripping into the tray beneath and by early evening the wonderful ice carving of a ballerina would be a blob.

Not that it was a problem for me. The bride wanted an ice sculpture, and she got one. I felt confident it was for her mother who'd been a ballerina in her youth, and I could appreciate that since it was how my young adult life started, too.

"I thought you would be outside with Lord Edward," I said when Mindy peeled off to meet with me.

"That's next on my agenda. Elizabeth said she wanted to leave the ice sculpture until the last moment as it's so warm today."

"Where is she?" I looked around but couldn't see her.

"Just checking with chef in the kitchen. The guests will be coming into the bar soon, so it's canape time."

Everything was ticking along as it should be.

"Right, well, you should head off to join your boyfriend." I pulled her into a hug. "Thank you for everything you've done today and in the weeks leading up to it. You're my favourite niece."

"I'm your only niece, Auntie, but you're welcome. If you need anything …"

"I won't," I insisted. Mindy was entitled to some fun and she'd put in the hours to justify having the rest of today off.

After she departed, I realised I should have asked her about Amber and Buster. Normally Buster comes to find me, but he had to be somewhere else because there was no sign of him. Amber is less inclined to seek me out unless she needs something from me, but I had hoped I might find her lurking somewhere in the ballroom.

Looking around as I checked the tables were set up exactly as per my instructions and hadn't been messed with, I found neither of my pets but did see Elizabeth. She was in the kitchen where she had a small army of servers assembled and was giving them clear instructions on how they were going to conduct themselves.

I doubted that was necessary. These were no ordinary rag tag gang of university students looking to earn a few extra quid during their summer break. They were all palace employees. Then I remembered that Cody Williams had also been posing as a member of the royal household staff and went to see how things were going.

Elizabeth finished just as I nudged my way through the door. I watched, staying back so I wouldn't intrude as they filed through the kitchen collecting silver trays loaded with bite-sized edible snacks. Like a river, they flowed into the bar area via a different door to the one I used. I could see the guests on the other side. Conversation created a din of noise, but the dinner gong would sound shortly to draw them into the banquet hall.

With Elizabeth now free, I approached her.

"Oh, Felicity. You're here. Jolly good. I've just sent out the canapes. The guests are being served cocktails and such in the bar, but chef knows to give them time enough only for one drink. With a party this size it will take fifteen minutes just to get them seated."

"The servers know to start bringing the back tables through first?"

Elizabeth nodded vigorously. "I must say I wish they were available for hire. I've never worked with a more dedicated and professional group. They don't question what they are told, and they all seem to know what I need them to do before I ask."

I guess I expected no less, but she was right, it was a welcome change to the rabble I so often found myself forced to manage.

Making a thoughtful face, Elizabeth said, "Mindy told me something cryptic about Primrose. In fact, she said she would take no further part in today's proceedings but wouldn't tell me why."

I took out my phone. "Do you recognise this bag?" I showed her two pictures. The first was the bag, the second the keyring attached to it.

Elizabeth pursed her lips and nodded along as though agreeing with herself. "That's Primrose's. I'm guessing she has done something to undermine you. That's it, isn't it?"

I put my phone away. "Something like that." I thought for a second and changed my mind about how much I should say. Innocent until proven guilty is all very well in court, but I needed to know what else Primrose might have done to upset my day. "Actually, Elizabeth, I think Primrose sabotaged the bouquets in the cathedral. Dozens of them had their water balloons pierced. There was water all over the floor and the blooms would have started to wilt if we hadn't got there quick enough."

"But you were able to save the day?"

I sagged a little at her turn of phrase. "We were able to save the flowers and mop up the mess. Mindy ... um, improvised with something to replace the water balloons, but my greater concern is what else Primrose might have done. She came here earlier when she was supposed to be managing the guests as they arrived."

Elizabeth showed surprise and lied through her teeth, "She did? What did she come here for? I didn't see her."

"Well, that's my point. I don't know what she came here for, but you will recall that she expected to be here today. I'm worried that she might have prepared something and that we won't know about it until it's too late."

"Yes, that is a concern. Can you have her arrested and questioned? Maybe she will cave." The deeper the wedge she drove between her two biggest rivals, the easier it would be to topple them both.

"No, I don't think so. I have no evidence to prove she did anything. If I approach the police, I will need something tangible to give them."

"Yes, I suppose you're right. Well, I should do another round, I guess. Triple check all the things I've already double checked."

It was boring work, but I wanted it done even though Mindy had only just done it. With so much going on, there had to be something no one had looked at yet.

With Elizabeth crossing the kitchen to do as she said she would, I asked, "Have you seen either of my pets?"

Chapter 51 – Lord Edward and Mindy

Lord Edward made small talk and introduced people to Mindy. "Yes, she's a commoner, but like Kate and my good friend Prince Marcus's darling Nora, there are fine women to be found among the masses."

Mindy chose not to remark on what felt like an insult, but would bring it up later when they were alone. What the heck was a commoner in this day and age? Nothing set Eddie apart from her physically or mentally. If anything, she would consider herself brighter, fitter, and stronger, at least pound for pound. So what set him above her? Birthright. She knew the answer and at once despised it. It was as though only the nobles could afford manners and therefore anyone not born to the nobility had to be riffraff.

Catching herself, Mindy chased those thoughts away. Not only were they perilously close to the same political ideals that drove Cody Williams to murder, but it wasn't how Eddie really viewed the world. At least she didn't think so. Hoping his out-of-character mannerisms and words were down to the present company, she cleared her mind to focus on enjoying the event.

A server came by with a tray of champagne. She caught the young woman's eye and took a glass when she paused. Mindy knew it to be the good stuff because she placed the order herself. The palace was picking up the bill and more than once advised her aunt to increase her budget (and profit margin) for elements they said would cost more than she had allowed.

Barely conscious of his date for the day, Lord Edward knew she had to be present and at his side. Plus, there were bonuses to be had from her company. That she would die today was a small comfort, and the sympathy as one of the few survivors would be something he could ride for years. He imagined himself on talk shows once all the dust had settled. As the heir to the throne and the world's most eligible bachelor, he wanted people to know him.

He would get an agent to make the talk show thing happen but doubted there would be much resistance. His looks would get him through the door and his natural wit and charm would do the rest.

As the couple they had been talking to, the Earl of Grantham's second son and his wife, drifted away, Eddie turned his attention to Mindy. She looked lovely in her dress; there was no denying that. The muscles in her arm moved in a sensuous way when she lifted it to bring the champagne glass to her lips. Had she been suitable queen material, he might have entertained keeping her around, but the daughter of a lawyer? Uurgh!

Besides, she was his patsy. She had no idea, but her fingerprints were on the murder weapon, both physically and in the paperwork trail. The poor girl was so innocent, so trusting, he almost felt that she deserved to be labelled as the regicide.

The secret no one else would know was that he found out about the wedding long before the world was made aware. Before Prince Marcus popped the question and before Felicity Philips became involved. In fact, he was the first to know.

THE ROYAL WEDDING

It happened one night after dinner at the palace. Lord Edward typically took his meals in one of the small rooms set out for dining near to the kitchen. Often, he ate alone, but on that occasion he had Prince Marcus for company. They were of a similar age, had known each other since they were toddlers, and both attended Harrow and then Oxford.

Much like Edward, the young prince had attracted women easily. He was good looking, trim, and a member of the royal family. Picking up girls required little more than turning up where there were some. However, he'd been dating Nora for some time and was thinking about proposing. He was yet to buy a ring but already knew he didn't want to get married in St Paul's Cathedral. The plan to kill his way to the throne popped into being the moment Prince Marcus said the word 'Canterbury'.

When they ate their meal and discussed the logistics of such an affair and if the palace would indulge him, Edward told him to plan for a wedding the following summer. It gave him a solid year. As it was, and largely due to Edward's own actions, the date was brought forward, but by then he'd already put in place that which was going to change the shape of the British Royal Family forever.

The date was brought forward in secrecy because Edward arranged the deaths of those royals who had elected not to attend the wedding. He was going to kill everyone ahead of him in the line of succession with the exception of his father.

The eleventh in line wasn't coming and that meant he had to die before the event. Had Edward not eliminated him already, the circle of protection surrounding him after today would have become impenetrable. The same was true for Edward's elder brother. He arranged his death first, just to get it out of the way.

At the time he thought his performance was masterful. Only afterward did he spot the holes in his illusion. His brother's body had no bullet holes in it though the flying, fire breathing dragon suit he wore very much did. The palace copper,

DI Munroe became suspicious at the time and still was. Edward hoped she would be in the hotel later when his device killed everyone.

Idly he touched the remote for it in his waistcoat pocket. He would have preferred to operate it using a timer, but that hadn't been possible and ultimately would have resulted in failure because they pulled the date forward.

Still, to all the world it would look like Mindy fitted the device and came to service it just a week ago. He'd installed it himself a year ago, long before he met Mindy. Seeing the opportunity to make the world believe she was behind the attack, he hacked the hotel's computer to add her name to the record. When the police looked, they would see her name recorded as the installer.

Then, last week, he disguised himself to return to the venue. He made no attempt to look like her – that would be ridiculous - but made sure he wouldn't be recognised if CCTV picked up his face. He signed in using her name, drove a car that was matched hers - it even had the same number plate (such an easy thing to acquire from a backstreet shop), and had the hotel's facilities manager take a photocopy of her driving licence which he'd swiped from her purse and returned a few days later. In what he thought to be a stroke of genius, he'd collected her prints on a plastic label which he stuck to the gas cylinder. The investigating team would find it and that would be that.

He took her hand and gave it a squeeze. It was time to introduce her to the King. After all, she only had a couple of hours to live.

Chapter 52 – Blue Moon and Patricia

An hour into the task, Tempest and Big Ben had investigated eight possible, yet distinctly unlikely, sources through which someone might have smuggled in a device of some kind. They had drawn a blank and were out of ideas.

Patricia, Jermaine, and Amanda had a minor scare when a police patrol spotted them in the basement and threatened to open fire if they didn't stop where they were. They complied and were able to calm things down by identifying themselves. They did not, however, find anything of interest in their search.

Patricia concluded that was because there was nothing to find. Not that it was a wild goose chase that could never bear fruit, but that they were looking in the wrong places or coming at it from the wrong angle.

When they regrouped, Barbie said, "We've gone back six months already. That's how long ago the venue was announced."

"Slightly further, actually," said Jane. "We're about seven months back now which is definitely before people knew."

Patricia's skull itched, a faint scratchy sensation at the back of her head that always occurred when she was onto something. Jane and Barbie were right in what they said, but also wrong at the same time.

"What about those who knew before it was announced?"

Tempest looked her way. "Like whom?"

Patricia shrugged both shoulders. "Now that I don't know, but it seems likely the bride and groom discussed it. Or one of them could have shared the idea with a friend. My point is there must be someone who knew before it was announced to the world."

Barbie agreed. "Patty's right. As always." She looked annoyed about it, but Patricia knew she was only teasing. "Okay, Jane," she grabbed Jane's shoulders to steer her back to the computer, "let's dig deeper and see if we find anything."

Chapter 53 – Felicity

I watched the guests beginning to fill the tables furthest from the raised portion on which the wedding party would sit. Combining my desire to check around the room for obvious signs of sabotage and the hope I might discover Amber and Buster under a table, I'd managed to kill enough time that Justin was gently beginning to clear the bar area.

I jumped when something brushed past my leg, but I knew it was Amber before I looked down to find her.

"Hello, Amber," I said, my pulse returning to its normal rhythm. "Anything to report?"

"I'm getting hungry. And I need to clean myself. There are cobwebs here."

A sad laugh escaped me. I should probably think it nice to have reliable characters in my life and there is no one more reliably self-centred than Amber. Then what she said caught up with me.

"Wait. There are cobwebs?" I looked around, my eyes wide. Every inch of the hotel had been scrubbed, repainted, or completely renovated since it was named as the venue six months ago. There shouldn't be a spider within a mile of the place.

"*Oh, don't fuss, Felicity. It was just one and I found it in the corner by one of the big plant pots.*"

I breathed a sigh of relief. No one was likely to spot it there.

"*But I got it on my fur and that won't do. If you would be so kind as to place me on the table I will take care of it.*"

Her request was so assured of my compliance that I almost did it. Catching myself as I reached for the chair, I said, "I rather think it is time to put you somewhere else, Amber. How about if I find you a snack and tuck you somewhere out of the way so you can wash yourself in peace?" It wasn't exactly a question; I was going to do it anyway. Bending at the waist, I scooped her from the floor. "Now, where is Buster?"

Cradled in my arms, Amber reached up with one paw to pat my face. "*Why would you ask about that mutt when you have me?*"

"Amber," I chided.

She looked away, unwilling to give me her attention. "*I haven't seen him since just after we got here.*"

It felt safe to assume he wasn't in the ballroom since he hadn't found me and wasn't currently bothering the guests as they filed in and around to find their tables. That left a lot of territory to cover, and a tinge of worry wormed through me. My dog is wonderful and I love him dearly, but he's not beyond causing chaos. He could follow his nose to the bar where dropped crumbs from canapes would have him snuffling around the carpet tripping people and generally creating trouble for yours truly.

I got the same report from Elizabeth who said she hadn't seen either of my pets at any point. Mindy might know but she was with Lord Edward now and I had sworn not to disturb her. Despite that, I was sure I would be able to catch her for ten seconds without ruining her day. Provided Buster wasn't messing with the guests, and I couldn't hear any loud complaints to suggest he was, then he was probably off playing superhero detective somewhere in the hotel. I would find him later.

A loud pop made me jump. It caught Amber by surprise too and in her fright she gripped hard with all her claws. I might have complained had the pop not been followed a moment later by a second and then a third as the first guests to reach the tables set off party poppers. They were the expensive kind you have to order in from a specialist, not the over-the-counter ones that cost tuppence.

They eject over a greater range with a louder pop and better confetti. They are not supposed to cause screaming. Laughter, yes. Screaming like a person is on fire, definitely not.

Catapulted into action, I spun around with Amber in my arms. Her claws were all the way through my dress now and digging into my chest and arms. She's never been a fan of loud noises and because Buster knows it she spends much of her life on edge waiting for my dog to get her again.

I expected to find the guests at the back of the room engaging in horseplay, but the reason for their screams wasn't fake. They *were* on fire.

Not engulfed by a fireball, but there were flames dancing across their hands and up their arms and they were freaking out.

Dumping Amber unceremoniously, I ran across the room. My niece, had she been present, would have got there first by leaping the tables and generally making it look like gravity was optional. I had to go around the obstacles in my path which meant the flames were out before I got to the victims.

"Goodness, are you all right?" I gasped.

Three men in their twenties, all with a drink inside them, had seen the poppers and thought it would be fun to set them off. That being their purpose I could hold no blame against them, but the moment they had, their hands went up as the tiny explosive inside created a spark that ignited the outer shell of the poppers.

"What do you think!" yelled a girlfriend, staring at me like I was mad to ask the question.

More people were coming; other guests drawn by the commotion. They crowded around as yet more guests filed in through the banquet room's grand entrance.

One of the affected party spoke with a clear head. "We need to get this looked at, Tailor. Let's get you all to the hotel reception where they can direct us to a first aid rep. The burns are minor, but they need dressing."

All around me the wedding guests were asking what had happened. Many were just arriving, drawn to the gaggle of people like moths to a flame.

I heard someone say, "What? These things?" followed by the crack of a popper going off and then more panicked yelling as yet another person caught fire.

The man, this one in his forties, remained where he was, staring at his flaming fingers with eyes so wide I thought his eyeballs might fall out. A blur of movement to his right turned out to be Tempest Michaels.

He tackled the man to the ground, using his jacket to smother the flames. Behind him Amanda and Big Ben arrived with Patricia and Jermaine. They needed about half a second to assess the situation and take charge.

Patricia whacked a hand against Jermaine's chest to get him moving. "Sweetie, please see to it that no further guests are directed this way for the next few minutes." He dashed away, heading for the bar.

Tempest aimed an arm at Big Ben. "Let's collect all these party poppers. Felicity, can you find a bag or something we can put them in, please?"

"Try not to touch them with your bare skin," said Amanda. "It looks like they've been dipped in something highly flammable but odourless." She was bent at the waist, leaning right over a nearby table with her face almost touching the tablecloth to get as close to the offending article as possible without actually touching it.

Tempest and Big Ben said, "Roger," in unison. I was about to dash off to get what Tempest asked for when Patricia produced one from her handbag. It was a standard supermarket carrier bag folded neatly so it tucked into one of the inside pockets. She opened it with a shake.

The Blue Moon team pulled latex gloves from their pockets, donning them with a shower of fine powder falling to the pristine carpet. I bit my tongue to stop myself from saying anything about the mess they were making.

The four men with burns were escorted from the room by their friends while the Blue Mooners went from table to table. They were careful to remove the party poppers without ruining the displays painstakingly arranged in the centre of each table, but what if the party poppers weren't the only thing Primrose had messed with?

I mean, it had to be her, right? This was another act of sabotage. The party poppers didn't come from the factory doused in an odourless flammable liquid.

As though attuned to my thoughts, Patricia said, "We should check the other items and pay special attention to the party favours."

At each table setting, placed just behind the name card, sat a box. Inside were special, one of a kind, cuff links for the gentlemen or earrings for the ladies. Designed and produced by Smallbridge Jewels and Timepieces in a commission placed before the owner of the firm went crazy and tried to kill me, they were commemorative pieces that would become family heirlooms.

Or be sold on eBay depending on the recipient.

I preferred to believe the guests at this wedding were of a higher standard, but whatever became of them it hadn't occurred to me to look inside the boxes. Had anyone else looked? Mindy would have gone through the room inspecting everything, but no one would have spotted the sabotaged party poppers.

Edging toward the table where Patricia stared at one of the boxes, I questioned whether I would find a set of cufflinks inside or a deadly scorpion or a small bomb or a photograph of the guest's rabbit boiling on the stove.

A tic started to twitch by my right eye. It was all happening again, but this time everyone would know about it. This would be on the front page of every paper in the world with a glossy centre section to really capture my failure.

Unable to take the tension, I yelled, "Aaaaaarghh!" and tore the top off the box.

Gasping for breath, I stared down at a pair of silver and gold cufflinks.

Patricia picked up the next box to find a set of earrings inside. I breathed a sigh of relief, but not content to assume we were safe, I kept going. The Blue Mooners joined in once they had all the party poppers. The guests in the room watched, saying very little.

Justin stuck his head around the door.

"Everything okay?" he asked. "Jermaine said there was a minor issue, and I should stop sending guests, but everyone's glasses are empty. I've sent the servers to get more champagne, but the budget will only stretch so far.

"Forget the budget," I snapped, not meaning to come across as harsh. "Sorry. I'm a little on edge. The budget doesn't matter. The cost can come out of my profit. Right now, I just want to come through this alive."

Justin nodded his understanding, but said, "They are also getting restless. The bride, typically, hasn't eaten yet today. Plus, the chef was planning to serve the starters already. We really need to get people inside soon."

I sucked some air through my teeth. "Give me five minutes and start sending people through. I'll explain the delay when we get time."

Justin ducked back out of the room. He was well versed enough to be able to control a hungry crowd and keep them going. It wasn't as though we had a choice.

With the party poppers gone, Amanda appeared with a vacuum cleaner to deal with the mess the first poppers made. The cardboard cases around the poppers hadn't set anything else on fire though there was a distinct smell of burnt paper and charred hair.

I thanked my helpers and apologised to the guests. I would speak with the burn victims individually later and prayed they were not being sent elsewhere for treatment. From what I saw the damage was minor. It crisped the hair on their knuckles, but the flames weren't big enough and didn't last long enough to burn through their flesh.

By the time the next wave of guests came through the banquet hall doors, the first ones were back in their seats. It was yet another minor disaster averted, and that was what troubled me most. Where was the big thing that was going to end the reception? What else did Primrose have planned?

Normally at a grand wedding, once the formal dinner had started, I would float between the kitchen and the banquet room. Today I was going to give myself a few moments to think. I left the servers to do their jobs, secure in the knowledge Justin could handle things and went to find my office.

Chapter 54 – Mindy and Edward

Edward knew he needed to keep his cool. Knew he needed to outwardly display no sign of the rising nerves he felt, but it was becoming a struggle, and he could see Mindy had noticed.

"Is everything okay, Eddie?" she'd asked more than once.

He brushed her off easily the first time, delivering an offhand comment about how the older ladies in the family so often joked that he would be next and here he was with the prettiest girl at the whole wedding. It dispelled her concerns for a while, but as time dragged on and they still weren't being called through to begin the formal meal, his worry only heightened.

What was the delay? Did the police know something? Had they found what he believed no one ever could or would? Edward told himself not to be ridiculous. If they had the slightest clue they would have evacuated the building already, but the niggling doubt was making him sweat.

Why did the human body do that? He wanted to display no outward sign of his fear, yet his organs conspired to betray him. His armpits felt like swamps. No one could see them inside his suit jacket, but he could feel perspiration on his brow. Was it showing on his collar?

When Mindy asked about him the second time, he feigned gastric issues. It wasn't the sort of thing he would ever tell a woman, but he believed it would alleviate her questions. Making excuses, he took himself to a restroom. Not the nearest one which would have too many other wedding guests in it, but another on the far side of the hotel behind the ball room.

Not that he needed the restroom, just some peace and quiet. He'd added a few drops of exenatide to his father's rum and coke knowing the small amount would not affect the taste, and that the effects would kick in less than an hour after ingestion. He just needed his dad to feel unwell. Research told him the drug, most typically used to treat type two diabetes, created feelings of nausea in almost all patients until they built up a tolerance for it. The small dose would do no lasting damage, but his father would either vomit or feel like he might. That was all he needed.

As his father's only living relative, he would have a perfect excuse to escort him from the premises. On his way out he would activate the device hidden deep within the hotel's air conditioning system and the rest really would be history.

Edward knew Mindy would insist on going with him, but he was ready to argue. The wedding clearly wasn't going according to plan, so if he was taking his father home, Mindy should return to helping Felicity. He would force the issue if he had to, secure in the knowledge she would be too dead shortly thereafter to say anything to anyone.

THE ROYAL WEDDING

Mindy watched Eddie. He said his stomach was bothering him, but she didn't think that was it. More than anything, he came across as nervous. He kept looking at his watch and had asked his father how he was feeling more than once.

The duke had what was supposed to be a glass of rum and coke in his hand but he had whispered in her ear when Eddie wasn't looking, that he was on heart meds and shouldn't be drinking. He hadn't told his son and didn't think today was the right time for it. Edward had one of the servers bring his father's favourite tipple, but the duke asked Mindy to surreptitiously swap it out for a Coke without the rum and claimed his son wouldn't notice.

She had to wait until Eddie went to the restroom but left the unwanted and untouched rum and coke at the bar. The barman had cleared it away the next time she looked.

There was something going on with her boyfriend. Mindy had no idea what it was, but she knew what DI Munroe wanted her to believe. Sipping her second glass of champagne, she kept her mouth shut and watched.

Chapter 55 – Felicity

Getting the hotel to assign me rooms my team could use as a base of operations was one of the first things we did when we first visited months ago. A pair of suites on the first floor with a door connecting them was where we set up just down a corridor from the banquet room so it was less than a sixty second walk to get from my desk back to the wedding reception.

Once inside, I closed the door behind me and rested against it. I felt bushed. It was always going to be a long, hard day, but I was going to have to find some energy from somewhere or I would struggle to get to the end still on my feet.

A second boobytrap had been triggered, this time by a guest, and I had no reason to believe that we were done.

Certain Primrose wouldn't answer and that even if she did there was no way she would admit to her crimes or tell me what disaster the wedding guests still faced, I thumbed her contact to connect us anyway.

The phone rang and rang, but as I expected, she didn't pick up. Frustrated, I sent her a message.

'The guests found the exploding party poppers before the top table were in the room. You managed to cause minor burns to the hands of four guests before the crisis was averted. I know you must have something else planned, so please tell me what it is before someone gets really hurt. I'm sure you won't and have probably convinced yourself that you won't get caught, but I can promise you will have the police and some of the country's leading sleuths coming after you when this day is finished.'

My finger hovered over the button before jabbing it hard with a hate-filled grimace on my face. I watched the screen for a few seconds, wondering if the three dots might appear to show me she was typing. When they didn't, I put it away and forced my brain to think.

The door to the room opened, startling me, and Elizabeth burst in.

"There you are! I heard some of the guests were injured. Vince told me the party poppers were rigged to catch fire when they went off."

I was standing over the desk, leaning on it with both arms as though that was the only thing keeping me upright. When I didn't speak, Elizabeth continued.

"You know it was Primrose who ordered those, right? I had nothing to do with it." Elizabeth had gone to great lengths researching, obtaining, and experimenting with different flammable liquids, gels and powders to find one that would be virtually invisible until it went off. Then she had to test soaking times. She wanted the outer case of the popper to be flammable but retain its integrity. It proved hard to get right, and after all that work all she achieved was a few scorched fingers.

The room was supposed to catch fire. Or the King was supposed to burn his eyebrows off. Or ... something. It was a lot of effort for a whole lot of nothing. Fortunately, the best one, the most assured one was yet to come. The ice sculpture was melting already and with the temperature rising now the banquet room was filled with people, it would only melt faster. She estimated the gas would begin to appear in less than an hour but could be no more exact than that.

"Have you spoken with the police?" she asked.

I pushed away from the desk to stand upright. I had thought I needed something tangible to offer the police as evidence, but perhaps that wasn't the case. Perhaps if they found her and brought her to the venue, she would be scared enough to reveal what else she had planned before it happened.

Dread, as much as anything else, pushed me to make the call. Elizabeth hovered in the doorway, but waiting the few seconds it would take to be put through to the local dispatch desk, I asked her to head back to the banquet hall. Someone had to be in charge.

There were dozens of officers on site at the hotel, but they all had assigned tasks, so I spoke with a person who put me through to a detective sergeant. He listened intently, asking questions, but didn't ask me to confirm who I was. When I asked why, I discovered he was at the cathedral. He was one of the additional officers pulled to the site after the drone attack and Cody's attempt on the life of the King.

He gave his name as DS Ross Mellon. He took what details I had for Primrose: her address and phone number and guaranteed a whole squad of officers would be looking for her within minutes. If she was in the country, they would find her.

Ending the call so he could get on with it, I actually felt a little bad. He hadn't said it, but I was left with the impression the police were smarting from the drone attack and how they were so completely ambushed by it. No one was hurt, but a lot of people were embarrassed and someone was going to lose their job.

Slumping into the chair at the desk, even though I knew I needed to be heading back to the banquet room, I found myself thinking about the party poppers. As

Elizabeth pointed out, it was a product Primrose took care of. She placed the order, she chased up the firm to ensure timely delivery and, thinking back on it now, she was the one who suggested them in the first place. Personally, I'm not a fan of them because they make so much mess, but I knew Nora wanted her wedding to be more like those of her friends.

But there was something about it all that just didn't sit right. Now, I have said on many occasions that I am not a sleuth. I have tried to figure out who or what could be behind the murder/theft/kidnapping and always get it completely wrong. Thus, I had no reason whatsoever to think I could figure it out this time.

For that matter, what was I trying to figure out? Primrose was so obviously behind it all. And that was what bothered me. Having turned the police on her, which was inevitable really, she would be caught, charged, possibly jailed, but very definitely ruined. Why would she risk all that just to get back at me?

Well, the leaked photographs of her with that male model for a start. She accused me, but I wasn't the one behind it. That alone suggested there had to be another player in the field.

But who else had the desire to ruin me? It had only ever been Primrose. There were other wedding planners playing second fiddle to me, or maybe third, fourth, and fifth fiddle was more accurate, but someone had to be number one.

The door opened again, this time with someone knocking as they came through it. I sagged with relief to see Vince.

"I need to see your phone, babe."

My right eyebrow hiked up my head. "My phone?" I picked it from the desk and held it up for him to take. "Why's that?"

"Because I thought about our earlier conversation. The one about it being cloned and that was how Primrose had those messages you never sent."

"Yeah." I wanted to know where this was going.

He didn't reply for a while. Focused on my phone, he was fiddling with an app on his own device. I was about to prompt him to explain when he said, "Nope."

"Nope?"

He handed the phone back to me. "When a person clones a phone, they essentially create a complete duplicate. The world can't tell the difference, right?"

"Right," I said, having no clue if he was or not.

"I just performed a 'find my phone' check using an app on my device. I was hoping it would just find the one in your hand, but there's a second ping, so we know someone really did clone it."

I blinked. "Back up a second. What does that mean? Did Primrose send fake messages to herself or not?"

"Well, that's more complicated to answer, but don't you see? Unless Primrose sent them to herself, they came from the person who is behind the sabotage."

Slowly, because I still wasn't sure I had fully grasped what he was trying to tell me, I asked, "How do we know which it is?"

"We locate it, darling. It's in this building!"

Chapter 56 – Amber and Buster

Buster's lip twitched and his eyes opened. They didn't stay open, though. He snapped them shut the moment light pierced the inside of his skull like an icepick being driven through his brain.

Keeping his eyes shut, he performed his 'where am I, what happened?' test. It involved gently snaking out his tongue to see what he was lying on. It turned out to be short pile carpet. That meant he was indoors and that was a good thing. Probably.

Trying to recall recent events, Buster needed a moment to remember that Mindy shut him in a room. Why did she do that? He couldn't figure it out. The only reason to get shut away was seriously bad dog behaviour and that didn't sound right at all.

A noise crept in through his ears. Something familiar. He knew what it was. Didn't he?

His head was pounding, the headache pummelling the inside of his skull one of epic proportions.

The sound came again, and this time it sounded like a word, "*Buster.*" That's me, he thought. I'm Buster. Why can I hear my name?

Groggily, he tried to open his eyes again, this time shifting his eyelids the smallest fraction so only a tiny amount of light shone through. He could stand it like that. Lifting his head, he looked around and tried to get his bearings. He was lying on his side in a room stuffed with files in packing boxes. His head was a few inches from the door. Buster thought he ought to get up, but the effort to rearrange his paws evaded him.

"*Buster?*"

This time, he realised what he was hearing and turned his head slightly toward the sound.

"*Amber?*"

"*Oh, thank goodness. I've been trying to get your attention for ages. Why are you so sleepy?*"

The cat was on the other side of the door, but did that mean he was trapped, or she was? Buster decided it had to be him who was stuck and as he thought that the memory of ramming the door came back.

He winced, and said, "*I rather think I knocked myself out. Mindy put me in here. I just don't remember why.*"

"*Well, we need to get you out. More things have been happening.*"

"*More things? Like what?*"

"*Hold on, Buster. I'm going to try to open this door.*" Amber looked up at the door handle. It was a long thin thing she could leap and grab. Provided the door wasn't locked, she expected to be able to open it. She had been doing the same with the doors at home for years. It drove Felicity wild. Especially when she was mating with Vince and wanted some privacy.

Telling himself he needed to get up, but certain his head would split in two if he so much as tried it, Buster stayed where he was.

Closing his eyes again, he asked, "*How did you find me?*"

Amber wiggled her back end and sprang upward, reaching the door handle with ease. The mechanism gave more resistance than she was used to but if she angled herself to push against the doorframe and leaned right out to the end for maximum leverage, she believed it would turn.

To answer Buster, she said, "*Are you kidding me? You're in there snoring and farting. I could hear you from a corridor away and could probably smell you if I was in France. What have you been eating?*"

Buster harrumphed. "*Nothing out of the ordinary.*"

With a grunt of effort, the handle turned. The latch shifted enough to clear the frame and with a kick Amber rode the door inward.

It travelled four inches and stopped when it hit something solid.

Buster wailed, "*Aaaaargh!*" and scrambled backward across the floor. He didn't want to move and now that he was the room started spinning, but his head hurt way too much for Amber to hit him with the door a second time.

Amber dropped to the floor and sauntered around the half open door.

"*Did you say something?*"

Buster groaned. He had his eyes shut tight again. He felt woozy and a little sick, but the fog had lifted and it imbued him with glorious purpose. Mindy shut him away because he was trying to get to Elizabeth. He was trying to get to Elizabeth because she was the saboteur.

"*I need you to take me to see Felicity,*" he said, keeping his voice to a whisper.

Amber accepted the request and went back out the door. She was two yards away when she sensed Buster wasn't following. She called him, and when he didn't appear she backtracked to find him in the exact same spot. He hadn't moved.

"*I feel a little off,*" Buster announced in his ever so soft voice. "*I might need a little help.*"

Expressing concern before she realised what she was doing, Amber went to Buster's side. "*Are you okay? You don't seem yourself.*"

"*I think I might be concussed*," Buster mumbled, trying not to dribble. "*I hit the door rather hard earlier.*"

"Hmm. Yes. You do have quite a large lump on your head."

Concentrating, Buster said, "*Amber, I need you to take a message to Felicity. You need to tell her that Elizabeth is the saboteur.*"

"What?"

"*Tell Felicity I saw Elizabeth in Scotland. She was at the hotel that caught on fire. I saw her. That's the thing that's been bothering me. I knew there was something important about Scotland, but I only figured it out a while ago.*"

"You're serious? How sure are you about this?"

"One hundred percent."

THE ROYAL WEDDING

Amber considered the news. Felicity needed to know, that much was clear, but Buster didn't look good. He was covered in white powder which made him look like the blow to his skull had knocked the pigment out of his skin. The lump on his skull sat dead centre between his ears and was the size of a boiled egg. Amber didn't know anything about concussions but wasn't happy to leave the dog where she found him.

Getting alongside him, she pushed her body against his so he could lean into her a little. "Come along, Buster. You can tell Felicity yourself. We'll take it slow. Okay?"

Buster sagged against the cat, letting her take a portion of his body weight. It made Amber regret her decision, but she nudged him to move a paw and they began a slow, staggering, tottering stumble to get out of the room and into the corridor.

They were on their way to save the day.

Slowly.

Very, very slowly.

Chapter 57 – Mindy and Eddie

Mindy pretended not to notice but Eddie had checked his watch five times in the last ten minutes and had asked his father how he was feeling four times. His left leg wouldn't stay still, jiggling up and down continually as though attached to an electric current.

His father had finished the 'rum' and coke a while back, draining the glass and switching to water. Eddie sent one of the palace servers to fetch a replacement even though his father said he didn't want one.

Thinking enough was enough and that she needed to call him out on why he was acting so weird, Mindy was about to open her mouth when Eddie asked her a question.

"Would you like a cocktail? I'm not a fan of this champagne. We could switch to cocktails." He delivered the suggestion with gusto and enthusiasm, doing his best to sell the idea.

Mindy frowned. "No, I don't want to drink a lot. I would like to remember this occasion. Eddie, what's going on?"

He tried a smile, but she could see the nerves trying to hide behind it.

"Why would anything be wrong? I'm just trying to have a good time with you, my dear."

"Really? Because you look like you might throw up and you keep asking your father how he's feeling."

Lord Edward had hoped it wouldn't come to this, but he was a planner who liked to have multiple contingencies in place. The problem with Mindy was how much she saw. For a teenager she was shockingly astute.

He bowed his head, sighed, and muttered, "Busted."

Mindy heard the word and felt her body tense. What did he mean? How was he busted? What was he up to that he could be busted doing?

Lord Edward looked up, found Mindy's eyes and dropped out of his chair onto one knee. From his inside jacket pocket his fumbling hands produced a ring.

Shocked, she jumped to her feet, shunting her chair back so hard it fell over. This was why he looked sick and nervous?

Around them, guests at other tables nudged each other to draw attention their way.

Heat rushed to Mindy's cheeks, and she looked around for help. What the heck was going on?

Lord Edward lifted his hands, one cradling the other with the ring leading the way. "Mindy, I know we haven't been dating all that long, but I know what I want.

I've known for a while. You noticed that I was sweating and looking nervous and that's all because of you. Because I'm so afraid you'll think I'm crazy and say no. But I don't want you to say no, Mindy. I love you and I want you to be my wife."

Mindy felt dizzy. All his weirdness was explained. He wasn't plotting anything other than to declare his love in a public setting. He'd bared his soul, exposing himself to ridicule and embarrassment if she turned him down.

Her eyes took in the ring and her mouth opened. The diamond was enormous. More knowledgeable than most due to her profession, even if she was just getting started, Mindy knew a ROCK from a rock, when she saw one. The ring in Eddie's hands would be measured in multiple carats, but a ring wasn't a reason to get married.

His imploring eyes bored into hers and she felt the world shrink around her. No one else existed. It was just the two of them.

"Yes." The word slipped from between her lips without bothering to consult her brain.

Lord Edward punched the air like a footballer celebrating a goal.

Just behind him and still seated, his father muttered, "Decorum, Edward."

But Lord Edward wasn't to be denied his moment of jubilation. He rose from the floor, grabbing Mindy around the waist to lift her into the air. Holding her so she was the highest, most visible person in the room, he whooped.

Mindy's cheeks burned. Everyone was looking their way and a ripple of polite applause became a crescendo as everyone in the room joined in. The groom got to his feet, congratulating his friend and when Mindy glanced that way she saw the King and Queen of England applauding her.

But Mindy knew it was a mistake. She was too young to be thinking about marriage. Even to someone as handsome and eligible as Lord Edward Chamberlain. Knowing now was not the time to discuss the subject, she let him lower her to the floor and kissed his expectant lips.

He slipped the ring onto her finger to another smattering of applause before finally retaking his seat. Face crimson, Mindy settled back into her chair. She hadn't wanted a drink before, and though she didn't exactly want one now, she needed a reason to leave the room.

The noise level of muted conversation returned though there was no denying the eyes looking their way, but Mindy waited a few minutes, then announced her intention to get that cocktail.

"Marvellous," Lord Edward replied, his hand still grasping hers. "Have you ever had a Long Island Iced Tea?"

Mindy had but said she hadn't. Delivering a kiss to his lips, she rose, her head a maelstrom of colliding thoughts, and made her way from the room. A server would have brought the drinks to their table, but Mindy needed a little air and a trip to the bar would provide that.

Acting as though reluctant to let her hand go, Lord Edward kissed it multiple times before begging, "Don't be too long."

Overwhelmed didn't even come close to how Mindy felt, and once again there were too many eyes following her when she made her way to the outer edge of the grand banquet room. Exiting through the nearest door, she paused on the other side to breathe.

Could she do it? Should she? The proposal came out of nowhere. She thought they were just dating and having fun. Fooling around really. Yes, she really liked him, but marriage? She needed time to think. Pushing away from the door to head for the bar, she glanced back at their table and froze.

All eyes were on the top table where the father of the bride had just risen to his feet. It was time for speeches, but that wasn't what Mindy was looking at. Her attention was on Eddie who had just squeezed something into his father's water and given it to him to drink.

She watched the duke take a sip and put it down. Eddie said something to his father and handed the glass back so he could take another.

What was she seeing?

Chapter 58 - Felicity

The news about the phone was a revelation. If it was in the building, then the saboteur was here and that meant it couldn't be Primrose. I checked my logic with Vince.

"Probably, yes."

"Why only probably?"

"Well, dear, what if Primrose *is* here in the building?"

I gasped. That hadn't occurred to me and now I needed to check. "Can your app find the other phone?"

"Sure."

"Please do that then. I'm going to head to the hotel lobby. The staff know Primrose well enough by now. I want to know if they have seen her. If she's here, then that seals it and she's the saboteur. I can scream for the police to search the building until they find her."

"Unless she has the phone on her. In which case I'll find her first." Vince made it sound like a positive thing, but the fluttering of fear in my gut soon quelled when I imagined Primrose trying to hurt Vince.

It had taken me a while to find out – actually he didn't reveal the truth until after our first night together, but Vince had been a boxer in his youth. Quite a good one, apparently. His size dictated he fight in the super heavyweight category, but after one professional bout, which he lost, he decided the restrictive life of a professional boxer wasn't for him.

Built like a tank with broad shoulders and a wide chest, Primrose could shoot him and still lose.

We left the room together, Vince turning left as he tried to orientate the map on his app and I went right towards the hotel's lobby.

"I'll let you know when I find the phone," he called over his shoulder, starting to walk away.

My feet twitched with indecision. I really wanted to ask if Primrose was here, but at the same time felt odd about sending Vince off alone.

"Go," he made shooing motions. "She's not going to be armed, darling."

Exhaling slowly, I told myself that speed was of the essence, so splitting up to get more done just made sense. I let him go and walked briskly to find someone from hotel management.

Chapter 59 - Barbie and Jane

That they were getting nowhere didn't need to be discussed. They had both moaned about the hotel's file management system and how awkward it was to cross reference the electronic data with the physical reports and invoices, but accepted it probably wasn't designed to be interrogated the way they were.

The point, really, was that they had to keep going back and forth between the computer in the office and the filing cabinets in a room along the corridor. After more than an hour of sending Patrica, Tempest, and the others to look at things that all turned out to be nothing, they were both holding back from voicing that they each thought they were now wasting their time.

As these things always go, it was just when Jane had decided enough was enough that she saw it.

Frowning at the screen, she zoomed in.

Barbie was in the filing room, leaning on a cabinet with her arms folded and her head resting on them. She was just about over the jet lag from flying into England from halfway around the world, but the lack of sleep was taking its toll, and she might have been asleep in minutes had Jane not called her.

"Hey, Barbie. I think I might have something."

With a deep breath, Barbie pushed herself upright and away from the cabinet to step into the corridor.

"Something interesting?" Jane hadn't made it sound like she thought it was all that.

A beat of silence passed before Jane spoke again.

"I need you to come take a look at this." Jane waited until Barbie appeared, the tall blonde yawning when she strolled unhurriedly into the office. She pushed back the chair to give Barbie room.

Curious, and hoping it might be something more tangible than the last twenty possibles, Barbie's eyes skipped over the page until she saw it.

"Wait. But that's …"

"Exactly," Jane agreed.

"Okay. Surely that's just coincidence."

Jane pushed with her feet to get the wheeled office chair back to the keyboard. "That's what I told myself, but then I remembered seeing it before." She backed out of the entry and opened a new one.

Barbie's breathing quickened. This really was something. Checking the date, she said, "That was just a couple of weeks ago."

Jane got to her feet. "Yeah, we need to check this out. Right now."

"Do we call the others?"

"Let's confirm it first. They've been running all over the hotel for more than an hour. If we are right, then we will need to evacuate the building and we'll need them for that."

Chapter 60 - Vince

The app on his phone led him to a room at the back of the hotel and that was suspicious in and of itself. The rooms Felicity had assigned to her party of wedding planners were all at the front and located as close to the ballroom and banquet hall as could be. If the cloned version of her phone was back here, it had to mean the person using it was trying to stay hidden.

Obviously, that made sense since they had to be up to no good, but the real question was who would he find when he opened the door?

Felicity believed the saboteur had to be Primrose and he understood why. Primrose was a good businesswoman in that she was cutthroat and ruthless and determined to get ahead of her competition and stay there. What went against her was the simple fact that Felicity was better at the whole wedding planner game.

Primrose used dirty tactics to score points against her biggest rival, but to the best of his knowledge, Felicity had chosen never to reciprocate. She played a fair game and won by using her superior knowledge and skills.

Putting all that to one side, Vince couldn't see Primrose dousing party poppers in something that would set fire to the hands of the people setting them off. She was cunning, maybe even conniving, but not so desperate that she would cause harm to get ahead.

That left a question to be answered because Vince didn't know who else it could be, only that he didn't think Felicity's dramas were due to Primrose.

Stopping outside the door, he put his phone away. The app assured him the cloned version of Felicity's phone was less than two yards away on the other side of the door. He didn't have a keycard to open it, which would have been easy enough to obtain, but he did have a large right foot.

Pivoting on his left, he drew back his knee and drove forward, smashing his foot through the lock. The door slammed open, creating the shock effect he wanted, but no cry of surprised terror echoed out from within.

Feeling a little anticlimactic – he'd hoped to find the saboteur with something incriminating in their hands – he stepped into the room.

The blow to the back of his head registered as a flash of blinding light. He felt no pain, but as his consciousness shut down and his legs gave way, he was dimly aware of a thing he was always telling his security operatives: check the corners. You must always check the corners.

Chapter 61 – Elizabeth

Elizabeth stood over the prone form of Vince Slater, the iron held above her head and ready to strike again if he so much as twitched. The angular plate on the base had left a mark on the base of his skull where she hit him. Creating energy by swinging the iron by its cord, the blow to his head had been sweeter than she thought possible.

Deciding he was out cold, she stepped away to place the iron in a bag. It wouldn't do to have it found by the police. Vince hadn't seen her face, but the way he'd entered the room gave her cause for concern.

Did he know something? If so, then how? Everything led back to either Primrose or Felicity. They'd made it easy for her. Both so used to being in charge of every element of the weddings they arranged, they were blithely unaware that she was carefully manipulating their decisions.

Felicity was very much in the lead role but refused to rule with an iron rod. She encouraged free thought in her team and that meant Elizabeth could suggest things like an ice sculpture to Primrose and rely on her to present it as her own idea.

Idea accepted, all she had to do then was volunteer to help Primrose with the arrangements.

They suspected nothing and that could not have been clearer today. So why was Felicity's lump of a boyfriend kicking in doors?

There could only be one explanation and that meant there was only one action she could now take. Kneeling so her legs straddled Vince's back, she wrapped her hands around his meaty neck and began to squeeze.

"Time to say goodbye, Mr Slater."

Chapter 62 – Felicity

"Yes, Mrs Green is here. She arrived about half an hour ago." The news came from the deputy manager, a woman in her mid-thirties called Janet Gilliland.

I had to fight not to react.

"Oh, super," I said in a tone that suggested it was anything but. "Did she ask for me?"

Janet's eyebrows did a little dance as she tried to decipher the question. "No, Mrs Philips. She didn't speak to me at all, actually. I happened to see her as she passed through the lobby. She looked to be in a hurry, just like this morning."

"Oh, yes, this morning. Did you speak with her then?"

"She asked about an ice-sculpture she was supposed to sign for. It arrived a short while after she did."

That was right. The message on her phone, the one I was supposed to have sent, told her to go to the hotel to sign for it even though Elizabeth was here.

I mumbled, "Thank you," and wandered away, taking out my phone to call Vince. Thumbing the button to connect us, I held the device to my ear and waited for him to answer.

But he didn't.

Primrose was here and Vince wasn't answering his phone.

My heart felt like a lead weight in my chest. For months there had been dead bodies in my life as crazy people decided the best way to solve their problems was through killing the person or persons who stood in their way. Was Primrose that crazy?

Panic washed over me like a cold wave, stilling my senses. Had Primrose returned to make sure the job was done? It hadn't occurred to me to have her removed from the list of approved persons to be granted access through the security checkpoint. The time of her arrival meant she must have come in before I called the police. They would realise where she was soon enough, but for now she was inside the hotel and ... what was I going to do if she'd hurt Vince?

My leaden feet had carried me back to the banquet room. I was outside the doors looking in when a shadow fell across me.

Unthinkingly, I had wandered around to the back of the banquet hall where I could enter virtually unseen by the guests. The speeches were on so almost everyone in the room faced the top table. It was the door I'd been using and had insisted my team use since the very start, so muscle memory was to blame as much as anything else.

I began to turn around, certain I already knew who was standing behind me. But as I rotated, time slowed down and my brain operated as if moving at high speed by comparison.

Primrose towered over me. Half a foot taller, she had always enjoyed looking down at me in a physical as well as a metaphorical sense. She wore the same dress as before, her heels giving her several extra inches she really didn't need. Her chest, two cup sizes bigger than mine, filled the space in front of my eyes, but I was looking at her hands. They were empty.

In the half second since I became aware of her presence behind me, I had gone back over everything I thought I knew. The cloned phone and the text messages, the party poppers that she suggested, the ice sculpture that she commissioned and then signed for, the bag with the keyring on it that could only be bought in Scotland … the leaked photographs. Someone timed revealing those to the press for the moment when it would do Primrose the most damage. She accused me, but if I hadn't done it, which I hadn't, then who else could have? It had to be someone who thought they would benefit from Primrose losing the royal wedding contract.

The contract came to me, but what if someone else thought they might get it …

I tilted my head back, looking up to meet her eyes. Her mouth was slightly open, and I could see she was breathing fast. Her eyes were a little dilated. She could see the truth too.

"It's Elizabeth!" we both blurted.

Chapter 63 – Jane and Barbie

Janet Gilliland, the hotel's deputy manager, nudged the mouse with her keyboard and made a small humming noise while navigating the hotel's facilities management system. Rick Haythorn, the facility manager wasn't someone she got on very well with. He acted as though his position was somehow more important than hers and generally refused to follow any instructions she gave him.

It was why she wasn't bothering to call him now and chose to try to answer the question herself.

"Yes, that's right. I have the record here. It was a routine maintenance appointment."

"For a system installed last year?" Jane pushed for further confirmation.

"That's correct."

"A system that adds fragrance to the air conditioning system?"

Janet looked down at her screen again, searching to find the information she needed. When she found the appropriate lines about the product, she looked up with a confident smile.

"That is what the paperwork says."

Jane and Barbie looked at each other and then back at the deputy manager. They both sniffed deeply. That there was no fragrance in the air didn't need any further demonstration.

"You need to show us where the air conditioning system is," said Barbie, her tone leaving no room for argument.

"The controls, the refrigerant, the motors … everything," added Jane.

Looking a little startled – the implications of what the women suggested but didn't express were horrifying – Janet clicked the mouse to log off the computer and came out from behind the lobby reception desk.

"I'll need to find our facilities manager," she said, leading them away from the direction of the wedding reception. "He'll know where all those things are." Janet thought it bad that she didn't.

With Barbie and Jane both telling her to hurry, they broke into a jog and she was a little breathless when they arrived at their destination.

Rick was behind his desk, his face glued to the screen and he jumped halfway out of his skin when three women burst through his door.

"Rick, these ladies need you to show them the air conditioning system."

Shutting off his screen so no one could see what he'd been looking at, Rick looked from Janet to Jane to Barbie, and then down a foot to Barbie's generous assets, his smile forming and then growing.

Barbie had seen it all before and had no time for nonsense.

The hotel's facilities manager was about to say something suave when the tanned blonde reached across his desk to grab the front of his shirt.

"I think someone planted a device in the air conditioning system and you signed off on the work. Take your eyes off my chest and show us where it is right now."

Yanked from his chair by the surprisingly strong woman, Rick spluttered, "The air conditioning system is in the basement. It's a restricted area reserved for hotel personnel." He didn't like that he'd been called out ogling the American woman.

Janet grabbed his arm. "Stop talking utter rubbish, Rick, and get moving!"

Feeling left out, Jane went around the desk to remove Rick's chair and propel him from behind. He attempted to squirm free but gave up almost immediately when he was forced to accept he wasn't strong enough. The skinny one, who had shockingly big hands for a girl, was far stronger than her slender frame would suggest. It was almost as though it was a man in the dress.

Frogmarched along corridors until they reached a locked door, Rick produced a set of keys. He'd given up fighting their demands and would show them what they wanted to see, but he knew they were wasting their time. The air conditioning system worked perfectly and always had.

The police had a team of specialists in to check the functionality of everything in the hotel less than a month ago and they returned to carry out the same tests twice in the last week.

He pointed that out and asked, "What is it you're hoping to find?"

The derision in his voice annoyed Barbie, but she said, "I would like to find nothing, but I suspect that won't be the case."

"And why is that?" Rick shot back. They had reached the bottom of the stairs where the vast space below the hotel was stacked with seasonal decorations of all kinds, spare equipment, spare glasses and plates, and goodness knows what else that senior management deemed too valuable to throw away. Poor Rick had to house it all in what he liked to think of as his space. He had a small gym with some free weights set up in one corner. Not that he'd used it in a while, but he liked the girls working at the hotel to know he had it.

Barbie hit the ground and continued walking. There was a generator to one side, there as backup in case of emergencies, no doubt, and a bunch of other equipment, about half of which she couldn't identify. Somewhere amongst it would be the air con system.

"Almost a year ago this hotel had an additional system fitted to add fragrance to the air being pumped through the ductwork, yes?"

"That's right." Rick wondered where this was going.

Barbie pressed on. "Are you aware that an engineer visited last week to check the system."

Rick's facial expression froze. Should he admit that he didn't know that?

"It doesn't matter, Rick, because chances are no one booked the appointment or carried out a check, so you wouldn't know about it."

"The point is," said Jane, picking up the narrative, "the name of the person on the paper for the installation and the check supposedly conducted last week is Mindy Walters."

Silence fell.

Rick broke it when he said, "Okay. So what? Who's Mindy Walters?"

"She's the assistant to the wedding planner managing everything upstairs. The name could be a coincidence, but I highly doubt it."

"So," said Barbie, stopping in front of what she believed to be the pump for the air conditioning system, "you need to show us everything to do with this system and you need to do it right now."

Chapter 64 – Felicity and Primrose

We stared at each other for a moment, each expecting the other to speak first. Inevitably we finally both started talking at the same time.

Waving my hands to stop her, I said, "Primrose, I'm sorry."

"Well, I should think so," she snapped, glaring at me. Thankfully, she relented after a moment. "Look, I get it, okay. I've been awful to you for years and I think Elizabeth knew she could take us both down if she made us fight each other. You really didn't leak those photographs of me, did you?"

"No, Primrose. I really didn't. The messages from me that weren't on my phone, they came from a clone. Vince went to look for it. It's in this hotel right now."

"Because it was Elizabeth," said Primrose. "That dirty underhanded cow is behind everything."

With a jolt I remembered the photograph and fumbled with my phone to get it on the screen.

THE ROYAL WEDDING

"Is this your bag?"

"That ugly thing?" Primrose turned her nose up. "That's Elizabeth's, Felicity. We've been working on top of one another for weeks. How do you not know that?"

I could have shrugged and said I was too busy preparing for the biggest event of my life to notice trivial details like who carries what bag, but I was too worried about Vince.

"I have to go," I said, moving to go around her. "Vince went looking for the cloned phone, but he's not answering now. I'm worried he found Elizabeth, and she's hurt him." I was going to set off to search the hotel, but Primrose stepped into my way.

"The ice sculpture," she said, giving no further context.

I drew in a breath to ask what she was talking about, but then it hit me. If Elizabeth was behind it all, she went out of her way to ensure Primrose signed for the ice sculpture when it arrived.

Turning around, I walked back to the door and peered through. Primrose came alongside me, leaning down so our heads were almost side by side.

The sculpture of a ballerina was beautiful. Light bounced off it but also seemed to pass inside where the ice froze it to make the figurine almost glow. Like a diamond with a billion facets, it sparkled. It was positioned to the right of the top table, right next to the route everyone had taken on their way into the banquet room.

Squinting, I pointed, "Is that ..."

"Gas!" Primrose shoved her way through the door, breaking into a run.

Chapter 65 – Albert and Rex

The truth of it was that Albert was bored. The invitation was an honour to receive and there had been no way to refuse attending. Confident that what he would remember from the day was his encounter with Cody Williams, and not the overly long speeches, Albert occupied his mind with thoughts of returning to his European trip.

The first few stops had not gone entirely as planned, which is to say they were unmitigated disasters he and Rex had survived by dint of blind luck. Despite that, he longed for the road and looked forward to packing his suitcase once more. He'd experienced the winter in the north of Europe but would go south when he returned. Italy would be lovely at this time of year, and he rather fancied sampling a pizza in Napoli.

Rex was asleep under the table. He'd eaten his fill, and it had been an exciting day so far, so he was more than ready for a nap. His feet twitched as he dream-chased a squirrel across the grass and up a tree. In real life the squirrel would have found a handy branch from which it could launch acorns and insults, but in the dream Rex ran up the tree trunk to continue the chase.

Albert looked around the room. The father of the bride, who had seemed nervous and very much out of his depth when he rose from his chair to find a sea of expectant faces looking his way, had stuttered a little when he began to speak. Hoping that might force the man to curtail his speech, Albert was disappointed to find the bride's father grew steadily more confident.

To be fair, his speech was amusing, his anecdotes about the bride all aimed to record their love rather than embarrass her which he'd heard all too many fathers do at such a key point in their daughter's life. Nevertheless, he was starting to drone on and Albert wondered if someone at the back end of the room might start to snore.

Not really paying attention to anything in particular, he just happened to be looking the right way when he saw Patricia Fisher run past outside. She was moving at speed with Barbie, Jermaine, and what looked like the Blue Moon team on her heels.

Albert chewed his bottom lip and argued with himself. There was something amiss. Watching to see if a squad of police officers might follow, Albert was shocked to see Felicity burst into the room.

Chapter 66 – Lord Edward

Albert Smith wasn't the only one to see Patricia Fisher and her friends running past the banquet hall doors. The urgency of their passage made him stare, questioning where they were going in such a hurry. He recognised who the middle-aged woman was; her face had been splashed across enough papers, but he didn't know why she was here.

And he very much didn't like it.

Getting to his feet, he made his excuses and aimed his feet toward the same door he'd seen Patricia Fisher run by. Time was pushing on and he'd expected to have already left by now. The drugs he put into his dad's rum and coke should have him doubled over with cramps or vomiting yet he was utterly unaffected.

Lord Edward assumed the old man simply ditched the rum and coke when he wasn't looking, but he'd administered a second dose and the drugs were in his body now. He would be cutting it fine, but there was still time to execute the plan. Probably. It helped that the father of the bride was such a bore with a definite love for his own voice.

The optimum time to deploy the toxic gas he'd fitted to the hotel's air conditioning system almost a year ago was during the speeches. That had been his plan since the start. With everyone sitting in their chairs, their focus on the top table, and only one person in the room speaking, he would be able to check all his targets were there before leaving.

He couldn't activate the device until he was clear of the building with his father. The hydrogen sulphide gas in the canister attached to the air con pump was seriously nasty stuff. Once inhaled the victim's death was ensured even if they managed to survive for a few minutes. A sufficiently high dose would cause instant collapse, but vented throughout the hotel, even the large cylinder he'd used would be 'watered' down. Regardless, no one in the building would survive.

Lord Edward harboured a minor concern that someone might get up from their seat in the minute or so it took him to get outside with his father, but it was a risk he had to take. If the King or one of the immediate heirs were to survive, another 'accident' a few years down the line would have to occur.

That was a problem for later. Right now he needed to know what a famous British sleuth was doing at the hotel.

He hurried in a sort of half crouch to the door, not wanting to distract the speech giver or draw attention to himself. Outside, he straightened and checked to his left. Mindy was yet to return from the bar and it wouldn't do to have her spot him sneaking around. The proposal strategy worked better than he'd expected, completely throwing off her suspicions and there was an added benefit he'd not anticipated.

When the police sifted through the bodies, doing their best to establish what happened, they would examine people's phones, building up a picture of who was where in the moments leading up to the fatal moment. They would undoubtedly find pictures showing Lord Edward leaving with his father, hence the sick ruse that would explain their exit from the building and miraculous survival. That was something he'd planned for. Counted on, even.

What they would also see was his proposal. Someone would leak the information and probably a photograph or two. Someone always did. The media outlets would pay handsomely for a tragedy story about the future King of England. He'd only just proposed to his girlfriend, and she died in the terrible attack.

Lord Edward stopped walking when the hole in his plan presented itself like a wet fish to the face. He'd framed Mindy as the culprit. Loaded into her laptop, which he'd conveniently borrowed a while back while she languished in his bath at the palace, was a message that would activate tonight. It was addressed to reporters at every newspaper in the country, but the whole world would see it soon enough.

It showed that Mindy held deep rooted anti-royalist views and saw her opportunity to bring them all down when Aunt Felicity's work thrust her into Lord Edward's orbit. She seduced him with her feminine wiles and plotted to murder.

The message, more a political manifesto than anything else, together with the physical evidence, including a dummy duplicate switch to activate the device which he would place in a deep recess of her handbag just before he left, would give the police no reason to look anywhere else.

Would his association with her cast a beam of suspicion in his direction? Lord Edward really couldn't tell but accepted it was too late to do anything about it.

Pushing on, he meandered in the direction he saw Patricia Fisher and friends run until he heard soft voices coming from the cellar. He was right. Someone had figured it out. He couldn't believe it. If they were in the cellar then they had to be looking at the gas canister.

Quelling his rising panic before it overtook his ability to think rationally, he looked about for something he could use to wedge under the door handle. A laugh burst from his lips when he spotted the keys still in the door and he had to clamp his hand over his mouth lest he be heard.

Locking the door, he pocketed the keys and walked away. No one had seen him, no one would know. Provided he set the device off soon, which was necessary anyway, no one would discover the people trapped in the cellar and they wouldn't have time to defuse it.

Feeling like he should whistle a happy tune for God truly was on his side, Lord Edward was almost back to the banquet room where he prayed his father was now beginning to feel iffy, when he ran into someone who complicated matters. "Mindy!"

Chapter 67 – Felicity and Primrose

Bursting through the back door to the banquet room, I ran after Primrose. The father of the bride was prattling on about something to do with Nora's childhood and a pony he couldn't really afford. All eyes were on him, and he might have been the only person in the room who saw us burst in.

Thin tendrils of smoke were coming from the ice sculpture. I didn't know what it was but could guess it was toxic. Elizabeth had gone for a big final statement that would kill or incapacitate anyone who breathed it in. There was no time to call the police to come help us. No time to evacuate the room. I could already see the gassy smoke was getting thicker. There still wasn't much of it, but there would be soon.

We were the only ones who could do anything about it.

Yelling, "Fire blanket!" I ran to the wall where health and safety dictated a fire extinguisher station was required. Next to it a first aid kit hung from a hook and beneath it was a fire blanket. I'd never seen one employed other than on one of those health and safety videos where they demonstrate what to do if a person has somehow caught themselves alight.

I ripped the box off the wall, shocked when the fire blanket, designed to smother the flames, fell into my hands.

Primrose was already running, weaving between the tables and drawing looks of bewilderment from everyone in the room.

The father of the bride had stop talking and the whole room was looking our way.

"Sorry!" I called. "Apologies, Your Majesties. Won't be a moment."

Holding the fire blanket between us, we held our breaths and threw it over the ice sculpture. It fell to the floor on both sides and stayed there when we gripped the trolley and started to push. Sitting on casters, it moved easily enough but was hard to steer.

I needed Primrose to angle her end around so we could fit through the door more easily, but she was driving with her stupidly long legs, and I could barely keep up. We hit the doors at an angle, blasting them aside with a clatter.

A glance back into the banquet hall just before the doors rebounded shut again, showed me a world filled with bemused expressions. A wispy trail of heavy smoke clung to the floor, dissipating even as I watched. Whether there was any danger or not, I had no way to tell but given that I was one half of the suicide team who chose to save the day, I had bigger concerns on my mind.

Smoke now roiled from beneath the fire blanket, pooling around our feet as we ran. None of it was coming through the material, but was I safe to draw a breath?

Hurtling into the hotel's lobby with its sleek reception desk, I was glad to find the area devoid of life. We were leaving clouds of the heavy smoke behind, and I feared for anyone who thought to follow us.

"The doors!" yelled Primrose, closing her mouth again the instant the words left her lips.

My lungs were screaming at me. I needed to draw breath, even if it was only a tiny thimble of air.

"The river!" I shouted in reply, barrelling through the hotel's automatic doors to arrive outside. I had sucked in the barest taste of fresh oxygen when I opened my mouth, and it wasn't enough. I was going to have to take a deep lungful soon, but the River Stour was right there.

The carpark at the front of the hotel, empty save for the police who were set up to keep the area secure, bordered the river on one side. It was thirty yards away, which doesn't sound like a lot, but I already had spots dancing in front of my eyes.

A low wall bordered it, which was perfect for us. If we could make it there the mere action of ramming the trolley into the wall would send the ice sculpture into the water beyond.

"Hey!" yelled a police officer.

I didn't have the time to look his way but could sense that there were now men and women in uniform running after us. They didn't need to see our faces or know who we were to be able to tell our activity registered high on the suspicious scale.

Ignoring them, I tilted my head back so my mouth was as far away from the gas as possible and sucked in a grateful breath of fresh air.

Primrose gasped, "Keep going!" while behind us the police yelled, "Stop!"

We were in heels and tight dresses and I'm in my late fifties. They were going to catch us, and the only question was whether we would get to the river before they could stop us.

Well, I supposed that wasn't the *only* question. I had a bunch of others such as, do I feel lightheaded and sick because I sucked in some of the deadly gas spilling into the air and I'm already too badly poisoned to survive, and what if this gas is the kind that kills you just by touching your skin.

With the sound of boots so close I was shocked I couldn't feel them running up my back, we reached the edge of the carpark and hit the wall.

The trolley stopped with a jarring crunch that hurt my wrists, elbows, and shoulders. The top was higher than the wall and tried to keep going, which meant the bottom flipped up to whack into my shins. I fell on top of it, bruising my ribs and ejecting whatever small amount of air I had left in my lungs.

The ice sculpture, still wrapped in the fire blanket plummeted over the side, hit the water with an almighty splash, and sunk beneath the waves with a plop that sent a plume of water into the air.

Primrose punched the air. "Woohoo!"

Then the cops slammed into her, bearing her to the ground as they piled on top.

Weirdly, no one touched me. At least it was weird until I realised why. I'd called the cops and set them on Primrose.

I could hear her squawking and protesting beneath the pile of bodies.

"No!" I shouted. "She's not the one! Get off her!"

A man in a bad suit said, "Mrs Philips?" He'd been running behind the guys and gals in uniform and was a little out of breath.

I was barely able to stand my body's oxygen supplies were so depleted, but I could guess who he was even before he introduced himself.

"DS Ross Mellon," he showed me his warrant card and sucked in some air. "I see you found her before I could."

I sagged against the trolley. "Yes, but I got it wrong. She's not behind it at all."

Chapter 68 – Barbie et al

"So what do you think?" asked Barbie, looking over Tempest's shoulder.

They were looking down at a gas canister that was attached via a pipe to the air conditioning system. The valve on top was a standard coupling but it was impossible to get to it.

Exhaling through his nose in a thoughtful manner, Tempest said, "I think we probably need to get everyone out of the building."

Gripped by dread, Patricia couldn't fault his cautious logic. They didn't know what they were looking at, the cylinder bore no labels whatsoever, yet they all doubted it was filled with happy smiles and baby laughter.

Barbie was already moving toward the stairs. "I'll do it."

Jermaine went with her, as did Big Ben – a forceful character if ever there was one. If they were right, then the contents of the cylinder would kill and there was no guessing how soon it might go off. They didn't have time for the police to check what they were telling them, so they were going to scream and shout and scare everyone out of the banquet room and then the building.

A few cries of, "There's a bomb! That ought to do it," said Big Ben.

The police would go nuts. They would all get arrested, but when the smoke cleared and a hazmat team was able to confirm the cylinder was indeed part of an elaborate plot to murder the royal family, all would be forgiven. Heck, there would probably be medals and knighthoods.

Reaching the door, Barbie grabbed the handle and threw her shoulder against the door. The handle didn't budge and her determination to exit resulted only in a bruise.

"It's locked," she announced, grunting with effort as she applied all her muscle to make the handle move.

Jermaine added his strength, but it wouldn't budge.

"Let me," growled Big Ben, lining up to ram it. He didn't have much of a run up, the landing at the top of the stairs was barely big enough for all three of them to occupy, but he gave it everything he had.

And bounced off.

Below them Patricia had seen the latest challenge and was attempting to defeat it by using her phone.

Sounding apologetic, Jane said, "There's no signal down here. Barbie had to go back to the ground floor to make the call to you."

Hearing her, Barbie took out her phone again. While Big Ben and Jermaine teamed up to drive their shoulders into the unyielding door, she moved her phone around, staring at the screen and daring it to show her just one tiny bar of signal.

On his knees next to the device, Tempest watched all that happen, accepted things for what they were, and turned his attention back to the cylinder.

"I guess I should see how complex this thing is. Maybe we can disconnect it."

Patricia didn't want to discourage him, but felt it necessary to ask, "Do you know anything about defusing weapons like this? Or about air conditioning systems? Or … well, anything that would help in this particular situation?"

Tempest nodded vigorously, his attention already focussed on the pipe running from the top of the cylinder.

"Yes, I know that this shouldn't be touched by anyone who doesn't know exactly what they are doing."

Chapter 69 – Mindy

Five minutes ago, Mindy had arrived in the bar to order the cocktails she had no interest in drinking, Mindy was surprised to find no one there to serve.

A barman appeared through a door behind the bar just a few moments later, an apology on his lips, and a question on his brow.

He expected her to place an order, but she was more interested to learn what might have happened. The man had a mop in his hands and the air around them carried a distinctly unpleasant note. Someone had been sick. It was too early for a wedding guest to be that inebriated – something she saw all too often in her line of work.

"Is everything okay?" she asked.

"Of course," the barman replied.

Mindy offered him a doubtful frown and left a silence she knew he would have to fill.

His cheeks colouring under her gaze – he had no clue who the pretty young woman was, but he was at a royal wedding, so she could be fifth in line to the throne for all he knew – he mumbled, "Um, one of the bar staff was taken sick."

"Sick as in they threw up." She cut her eyes very deliberately to the mop in his hands.

"Yes. Um, sorry. Now what can I get you?" He placed the mop back into the bucket. He would finish giving the floor a second go over when she was gone.

"We'll get to that." Mindy wasn't sure how to phrase the question in her head. Less than a minute ago she had watched her fiancé (goodness it felt weird using that term) tip something into his father's drink. Earlier he'd insisted his father have a rum and coke when it was clear he didn't want one and then spent the next hour asking if he was feeling okay. Now she had a sick barman …

"Did he drink anything?"

The barman jinked an eyebrow. "Excuse me?"

"The man who got sick suddenly. Did he drink anything?" She knew from experience that bar staff, some at least, were wont to minesweep drinks at the end of a night. An untouched rum and coke might prove a tempting tipple to a person inclined to drink on the job.

The barman facing her looked guilty, and though his lips moved, no words came out as he struggled to find something to say.

"He had a rum and coke, didn't he?" She was guessing and didn't like what being right could mean.

The barman said, "Um."

Mindy turned her head to look back in the direction of the banquet room.

Chapter 70 - Elizabeth and Vince

Her hands aching and out of breath from the effort of trying to strangle Vince, Elizabeth accepted defeat. The man's neck was just too big. Or her hands were too small. Or she just wasn't strong enough. Whatever the case, after ten minutes of trying to squeeze the life out of him, she'd been forced to give up.

Massaging her knuckles, she looked around for something else she could use. The cord on the iron could make a half decent garrot. Or she could use the iron to bash his skull in. The latter tantalised with the promise of cathartic release, but the likelihood of blood splatter on her clothes struck it from the list. The cord for the iron would avoid that particular issue but her hands ached and she doubted strangling him with a thick electrical lead would prove much easier.

No, she needed something sharp and all she had was a small pair of scissors. Great for trimming one's fingernails, but not a whole lot of use for opening an artery.

Collecting her things and wiping down a few surfaces she knew she must have touched, Elizabeth backed out of the room. There was a fire station around the corner with a fire axe behind a pane of very breakable glass. That would do the trick nicely.

"*Gotcha*," said Buster.

Chapter 71 – Albert and Rex

Rex had been enjoying a fun dream when his human woke him with repeated gentle taps to his shoulder. Blearily lifting his head, Rex could only see Albert's legs from the knees down and his right arm, the hand of which was still poking him.

Rolling onto his chest, Rex nudged the hand away and crawled forward to poke his head out from under the tablecloth.

Racked with indecision, an unusual trait for Albert Smith, five minutes had passed since he saw Patricia Fisher and the rest run past outside the banquet hall. Were he not sitting so close to the front of the room and the top table with the King, Queen, and a prince all within spitting distance, he would have already left to pursue them. Instead, because it felt awkward to get up and leave, he'd stayed in his chair and hoped his friends would wander back past the doors looking distinctly calmer.

But they hadn't, and his sense that something had to be off grew with each passing moment. Unwilling to wait any longer, when Rex popped his head out from under the tablecloth, he used his head to indicate that they were leaving.

"Walkies," he whispered, making his voice just loud enough that the people around him at the table would know he was going. He figured they would assume the old man had a weak bladder and was using the dog to disguise his need to find a restroom.

Striding boldly and keeping his eyes dead ahead so he wouldn't be able to see the father of the bride or anyone else at the top table tracking his exit, Albert let Rex lead him from the room.

Outside he turned right, setting off in the direction he saw Patricia and pals running. He had no clue where they might have been going or might now be but expected his ears would guide him. If there was drama occurring, it was unlikely to be quiet.

Chapter 72 - Mindy and Lord Edward

When she left the bar on her way back to the banquet hall, Mindy did her best not to jump to conclusions. Eddie was up to something, of that she was certain, but that didn't mean he was planning to kill a whole load of the royal family.

Did it?

Cassie believed he was behind his brother's death and held an unwavering belief that the royal family was in peril. So many of them had died in recent months that Mindy understood why the conspiracy theorists were getting so much airtime.

Eddie put something in his father's drink, but that didn't make him a killer. She couldn't dismiss it, though. She needed to know what was going on. She couldn't prove the barman got sick because he drank the rum and coke and didn't know for sure Eddie had put anything in it.

But she would know if he lied to her, so Mindy was going to ask him. That was going to be awkward at the table where Eddie's father would undoubtedly hear –

the man had ears like an owl, but on her way back to the banquet room, she ran into Eddie as he was leaving.

Startled to see her, he blurted, "Mindy!"

"Where are you going?" she asked.

Sagging as though embarrassed to reveal the truth, he said, "The restroom, my love."

Her eyes narrowed slightly at the obvious lie. "That's the other direction," she pointed out. "Where have you been?"

His gut now clenching – the stupid girl always had too many questions – Lord Edward tried to change the subject. He cast his eyes down to her hands. "Were you not able to get the cocktails?"

Mindy had forgotten all about them. "No," she said, still eyeing him curiously. Yet again he was acting strange. "They didn't have one of the ingredients," she lied. "I was coming back to ask you what else you might like."

Lord Edward's mind raced. He doubted very much there was a bar in the country that couldn't make a Long Island Iced Tea. It used such readily available ingredients, but why would Mindy lie about it?

Thinking fast, he hit her with a devilish smile and closed the distance between them. She felt rigid when he put his arms around her, pulling her close – she had never been like that before. She suspected something and he needed to act right now.

"Darling," he whispered in his best bedroom voice. "I'm feeling rather naughty. Now that we're engaged, how about we find a private spot where we can …" He didn't need to finish the sentence; his intentions were obvious enough.

Mindy bit his ear and laughed playfully. "You are terrible, Lord Edward. What sort of girl do you take me for?"

Shifting his hands away from her waist, he grabbed her right hand to pull her along behind him as he set off. Tucked away in a restroom, he would overpower her and leave her unconscious. Whether his dad was sick or not, they were leaving the building in five minutes, and he would activate the device the second they were outside. Mindy would never regain consciousness and nothing in his plan would need to change.

Mindy let Eddie lead her away from the banquet room. She was sick to her gut, but there was no denying his odd behaviour now. One moment he's nervous as anything, the next he's proposing, then he's sneaking around and now he wants to have sex. She was going to let him take her to a restroom or wherever it was he thought they ought to go and once inside she was going to bend his right arm to breaking point. He would answer her questions and if she was right and he was up to something, she would walk him right out to the police herself.

It would break her heart, but she would do it. Lord Edward Chamberlain was too good for her. That was the truth, and she knew it. He'd picked her when he could have had anyone and there had to be a reason behind it.

"In here, darling," he whispered when they came to a men's toilet.

They were well away from the banquet hall where they were less likely to be disturbed. Going through the door Mindy steeled herself. If she was wrong would their relationship survive her doubt? Still second guessing herself, she felt something hard touch her neck and all her lights went out.

Lord Edward looked down at Mindy's slumped form. She really did have a great body and the dress showed it off magnificently. Like a gunman in the wild west, he lifted the stun gun to his lips and blew across the electrodes as though clearing away the smoke. He'd thought getting a weapon through security would be impossible until he found one that looked just like a mobile phone. Designed by an American, it was expensive and illegal to own in Britain, but worth the risk and every penny he'd spent to obtain it.

Removing the spare transmitter from an inside pocket, he slipped it into Mindy's hand and closed her fingers around it. Backing out the door, he hurried away. Now there really was no time to lose.

Chapter 73 – Elizabeth

Elizabeth turned to find Felicity's cat and dog looking at her. The dog looked like his eyes weren't lining up correctly, but he bared his teeth all the same.

"Shoo," said Elizabeth, making 'go away' motions.

"*I think someone has been rather naughty*," said Amber.

Buster took a tentative step forward, moving without Amber's assistance for the first time since she found him.

"*I think someone has been downright criminal*," he remarked.

Elizabeth saw the animals stalking toward her. The cat meowed and the dog woofed and though it was ridiculous, it sounded as though they were communicating. She needed to get the fire axe to deal with Vince, but it could be used to make short work of a cat and a dog too. Pets had never been her thing. Not since her guinea pig died when she was eight had she even entertained owning something that would get old and die on her.

Yet Felicity took her animals everywhere and clearly loved them very dearly. Well, their loss would be another cruel blow Elizabeth was only too happy to deliver.

"Go on, get!" Elizabeth stomped her right foot, thinking that might send the pets scurrying.

Taking another pace, Buster said, "*I think it's time Devil Dog ...*" he paused for Amber.

"*And Fatal Feline,*" she filled the gap.

"*Brought righteous justice to the wicked.*" He didn't feel up to a fight and worried ramming her legs with his head might leave him in a worse state than her. But it had to be done. Dropping his head into attack position, Buster leapt forward. "*Dun, dun ...*"

Amber screeched, "*Dah!*"

A squeal of fright burst from Elizabeth. The cat and dog were coming for her. Sure, they were tiny compared with her, but they had teeth and claws and would tear her flesh if they got to her. Spinning off her heels, she sprinted away.

Buster and Amber gave chase, the cat giving the dog an occasional nudge to keep him going in a straight line when he veered off.

"*This is actually kinda fun,*" said Amber.

"*Haven't I always told you that?*" Buster replied, hitting the back of Elizabeth's legs so they tangled and she fell. Wisely, he'd chosen not to use his skull, employing a shoulder instead to side barge one leg into the other.

With the pets scampering out of the way like lumberjacks avoiding a falling tree, Elizabeth tumbled out of control to the carpet. Skidding along it, she scored multiple friction burns but came to rest directly under the fire axe cabinet.

Kicking up with both legs, she smashed the glass. A shard that stayed in the frame sliced into her leg, but she didn't even notice the blood start to flow as she snatched the weapon from its cradle.

Amber had been about to leap, aiming to land right on Elizabeth's face, and only narrowly avoided the head of the axe when Elizabeth swung it wildly to chop her in half.

The axe head bit into the carpet and the wooden floorboards below. She yanked it free and clambered to her feet.

"What are you going to do now, eh?" she challenged the cat and dog. They had backed off, but only to get out of range.

Hefting the weapon, Elizabeth knew throwing it would kill at least one of the animals. The corridor was too narrow for both to escape. They'd picked the fight but now she had the upper hand.

Grinning madly, blood flowing freely down her cut leg, Elizabeth raised the axe and pulled it back.

And there it stayed.

Confused, she looked around to see what she could have hooked it on.

Rex wagged his tail.

The blunt end of the axe head was in his mouth, and he wasn't about to let go.

Behind him stood an old man who was clearly one of the wedding guests. Elizabeth had to dredge her memory to conjure his name – Felicity had made them all memorise the entire guest list in the build up to today.

Albert said, "I think perhaps you should put that down before someone gets hurt."

Chapter 74 – Tempest and Patricia

Barbie and Jermaine had taken to shouting at the door. Their only way out, the only way they could raise the alarm and save everyone at the wedding, was to attract attention. Yet that wasn't happening.

Rick the facilities manager and Janet the deputy manager were with Tempest at the control panel for the air conditioning. The cylinder stood like a threat, menacing and silent. No one knew how to disconnect the cylinder safely.

"I think this is a radio receiver," Tempest pointed to a small device fitted in the pipe leading away from the top of the cylinder. "If I'm right, what it's attached to is a switch so someone with a transmitter can operate the device remotely."

Big Ben chipped in, "But they would need to be close."

Patricia asked, "How close?"

Neither of the ex-army guys knew and neither did Amanda, but they all concluded a person would have to be in the building or at least in the grounds for it to work.

"Wait a minute," said Jane. "We can't get a phone signal down here. How is it that a radio wave will work?"

"Different kind of signal. To get from your phone, the signal has to bounce off a relay tower miles away to then go onwards to whomever you are calling. That's true even if they are right next to you. The signal from the tower is getting lost among all the concrete and steelwork and everything else that makes up this building. A signal from a radio transmitter goes directly outwards in every direction. It will find this receiver with no trouble at all."

Patricia asked, "How sure are you?"

Tempest grimaced. "Not one hundred percent but do you want to bet your life that I'm wrong?"

Patricia didn't doubt Tempest got things wrong from time to time, everyone does, but she was yet to ever personally witness it happening.

Rick, sounding terrified, asked, "What happens when someone activates the switch?"

Tempest scratched at an itch on his chin. "Well, the cylinder is pressurised, so when the switch opens, the gas will flow into the air conditioning unit which is pumping air through the hotel. Assuming whatever is in here is toxic, in seconds the folks outside will be breathing it."

"We're looking at a mass casualty event," said Big Ben grimly.

"Including the whole of the royal family," added Patricia.

"Can we just disconnect it?" asked Janet, speaking for the first time in minutes.

Tempest nodded. He knew they could. It was the first thought he had, but it came with a dire consequence.

Pointing to the cylinder, he said, "I can rip the hose right off at the air con unit, but if I do that and the switch activates, either due to a failsafe I can't see or because the person with the transmitter decides it's time, the poison gas will be sucked through the hole and into the ventilation shafts anyway. It will probably be a weaker mixture because the bulk of it will fill the cellar, but it might still be enough to kill everyone at the wedding."

"But what about us?" asked Rick. "That's going to kill us. So we die and very possibly everybody else upstairs dies anyway."

Tempest nodded again. "The alternative …"

"Thank the Lord," said Rick, breathing a sigh of relief. "I knew there had to be a better plan than that."

"Alternatively," Tempest continued, "I can rip the hose off at the top of the cylinder and the integrity of the ventilation system won't be compromised."

Silence fell.

Until Rick blurted, "How is that any better! We'll still all be dead!"

Patricia exhaled a hard breath and said, "But we'll be the only ones."

Amanda crouched next to Tempest, putting her arm around him. They had just started to plan their wedding following her proposal a couple of weeks ago.

"We're dead either way," she said. "At least we can save the royal family."

Rick surged forward, trying to get to the cylinder. "No! If you just leave it alone the gas won't come in here at all. The ventilation system doesn't touch the cellar."

Big Ben caught him, pinning the struggling man as gently as he could.

Tempest looked around.

Barbie and Jermaine, having heard what was being discussed, had given up banging on the door and shouting for attention. They joined the others standing around the cylinder. A grimy cellar below a hotel was a poor place to die, but the location didn't matter, only their actions would count.

It was them or hundreds of guests and staff upstairs. None of them wanted these to be their last moments, but there really was no other choice.

Reaching forward, Tempest placed his hands on the pipe. Rick continued to struggle but he was no match for Big Ben.

No one said anything when they saw the muscles in his shoulders bunch.

Jane asked, "What does that valve on the top do?"

Chapter 75 – Felicity and Primrose

Primrose's dress was ruined, and she was having a hard time forgiving me for setting the police on her. I mean, she understood why I did, but that seemed to be small comfort.

Once I'd convinced the police officers the real threat was inside and they needed to find Elizabeth Keats before she could do any more harm, they rushed to the hotel and went inside. Led by DS Ross Mellon, a team of about twenty cops, almost all in uniform, went looking for the third wedding planner.

Limping a little from being thrown to the ground and jumped on, Primrose hobbled along next to me as we made our way back to the hotel lobby. I couldn't guess what the gas coming from the ice sculpture could have been, but the cops seemed to think it was dry ice.

The completely innocent substance, great for spooky Halloween events and special effects on movie sets, would have done the wedding guests no harm at all. I couldn't have known that, and it would have caused a disturbance because no one knew to expect it. That was probably the point.

Whatever the case, we had averted the crisis, and as we walked back through the hotel lobby, which was still deserted, the hotel staff avoiding it for some reason, I could hear the speeches still going on.

Was the father of the bride still going? It was a factor I had no ability to control, so I hoped the guests were okay and he wasn't too boring. I would send the servers in to refresh glasses shortly. In all the excitement and confusion, I couldn't be sure when they last served drinks.

I needed to check on the kitchen and thank the chef anyway. His team had outdone themselves.

Nearing the doors, I heard a dog bark. And then another. One sounded distinctly like Buster.

Chapter 76 – Elizabeth and Lord Edward

Elizabeth shoved the axe away, pushing the German Shepherd backwards as she fought to gain a little room. The old man behind the large dog was Albert Smith. She knew his face from the papers, and she'd read the incredible story that put him there.

The old man she believed she could deal with. How strong could he be at his age? But the dog was an entirely different proposition. One bite from Rex would be all it took, so she ran.

The bulldog snapped his teeth at her feet when she leapt high to get over him, and she could hear both dogs barking as they gave pursuit. There were fire doors ahead, the kind they fit in long corridors to create a barrier so the whole place doesn't go up so quickly and people can escape. They were triggered by the fire alarm system but could be closed manually.

Slamming the wall-mounted button as she ran past it, Elizabeth glanced over her shoulder to be sure the pets would be trapped on the other side and consequently didn't see the obstacle that was suddenly in her path.

THE ROYAL WEDDING

Lord Edward had returned to the banquet hall to find his father's pallor turning grey. He didn't look well at all. He had breathed a sigh of relief, hooked a hand under the old man's shoulder, and told him they were going outside for a breath of fresh air.

The duke didn't resist, allowing his frailty to show when his son helped him to stand and then escorted him from the room.

Lord Edward got a few sympathetic looks from those who caught his eye, but he didn't bother to return them. They were all mere moments from death. He didn't know how long it would take for the hydrogen sulphide to get through the ventilation system, but 'not very long' covered it well enough.

Wishing his father could stumble a little faster, Lord Edward took the transmitter from his pocket. He would destroy the device as soon as he was sure it had worked and the pieces would go into the river where they wouldn't even be looked for, let alone found.

He was moments from victory when a woman ran headlong into him. The air left his lungs with a strangled whoosh, the impact bowling him over. His father collapsed, Lord Edward watching him crumple into a heap as he hit the floor and rolled.

Scrambling, even though he was gasping for breath and wanted to stay down, Lord Edward got his feet back under his body and was getting up when movement caught his eye.

Just the same as he was, the woman who ran into him was scrambling to get back to her feet, but that wasn't what got his attention. The woman was insignificant. However, coming through a set of fire doors twenty yards behind her, Sir Albert Smith presented a greater problem. Or rather, his dog did.

"Elizabeth!" shouted a voice to his left.

Lord Edward swung his head to find Felicity coming from the direction of the banquet room. She was in the corridor that ran around the outside of it. She had Primrose with her, though bizarrely the taller, younger woman looked like she'd just been in a fight.

Hearing her name, the woman who knocked him down, squealed in fright and started running again. She didn't get far.

Lord Edward knew Felicity's pets through his relationship with Mindy but was shocked to see them chase down the assistant wedding planner.

Elizabeth's feet went out from under her when Buster ran through the back of her heels. The cat landed on her face and clung to it with all her claws.

Elizabeth screamed.

Buster, still feeling woozy, but confident he would be able to rest soon, turned around, his little legs digging into the short-pile carpet to get him facing the right way again. Rex understood Buster and Amber had been chasing the woman and had deferred to them, following in a backup capacity should he be needed.

"*Deploying Devil Dog belly flop!*" Buster barked, leaping to land heavily on Elizabeth's midriff.

Elizabeth exhaled so sharply she almost blew Amber off her face.

It all happened in the blink of an eye as Lord Edward clambered to his feet. It was time to go. There was nothing more he could do to prevent the fallout that might come. If he didn't go now and activate the gas, it would be too late.

But the transmitter was no longer in his hand.

"What's this?" asked his father.

Lord Edward snatched it from his dad's fingers. He wanted to save the old man. It would all look so much cleaner if the duke became the next king before Edward inherited the throne upon his death, but there was no time now.

With the device gripped firmly in his fist, Lord Edward ran. He had one purpose now. To get outside and press the trigger. It was right ahead. Just a few yards more. There were people chasing him, but none who would catch him. Once he was outside, he would lean on the door to keep them inside and watch them asphyxiate from the deadly gas.

He was right at the back of the hotel. No one would see him and once everyone was dead he could make up whatever story he wanted.

DI Cassie Munroe clotheslined him as he went out the door.

Chapter 77 – Lord Edward and DI Cassie Munroe

The stiff arm had been aimed at his throat, so when he hit it his head stopped and everything else kept going. Lord Edward came down with a crunch and the transmitter flew from his hand.

Cassie straddled his back, reaching to grasp his right arm so she could cuff him.

Filled with rage that yet another person was trying to stop him in his moment of victory, Lord Edward flipped over, rolling to crush Cassie under his back. He threw a hard elbow backward into her, snarling with satisfaction when it dug into her ribs.

She still had hold of his arm, but she wasn't getting a cuff onto him any time soon.

Flipping over so he was on top, he grabbed her jacket collars and tried to smash her head against the ground.

"Hey," said Mindy, using a sweet voice to get his attention. The moment he looked up she kicked him in the side of the head, spinning off one foot to create speed.

THE ROYAL WEDDING

The kick snapped his head to the right and the force of it knocked him off Cassie. He went with the blow, rolling across the ground to put some distance between him and everyone else.

People were pouring out of the door he'd planned to hold shut. Patricia Fisher was there, so too Sir Albert Smith and his dog. The dog, whatever the heck its name was, was poised to lunge and was only held in check by Sir Albert.

A whole bunch of people he didn't recognise were with them, including two people in suits who looked like they worked at the hotel. Felicity was there along with Primrose and the damned bulldog and cat were by their feet.

Surrounded and backing away, Lord Edward spotted the transmitter. Lunging, he grabbed it. He was caught, he knew that, but if he killed everyone inside the hotel he would still be the rightful King of England.

On his knees with his feet beneath him, Lord Edward spat blood on the ground and smiled at the faces coming his way.

Pressing the trigger, he said, "I win."

No one reacted.

He looked down at the transmitter. Surely it was working.

"Sorry, old boy," said Tempest. "You put a valve on top of the cylinder. That allowed us to close off the outlet so even if the switch just opened the pipe leading to the ventilation system, the gas can't get there."

Lord Edward blinked. "What?"

Closest to him and looking like she could kill, Mindy threw the diamond ring so it arced high into the air to fall towards Eddie's hands.

"Consider this a divorce," she quipped. The spin kick caught the ring just as it passed Eddie's face, driving the hunk of diamond into his teeth with her foot.

His head snapped back, whiplash tearing the muscles in his neck as he collapsed to the ground.

Mindy's leg continued the rotation, coming back to earth as she settled into a classic fighter's pose. There was no need to follow up, though. Lord Edward was out for the count.

Big Ben sniggered, "That was an Arnold Schwarzenegger line."

Mindy let a sad smile play across her lips. She had liked Eddie. She'd given herself to him but had never really believed in their relationship. For months, she had awoken each day expecting the call to say he was splitting up with her, but it never came. The proposal came as an absolute shock, but their engagement lasted less than an hour which had to be some kind of record.

Now back on her feet DI Munroe, the only serving police officer present, walked over to check Lord Edward's pulse. He was still alive despite the mashed mess his lips had become. He looked to be missing a couple of teeth.

She cuffed him and pulled out her radio, doing so just as uniformed police officers came out through the same door everyone else had used.

Holding up her warrant card, she identified herself and started to explain.

Patricia touched Albert's arm.

"Thank you for letting us out of the cellar."

"Yes," echoed Tempest. "Thank you indeed."

Albert nodded to accept their thanks and said, "That fellow dropped a bunch of keys before he ran outside. I'm not sure he even noticed, but when I heard you all hammering on the door to be let out, I figured the key marked 'Cellar' was probably the one I wanted."

Coming from behind them, Felicity placed a hand on each of their shoulders. Popping her head between theirs as they turned inward to see who was there, she said, "Anyone for a drink? I'm not sure I can go another minute without a healthy dose of gin in my bloodstream."

"Hear, hear," said Patricia, winking at Jermaine.

With the police taking over and a whole pile of questions to answer, plus the need to show them the cylinder of as yet unidentified gas, the whole rag-tag team traipsed back to the hotel bar where there was a bottle of gin with a very short life expectancy.

Chapter 78 – Three Days Later

So far as the outside world knew, the reception for Prince Marcus and Nora Morley had gone without a hitch. We were all questioned at length by the police when Tempest showed them the cylinder of gas. Mindy's name was all over the paperwork for the device with a trail of evidence going back to before I even hired her.

That it was bogus was never really in question, but the police conducted their due diligence to be sure. Lord Edward was locked away somewhere, and I doubted he would ever see the outside world again.

Elizabeth was likewise remanded in custody awaiting a trial. The police found evidence to show she had been in Scotland. They were yet to confirm she was ever in the Loch Richmond Hotel and Spa, but that was just a matter of time. It was her behind the attack on Justin, and probably she who started the fire that consumed the building. In a confession to the interviewing detective superintendent acting as senior investigating officer for the case, Elizabeth's part of it at least, she ranted about how she should have been the one to win the royal wedding contract and how everything could have been avoided if the palace had been sensible in the first place.

She admitted to leaking the pictures of Primrose, which put another part of the mystery to bed. She also explained how she had secretly paid the sculptor to add a piece of dry ice inside his masterpiece. Positioned at the back where no one would see it, it was covered by a layer of real ice so it would begin to deliver the thick, heavy smoke only once the sculpture began to melt. There was nothing illegal about it, but she also rigged the party poppers to catch fire, tried to kill Vince, and was found wielding a fire axe by Sir Albert. She would spend years in jail.

A third set of investigators were dealing with Cody Williams and his co-conspirators and their plot against the King. In their confessions it was revealed the only reason the drones were filled with water was down to their lack of connections. They wanted to fill them with something harmful but everything they tried ate right through the plastic tanks and using metal tanks that could withstand the corrosive nature of the liquids they tried to employ made the drones too heavy to get off the ground.

The drone pilots would all serve long sentences at his majesty's pleasure and Cody Williams, though famous now, was going to do hard time. The women he stabbed in and around the cathedral grounds were all recovering, though he was being charged with three counts of attempted murder just for them. I wondered if they would ever let him out.

Vince was at home convalescing. The blow to his head had cracked his skull, but aside from a bad concussion, he was okay. They had allowed him to return home this morning and I was packing some things to move in with him. Just for a while.

Buster and Amber … well, they had found a new relationship built on mutual appreciation. In the last three days Buster hadn't snuck up on the cat once. He hadn't sneakily farted under her nose when she was asleep and neither of them had threatened to kill each other since the day of the royal wedding.

I even found them curled up asleep together on the sofa yesterday evening.

The royal wedding was behind me and as predicted I had enquiries falling from the sky. I could pick and choose which weddings I would arrange but for now I was taking a break. I believed I deserved one.

Patricia had returned to her cruise ship, flying out with Jermaine and Barbie yesterday afternoon. I would miss her but suspected our paths would cross again.

When I last saw Albert, he was talking about going back on the road. He had itchy feet the same way I had in the months after my Archie died. Albert's house was filled with memories of his wife and he longed to be free of them.

But he wasn't leaving just yet and we had a date in the diary for lunch next week.

Tempest and the Blue Moon team went back to their regular work as paranormal investigators after the dust settled. Patricia told me all about how they were going to sacrifice their lives to save the royal family and everyone else in the hotel. They were all very noble people, and it was my honour to know them.

DI Cassie Munroe was being honoured for her part in stopping Lord Edward's attempt to murder everyone at the wedding. Tempest and Patricia used their connections to make sure the press knew who the real hero was. As I understood it, Commissioner Blunt tried to claim she was working under his authority and was now under investigation himself. The Police Department of Professional Standards were taking great interest in Cassie's report that she was side-lined after he terminated their relationship.

His wife had left him, and his career was going to stall. That wouldn't impact him too badly and he would likely still get his pension. Worse yet, having accused such a senior police officer, Cassie would live with a black mark against her name to make things worse than they had been before.

Mercifully, the people at the palace wanted her and she had already submitted her notice to the police. She was going to join the security team at the palace, taking on a senior role that she rightly deserved.

As for Primrose, we shook hands when it was all done, and she went back to her life. I made sure the industry knew she was partly responsible for the wedding of the year, highlighting how she kept a cool head despite all that transpired. Via the grapevine I heard she was taking record numbers of bookings. I couldn't say for certain that our rivalry was at an end, but there was at least a ceasefire for now.

I drained my mug of tea and set it in the dishwasher just as Mindy came into the kitchen.

"All set?" she asked.

I had a small suitcase and a couple of overnight bags plus my iPad. The decision to leave my laptop behind was very deliberate. If I didn't have it, I couldn't work. More than anything, I needed some mental downtime.

I scrunched up my face, questioning what I might have forgotten. Whatever it was wouldn't matter. I could come back for it or buy a new one close to Vince's house if it was really that desperate.

Nodding to myself, I said, "I think so. You're all set here?"

Mindy grinned. "Yeah, me and the pets are going to watch movies and eat pizza." Her youthful resilience shone through in a way I could not recall ever possessing myself. I learned about Lord Edward's proposal only in the aftermath of the wedding reception. It wasn't even Mindy who told me. I learned about it from one of the guests.

I had thought she was in love with him, but Mindy assured me she was too young to tolerate such a deep emotion. Certain she was hurting at some level, I chose to give her space to work it out for herself. Had she needed any further proof that Lord Edward saw her as nothing but a pawn, an email, seemingly written by her, was sitting on her laptop. The police found it minutes before it was due to be sent to dozens of media outlets. That her boyfriend wrote it was never in question.

Buster wandered in, pausing halfway across the kitchen to use a back leg to scratch his head.

"*Mindy said we're going to watch movies*," he boasted, like a kid whose dad has let them stay up late and thinks mum should know. "*I wonder what we are going to watch first.*"

Eyes on her phone, Mindy said, "One of the Marvel movies."

It took a second for the penny to drop, but when it did her head snapped up, her eyes met mine, and she said, "Holy sh …"

The last word was drowned out when Buster barked, "*Oh, yeah!*"

The End

Author's Notes:

Dear Reader,

On this occasion I must thank you for reading not only to the end of the book and beyond but to the end of the series. I set out to deliver a ten-book arc that would introduce a concept (the royal wedding) early on and to weave a subplot throughout the books that would wrap up the series in a climatic manner.

Only you can determine if I succeeded, but I am happy with the end result.

To achieve the effect I desired, I drew in subplots from other series and had to take a long run up to sow the seeds in other books. Albert Smith has his own stories, of course. You first met him in *Wedding Ceremony Woes*, the fifth book in Felicity's series. At the time of writing, he has more than twenty adventures under his belt and has appeared in this series as well as Patricia Fisher's.

Patricia Fisher is another crossover character. With more than thirty titles of her own, it was in her twentieth book that Felicity first appeared. Felicity has played a major role in the Patricia Fisher stories on three occasions but has popped up in conversation multiple times.

Then there is the team from Blue Moon Investigations. When I wrote Sparks in the Darkness, in which you first meet Lord Edward and DI Cassie Munroe, I wasn't trying to plant a seed for the Felicity Philips books, but once it was out there I saw the opportunity to include it. Tempest and friends appear in *A Dress to Die For*, the fourth book in this series where they help expose a prank Primrose is playing on Felicity. Their office is just along Rochester High Street from Felicity's boutique, so it was only natural she turned to them when her spooky problem arose.

I talk of Buckingham Palace and the household staff in some detail. This is because I have enjoyed the pleasure of being hosted there for a cocktail party. I'm not claiming to know the royals, but my time as an army officer exposed me to the opportunity and I was swift to accept. Not for myself, exactly, but because I believed it would make my wife smile. Which it did. I have a framed canvas of her with a guardsman in the background on the wall in our kitchen where I can see it every day.

This is only the second time I have finished a series of books. The previous one was an urban fantasy tale called The Realm of False Gods. It remains my bestselling series, and I attribute much of the success to the fact that readers can start the tale knowing they won't be forced to wait five years to find out how it ends.

The same can now be said for this series and I'm glad I chose to wrap it up.

This is the end of Felicity Philips, but she will reappear in books led by Albert or Patricia, and I find myself toying with the idea of a spin-off series featuring Amber and Buster. I'm taking a break from them for now so I can explore other ideas. I have a lot of them.

It is early summer as I wrap up this final note. My children are ten and five and school has just broken up for the summer. I'm delving straight into the next book,

THE ROYAL WEDDING

another last in series, and will have to negotiate writing it around days out and other activities.

Take care.

Steve Higgs

Printed in Dunstable, United Kingdom